The ORPHAN *of* TORUNDI

The ORPHAN *of* TORUNDI

J.L. McCREEDY

PENELOPE PIPP PUBLISHING

To frog bands and dreams and this adventure called life.

And to my husband.

Published by Penelope Pipp Publishing, McHenry, MS, U.S.A.

www.penelopepipp.com

ISBN-13 (pbk): 978-0-9882369-2-9
ISBN-13 (e-book): 978-0-9882369-3-6
Library of Congress Control Number: 2014948671

CONTENTS

1. SPILLED ORCHIDS

The narrow steps glint silver in the sunlight. I take the first one, knowing it leads me from everything I have ever known.

I plant both feet on the grooved metal, then pause to look up at the cockpit of the tiny, white plane. I do not know the man who sits there, but I am told he is a pilot for some environmental group in nearby Papua New Guinea. He has agreed to take Miss Trudy and me to the closest international airport. From there, we'll fly to Singapore before parting ways. She is off to New York for a short furlough and I … well, I guess I am more or less headed to exile.

"Don't forget to look for Mr. King when you arrive, Sam," Dr. Jean calls, and then he stares at the ground.

I take the second step, then another. The green runway spreads below me and the smell of cut wild grass still lingers in the air. The Dyeens cleared the field especially for my departure. I saw them do it. I wondered at the time if that's how executioners feel: obligated, dutiful, morose. I look at them now as they line the runway, heads up and silent. Stoic. I don't think they understand what is happening any more than I do.

And I can't quite place *why* this is happening. Three weeks ago, I was helping Dr. Jean at the mission. Just like always. Clinic hours in the morning, pharmaceutical research in the afternoon. Only that day, we worked in the clinic until early evening because of an outbreak of dysentery in the village, probably from something floating downstream in the Mokanan.

Everything here traces back to the Mokanan. It is where the Dyeens bathe, swim, fish and gather water. It is how they travel, too. They even say their precious river flows over a bed of diamonds. In my almost-seventeen years here, all I've ever seen is mud. But they believe it, and they say that the Great Spirit takes the form of a crocodile in search of these gems, and when a diamond is found, it is turned into a star. Now I have seen a crocodile or two in my lifetime. And as for stars? Our nights explode with them.

Or used to; for me, anyway.

I have two more steps before I reach the plane's doorway. It looks so perfectly ordinary, boring even. How can something so nondescript swallow a person whole like that, sever one from their life? It's the ultimate insult. No, that isn't quite right. Not knowing *why* I'm being sent away is the ultimate insult.

I think it has something to do with that day, three weeks ago, when the outbreak of dysentery disrupted our routine in the clinic. I remember everything about that day now. I wonder if we all store strings of minutia like that, just waiting to be recalled, to be turned over and over until every recollection rips a frayed little place in your head. Snuggles in, comfortable-like. Each memory so close it feels like it just happened.

And *it* happened, or rather began to happen, at around five-thirty in the evening that day. I'd snuck out of the clinic while Dr. Jean was mid-patient, calling through the doorway that I was going to search for some *Lai* root. I knew the root wouldn't cure a hundred moaning Dyeens of their stomach woes, but it might at least help with the symptoms. Besides, I couldn't take the smell anymore. The Dyeens are family to me, but there is a certain scent to dysentery that I would rather avoid.

The clinic – and the rest of our mission – lies between the banks of the Mokanan and the rain forest beyond, so it only took a few minutes before I was under the forest's shadowy eaves. I remember the coolness washing over me, the earthy, damp smell folding over my skin, and then the sound of the blue-horned cicada – Torundi's very own species – vibrating from the treetops. I remember thinking that in three days its call would end. Eighteen months would pass before it began again.

I walked deeper and deeper into the forest that evening, squinting into the shadows for the glossy sheen of the *Lai* leaf. I couldn't find any at first, so I began picking wild orchids along the way: violet and cream and blood, rusty red. I planned on leaving them at the mission cemetery where my mother is buried. I've always imagined that, if she were still alive, she'd like orchids. Maybe they'd even be her favorite. I remember thinking about that as I stared down at my gathered bouquet.

And that's when it *really* happened:

The sudden stillness in the air. My skin prickling with the sensation that I was not alone. The amber eyes locking on mine from not ten feet away, floating in a spotted face. Then my pulse blooming hot, exploding inside my ears, because I knew it at once: the clouded leopard. It looked hungry. It is rare, but not unheard of, for a leopard to attack a human.

I did not want to find out what that was like.

Also? I remember thinking that Pak Siaosi would have a fit. After years of teaching me. Of showing me how to use a *sumpit*; how to track, how to shoot when necessary, how to listen so your feet and your skin work as much as your eyes and ears; to always be aware. And instead, there I was in the middle of the rain forest, utterly unprepared.

The leopard knew it, too. It stared back at me. Calm. Anticipating.

I felt so stupid.

The animal moved forward again, curling back its mouth to expose long canines. I remember the effort it took to breathe evenly, to keep my gaze steady. Slowly I raised my arms in order to look as big and imposing as I possibly could. And then I yelled with as much fierceness as I could muster.

Impressive, right? My jungle savvy and all that. If Torundi had a newspaper (this is probably unnecessary, but just in case, I should explain that – aside from the sultan's palace and our mission's generator and solar cells – Torundi doesn't even have electricity, much less a newspaper) the headlines might read "Girl Vanquishes Carnivorous Jungle Cat with Ferocious Roar" … or something along those lines.

I would love nothing more than to report that this is in fact what happened, minus the newspaper headline, of course. That I scared the leopard off. That I returned to the mission, festooned my mother's grave with my warrior bouquet, tucked into my room with little ado and finished the evening with some killer origami.

It could have happened that way, right? I wish like hell that it had. If it had gone down differently that evening in the rain forest three weeks ago, I am fairly certain I would be assisting Dr. Jean in the clinic at this moment instead of climbing the steps to a plane.

I am at the doorway now. I turn to take one last look at everything that is my life waiting below. Pak Siaosi stands closest, dressed in full ceremonial garb as a last tribute. Magnificent feathers rise from his head and bracelets of shell, boars' teeth and beads encircle his bare, tattooed arms. His chest is bare, too, but around his waist a kilt of sorts made of thick, woven fibers drapes to mid-thigh. Even at sixty, his frame is lean and wiry. Proud. But his eyes, normally glinting with a sly sort of humor, are solemn today.

Leila's there, too, holding a woven basket that cradles her

infant son. Leila's my closest childhood friend other than Paolo. She's two months younger than me.

And then there's Paolo, to whom I've not said more than ten words in the last year. He's standing next to Leila's husband, and this surprises me. I hadn't expected him to come. His gaze holds mine for a moment. I want to call out to him, to at least say goodbye. But then, before I've found my voice, Paolo turns and walks away.

I wish I could do that, too. Just walk away.

If only I could walk away from today and go back to how things were; if only things had gone differently that evening when I faced the clouded leopard ....

But life is full of *ifs*. Some of them haunt me every day, reminding me that others have not been so lucky. *If* my mother hadn't been so brave, for example, I probably would have died with her in the rain forest shortly after I was born. And *if* I had been born a boy, I most likely would not have survived the sultan's terrible purge that occurred only a year or so after my birth. I would have joined the little mounds of earth that dot the graveyards here instead. And *if* the King and Queen of Torundi had only born an heir, their passing would not have resulted in Sultan Djadrani taking power in the first place. This is a fact that scars every village in Torundi, every family.

And now for a far less consequential *if*, but one that alters the course of my life all the same. Because instead of the random *ifs* that *could* have happened that evening in the rain forest, something far less ideal actually did. To be more precise, just as I released my roar designed to terrorize and intimidate that leopard, something crashed from the banyan tree overhead. I didn't realize how significant that was at first. I thought it was just a limb or something. A reasonable assumption to make when one is wandering alone through a jungle, isn't it?

But it turns out, it wasn't a limb. It was a man. A strange-enough fact on its own, but when I add that the man was a foreigner, it becomes downright perplexing. I did not catch much more of the stranger's appearance than a flash of his eyes, however, before he yelled at me to run. He even said it in Torundi.

"Lari!" he said, just as the leopard ripped its claws down his back.

For a moment I think I just blinked from the man to the leopard to the strewn colors that now covered the brown earth at my feet. I remember wondering when I'd dropped my bundle of orchids, and then immediately realizing how idiotic that was because a *man* was being *mauled* to death. I lunged for something, anything, and my hands grabbed at a stick. I must have thought I was going to hit the leopard with it, but the man turned to me.

"RUN!" he shouted again. *"Now*, damn it!"

"But you—"

"GO!"

I staggered backward and the movement helped return me to my senses. "Of-of course, yes, I'll get help," I managed to say, and then I dropped my stick and sprinted back to the mission.

It only took about five minutes for me to reach the clinic. I found Dr. Jean at his desk, glaring at a letter in his hands. He shuffled it into a drawer.

"What on earth?" he began.

I panted out what happened, but to my surprise Dr. Jean just sat there. I remember that specifically. Maybe his face turned a little white, but otherwise, he just *sat* there.

"Don't just stare at me!" I tried again. "We've got to help him! I'll get my *sumpit* and Pak Siaosi, too," I quickly added, because everyone knows he's the best. Pak Siaosi can hit a single rambutan from sixty feet away. "Hurry, we've got to go!"

He was so still, the way he looked back at me. And then he said the most peculiar thing. He said:

"What color were his eyes?"

I couldn't believe it. I mean, a foreigner in Torundi is a rare sight, granted. Rarer than hen's teeth as Nurse Kathy might say. And a foreigner falling out of a tree in the middle of the rain forest to then do battle with a clouded leopard is so bizarre that even I recognized the potential delusion. But still, at that moment, and of all people, Dr. Jean had asked the wrong kind of question.

"Are you even *listening* to me?" I shouted impatiently. "There's a man out there who needs our help!"

Dr. Jean pressed his mouth together, his lips forming a hard, white line. Exasperated, I ran toward the door. "Fine, I'm going—"

"Sam!" Suddenly Dr. Jean was at my side, catching my wrist in his hand. That probably should have been my first clue that all was not well with my world; that there were schemes itching beneath that calm facade that were finally wiggling free. But all I was aware of at the time was being shoved into a dirty linens basket, my arms and legs grabbing at the air like a flipped turtle. "You are staying put. *I'll* go find him!" he growled. And with that, he stalked out the door and slammed it shut.

A lock clicked. Through the bamboo walls of the clinic, I heard several men gathering in curiosity outside. They must have heard my protests because one of them called to me.

"Apa Mata Hantu?" he asked.

Then I heard Dr. Jean explaining about the foreigner in the forest and the clouded leopard. The latter part certainly caught everyone's attention because the leopard is a peerless prize. In fact, the sultan had declared it against Torundi law to hunt them unless one had proven a threat, so the circumstance afforded a rare opportunity. The men organized themselves immediately, speaking in low, quick tones with that precision that makes the Dyeens such excellent hunters. Seconds later, I heard the swift sound of footsteps running toward the jungle, followed by Dr. Jean's reticent tread.

So there I was, struggling inside a dirty linens basket while the hunt for my Tarzan-wannabe and the clouded leopard began. What happens next is, I am confident, all ripple effect. I am sure of it. The question remains: *Why?* That's the sticking point. I run it over and over. The jungle encounter, returning to the mission, Dr. Jean taking off with the Dyeens while leaving me locked in the clinic. Nothing clicks into place other than the fact that I'd had the misfortune of encountering that foreigner. If he'd just stayed in his tree while I did my thing with the leopard, I think I'd be happily working in the clinic this morning instead of climbing the steps to a plane. Or maybe I'd just be dead.

So, anyway. Back to that day. I did extract myself from the basket after several attempts that I'd rather not describe. The door was still locked, of course. It was dark by the time I managed to crawl through the rafters, an unfortunate fact that probably had something to do with why I dropped straight into a rain barrel filled with rotten leaves. As one might imagine, I was in rare form when I finally marched through the mission's open-air common room.

"Hoo-hoo!" cackled Miss Trudy as I sloshed past her.

She was in the middle of one of her bizarre experiments, I could tell. She looked up from the pile of coconut husks beside her, pushed back her wire-frame glasses and said, "What's happened to *you?*"

"False imprisonment."

"Dr. Jean?" she guessed cheerily. "He's still not back, so if you are planning retribution, I'm in!" But then she grew distracted by a husk that roared into flames. With a shriek, she was off to the kitchen for a bucket of water. I skulked into my room and grabbed a towel, listening to Trudy's exclamations intermixed with hissing coconut shards. I wondered what she'd soaked them in this time. No telling, but one of these days she was going to burn down the mission, I just knew it.

Would serve Dr. Jean right.

I headed straight to the bathroom and took a long, hot shower. Steam billowed from the tile floor as I stood there, sweating rage. I remember wondering why on earth Dr. Jean cared more about *who* was in danger rather than just helping. And asking about eye color? Ridiculous.

I couldn't figure it out. And I certainly had no idea that, in a way, the shower I was taking would be my last. My last where I could look down at my feet and take it for granted that they would return to this spot the next day and the next and the next. Or that I'd always have my room to go to, my bed to sleep in. It is incredible to realize, really, how a person can be so clueless when fate is sharpening its knives.

So I'm standing there in the shower that evening with no inkling whatsoever that the next day Dr. Jean would announce my exile to an international American boarding school three weeks hence. He'd speak in cheery tones while signing mission thank you notes with his favorite fountain pen – wispy strands of letters that used to look kind of magical to me – but all I would see were the scratchings of something terrible. It would take several minutes for his words to sink in.

He would say things like, "Honestly, Sam, it will be great for you. You're practically a nun here – all you do is work and research – you need to see how the rest of the world lives! A friend of mine helped arrange for your tuition – we thought you'd be delighted by the surprise!" And then, "The school's in *Penang, Malaysia*, Sam! It's a tourist resort paradise! I'm jealous, actually. In just three weeks, you'll be making friends and going to the beach while we're stuck here researching medicinal properties of Tuafi leaves!"

I would watch him speak, fighting back the panic, the hot swell of things I couldn't understand. Any protest would be countered by calm definitiveness best executed by those who bear all of the control and none of the loss. For a moment I would consider running away, but then quickly realize the impracticality. I had no family to turn to. Torundi wasn't exactly accommodating and life at the mission was all I'd ever known. And I'd only be a burden if I stayed with the Dyeens. So then, after several more stunned minutes, I would say the only thing I could think of.

"Did you find the man?" I asked.

Dr. Jean frowned, put down his pen and looked away.

"No," he said with a tone to his voice that I couldn't place. Like aggravation, but with something more noxious laced underneath. A tone I'd consider over and over for the next three weeks until I knew, somehow, that his answer was tied to my current banishment. "There wasn't a sign of him anywhere. Or of the leopard."

Thus concludes my account of that fateful day and the repercussions that followed. You'd think I would have sensed it that evening when I took my shower, that I would have suspected *something*. Instead, as I watched the steam crawl over the tile floor that night, I remember thinking I had to give Dr. Jean points for one thing: the solar water heater. Until two years ago, cold dipping baths had been the norm at the mission. Dr. Jean was the one who got the solar stuff here. And satellite internet. Truth be told, he was the one who'd set up everything here, in the middle of a remote, jungle island floating between Oceania and Southeast Asia. Go figure.

That was actually my thought that night.

So, fast-forward three weeks to where I stand presently, in the doorway of a tiny white plane. With everything Dr. Jean has brought to Torundi, I suppose it is fitting that he is now the one who is sending something away.

Miss Trudy is behind me now. "Sam, we've really got to go," she says.

"Yes," I say, and then I duck inside the stuffy interior.

2. PACA

Steel clicks into steel.

A question floats in my head, ignoring the seat belt's cold metal, growing like a mushroom in the dark. And the question is this:

What do you call those moments in life when you know what lies ahead will change you into a different person, whether you want it to or not? Maybe you will be better, maybe you will be less, but you will most definitely be different. Just like that.

Is there a word or a phrase that is more succinct, less generic than A Life-Changing Moment? It seems so trite, that phrase. Too dismissive of the effect – as of yet unidentified – that inevitably flows in its wake. Like summing up the death of a loved one with some vacuous condolence like "It was meant to be" or "She's in a better place now."

Who decided that, anyway?

I have no answer.

So I sit in the plane.

It lifts into the air, now vibrating through the clouds with a smell of old nylon and stale exhaust. I wonder if Ibu Heti is over her cold yet, or if Nurse Kathy will remember that Nonya is supposed to receive her vaccine tomorrow. I feel slightly nauseated. The sky is a merry, baby blue.

We arrive in Singapore, where I have a two-hour layover until my connecting flight will bring me to Penang, Malaysia. Trudy escorts me to my departure gate as I stumble along after her, staring in bewilderment at the shiny tiled floors, the elaborate fountains and the duty-free shops that rise up behind glass walls, sparkling like gemstones. The airport looks more like a futuristic shopping mall than a transportation hub, but then again, what do I know? Before now, I've only seen this type of thing in movies.

We pass another shop window and I gaze at it vacantly, seeing my mournful reflection staring back. A full mouth. Brown, shoulder-length hair that is neither straight nor curly but instead waves and twists on a whim. A pretty standard-looking nose, although the bridge is wider than most. If pinched noses are what's considered attractive, then I'm out of luck.

But it's my skin – a shade or two darker than my adopted mission family and a shade or two lighter than everyone else –

that stands out the most. At least it does in Torundi. And my eyes, too. The Dyeens call me *Mata Hantu* because of them. They are light, ghost-like. A color between honey and grey. I know that my mother's eyes were most likely brown. What color are my father's then? Blue? Grey? Green?

"There's no need to send you off like this, as if you actually need some boarding school-sanctioned education!" Trudy bursts out.

I turn from my reflection, surprised. Trudy is an unusually tall woman, just over six feet, so I literally have to look up to her. She's been with the mission, Global Medicine Solutions, since I was a kid, coming for a summer of research and falling in love with the Dyeens so much that she decided to stay for good. Thanks to her, Dr. Jean and Nurse Kathy – who's about as old as the hills at this point – GMS has been running full steam ever since, researching the medicinal properties of indigenous plants while providing health care and education to anyone on the island who wants it. Dr. Jean handles most of the pharmaceutical research … and up until now, so had I.

But I'm not going to think about the mission. I look up at Trudy instead. Even in her frumpy clothes, there's something about her that's pretty. Well, maybe the right word would be handsome but, in any case, she's the closest thing I have to an older sister and, at this particular moment, seeing her upset at my departure fills me with relief.

"But I thought you agreed I should go," I say.

"Succotash!" she snaps, shoving back her glasses. "I was coerced; he said it would make it easier for you if we all pretended, allowed you to make a clean break, so to speak. But this is all on him, and I can't pretend anymore. We've been ganged up on! And why are we not even supposed to *write* each other while you're away? That's ridiculous! When I get back from furlough, I'm demanding some answers!"

"A little late for that."

"As it stands, you can already pass any standardized test," she continues as if not hearing me. "All that dribble about what universities need to see on your record? Poo!" An announcement for a New York departure blares in English, cutting off her tirade. A look of distress floods her face. "That's my flight," she says. "It's boarding now … I'll have to leave you here …."

"Okay."

"Oh, Sam, I'm so sorry," she wails, hugging me close.

I try to smile. "Hey, don't forget, I want that picture of you outside Tiffany's."

"It'll be waiting for you at Christmas – I'll even hold a cigarette for you, just like Holly Golightly," she sniffs, tearing up. It is one of our favorite movies, *Breakfast at Tiffany's*. We'd watch it on rainy days when there was nothing else to do, much to the mockery of a certain resident male physician. Trudy wipes her eyes. "In fact, I might even smoke it, just to piss him off; then I'll frame that picture and hang it in the common room!" She glares. "This is so unfair! And what about the rest of us? Who am I going to practice my jujitsu with?"

"I know who you can practice it *on.*" The speaker blares once more, announcing the final boarding call. "You'd better go. See you in four months," I say, and then I walk toward my gate, my vision blurring as I pick out an empty seat. Trudy calls my name, saying something about origami paper from New York, I think, and I wave without turning, not trusting my reaction if I were to look back at her.

When I finally land in Penang, I follow the line of arriving passengers through Immigration. Judging from the official's face, my Torundi passport is an unprecedented sight. I think he wonders if it's real. He makes a phone call and then consults with an individual whom I presume is some sort of supervisor. I'm stamped through.

Soon I find myself in the baggage claim area, where my suitcase is already waiting. A few bureaucratic procedures later, I'm officially outside the arrival gate where I'm swallowed whole by the heat. And it's *hot* – much hotter than Torundi. Muggy, too. I can actually see my hair frizz as I stand there.

I look around, battling for a full breath of air, when a man marches up to me and introduces himself as Mr. King, the school principal. Well, at least that was easy enough. He must have had a picture of me already because he doesn't ask who I am; he just escorts me to a bus filled with students of all ages. They stare curiously as I board. I nod back, find a seat next to an empty one, and then the bus cranks up with a groan that could resurrect carbon matter.

Soon we're rattling down streets that curve between

colorful shops, buzzing traffic and alternating seascapes. People and cars are everywhere. And that's when it hits me:

The posh planes, the shiny airports, the dainty, immaculately dressed flight attendants who all looked like the most gorgeous humans on earth … they were nothing compared to this. Everything up to this point seemed contained, fake somehow. Like a science fiction movie. But *this!*

I stare out of my window in utter bafflement, fighting the spasms of panic that make me want to throw up. My forehead is sweating; my arms, too. Everything is upside down. This place could not be more opposite from my quiet, undeveloped world of Torundi. And I know that I'm totally screwed.

The bus continues on, indifferent to my panic. I am still sitting there like a lobotomized Bambi when it finally turns down a road labeled "Tanjung Bungah." I already know this road as the address of my new educational confinement. I've done so many online searches during my last three weeks in Torundi that the address is burned into memory. And sure enough, a few minutes later, the bus rattles left toward a complex surrounded by imposing, cement walls. A wide gate yawns open and the bus rumbles through it, passing a guard who waves at the passengers inside. Excited chatter erupts all around me, but I feel as if I'm watching everything from somewhere else. Hell, maybe.

Overhead, I note an arch connected to each side of the gate embossed with large, metal letters that read "Penang American Christian Academy."

So, this is it.

Good God, what has Dr. Jean done?

I take a deep breath and close my eyes for just a moment. I will not sink into that debilitating realm of self-pity. I will not cry. Besides, Trudy's outburst at the airport gave me plenty to think about.

And now, I have a plan.

The bus rolls to a stop in front of a two-story, white concrete structure. It looks like an enormous confinement cell, but a sign indicates that it's the student center. Close enough. I heave from my seat and follow the line of students tumbling out of the bus. Everyone's grinning and generally looking happy to arrive here. I look around and wonder why.

Now, granted, I've spent my entire life next to riverside villagers whose idea of good architecture involves interlacing palm fronds for their rooftops, but still, even *I* know this is a sad-looking affair.

Dilapidated, single-story buildings line the campus on all sides. The adjective "ugly" may be derided by some as an unimaginative word, but upon seeing this place, I finally appreciate its value. It's almost like an onomatopoeia, except instead of a sound, it's just the bare, gangly little word that illustrates. Because, really, what does u-g-l-y look like? You probably don't know exactly. You've got an idea – perhaps something that isn't necessarily abhorrent, but it doesn't have much to redeem itself either; it is tired and unoriginal and drab. You've got an idea but not an actual vision of the word. And that's because you've never been *here*.

In the middle of the campus, directly in front of where I now stand, sun-bleached basketball and tennis courts provide the center attraction and are surrounded by sagging, wire fencing that's been patched up a few times. Beyond that, to the far north side of the campus where grass grows in forlorn yellow clumps, several cement stairways lead from the bluff overlooking the sea to a lower level. The bluff itself is scattered with random trees, benches and swings. It is the only welcoming element I can discern.

"You must be Sam," comes a voice to my left.

It is another one of those moments. One where you're struggling to navigate through a reality that your mind still can not accept – not just yet, you need a little more time – and then Bam! People! They don't observe the quiet order of reconciliation. They don't acknowledge an inner world that is not a part of their own. They barge in, push around, demand to be noticed.

"Yes," I hear myself say. My eyes move in slow motion. It takes an inordinate amount of time before I realize that I am looking at a blonde girl with big, cow-brown eyes. She's smiling at me.

"I'm EJ," she announces.

She's so cheerful about it.

"Well, it's Ellen Jane Brown, but everyone just calls me EJ. We're roommates – you, me and Tess. I've been here three years. My parents are missionaries in Thailand, although we're *really* from *California.*" She throws back her long hair and looks at me. She's so pretty. I feel like I'm simultaneously eight years old and eighty … with all the disadvantages of both. "I was on the swim team there and everything; I'm an excellent swimmer, but there's nothing like that here. PACA's too cheap for a *real* pool … ."

She prattles on, now saying something about an older brother who's apparently a soil tester in France, something about eating sun-dried tomatoes – I think that had to do with a visit to see her brother – and then a college in California called Pepperdine; all this without taking a single breath. "That your bag?"

"Um. Yes."

I wrestle it forward on its wobbly wheels as EJ pulls me toward a ramshackle building, still talking.

"You won't believe this, but our dorm used to be horse stables!" I stumble after her, thinking that horses deserve better. "This whole campus was actually a military base during World War Two."

"That explains it."

"What?" EJ stomps up some steps.

"The campus," I answer. "It looks like a prison."

"Close enough," she chirps, and then she slings open the third door on the left and tugs me inside. "Sam, meet Tess."

I blink, trying to adjust to the sudden change in light. I'm standing in a small room with white-washed cement walls and a cement floor waxed to a rusty-red color. A bunk bed and a single twin take up most of the space. An open door in the back leads to a small, tiled bathroom.

"Oh, it's so hot," moans the Tess voice.

My eyes are still adjusting, but then I spot an exceptionally sunburned girl sprawled over the twin bed. Her long, black hair is mostly pulled into a bunch that wobbles above her forehead. She opens her eyes for a moment before closing them again, as if closing one's eyes somehow helps with the heat.

"Hey, Sam." She flutters a tomato-hued arm in the air. "Looks like you get the top bunk. Welcome to the inferno."

"Thanks," I say, but it sounds more like a question. I guess it should because, in fact, I am having a hard time believing any of this is actually happening. It seems impossible to be transplanted so efficiently from one's idyllic island to this place. There should be a law against it, or at least guidelines. Even goldfish get acclimated first.

By now, Tess has sweated herself to a sitting position. "I'm relieved you're here, Sam," she says, rolling her eyes at EJ as I busy myself with my suitcase. "I've been putting up with *that* on my own for three long years now. And before she resumes her inevitable, fascinating life story, may I take this reprieve to ask about you? We heard you were from the Kingdom of Torundi! We had to *look it up!* I mean, what on earth does your family *do* there?"

"Isn't it super remote?" EJ adds, and from the tone of her voice, I gather my origins have already become a subject of intrigue. I would laugh if I were not so miserable. "We weren't sure what to expect. I mean, it's basically National Geographic material, right? Like, isn't it cannibalistic or something?"

"Oh. My. *God!*" moans Tess, turning to me. "Sorry, Sam. There's absolutely no filter on her."

I shrug. "No cannibals."

"O-o-h," Tess and EJ breathe out together. They look back at me, expectant.

"And your family?" says Tess. She has bright blue eyes, round as lollipops. *Her* family is like one of those old TV shows from the fifties, I'm pretty sure. Cheerful, good-looking mom and dad. Slightly rapscallion younger siblings. Church on Sundays. Cherry pie.

I unzip the rest of my suitcase, not even caring. I already know I am woefully out of place here. My research has informed me that PACA is for the offspring of affluent business people stationed locally and for the coddled children of missionaries stationed elsewhere, neither of which I am. Our mission has no "aries" about it; it's a pharmaceutical research one, and religion has nothing to do with our cause. And then there's the matter of my family, for which I can not exactly account.

I rummage around in my suitcase. It's like a bandage. Just get it over with already.

"I don't have a family," I say, going straight for the jugular. Evangelical boarding schools are not particularly known for their tolerance, and children born out of marriage – as normal as it may be in the rest of our world – are clearly not the clientele of PACA. I know this.

"My mother was from one of the villages; she passed away right after my birth. And my father was some tourist that must have had an *awfully good time* on his two-week Torundi visa all those years ago ...." I snort-laugh (nervous habit, unfortunately), but I can feel the instant unease. "No idea where he is now, so I've been raised by the mission ever since." I quickly finish and peek up to catch their expressions. Yep. I should have stuck with the cannibals. "What about you, Tess?"

A graceless transition, certainly, but at least it works. Tess takes her cue and begins a lament of her miserable summer in Jakarta, Indonesia, and how much she misses their old post in Timor. I pull out the hiking boots Trudy gave me last year for Christmas while Tess shifts into a bizarre anecdote about her younger brother and sister, who are still at home. Sounds like my theory is spot on. Two cherubic siblings who dabble in random hobbies like volcano spelunking and the acquisition of exoskeletal beasts. A mother who is horrified upon discovering a shoebox of live scorpions in the closet. A dad who thinks it's funny. Tess pauses as another girl pops into the doorway.

"Hey guys, want to go to Hillside? Aunt Janie said we could go."

Tess lifts a hand in her direction but turns to me. "We're not allowed to leave campus without getting permission first," she explains dourly. "And we have to call all dorm parents our aunts and uncles. And we can't leave PACA without at least one other female as accompaniment. Yes, it's really that bad – I could *not* make this stuff up. And don't get me started on the socializing rules. This is Sandy."

"New girl from Torundi, right?" The girl at the doorway – A.K.A. Sandy – glances from me to my suitcase. "That's all you brought? One suitcase?"

"Well, it explains the clothes," mutters EJ.

"The suitcase?" says Sandy.

"No, Torundi," says EJ.

Suddenly, they're all staring at me. I follow their gaze, which stops at my current outfit, and instantly realize the problem. But what's a girl to do when your wardrobe is made up entirely of donated items? Those church ladies should think about that before they send their fashion rejects to orphans in the Pacific.

"Ignore those two," says Tess. "I think your granny skirt is kind of retro. Besides, you keep dressing like that, and you'll be golden with the staff. They freak out if they so much as see a kneecap."

"Hillside," barks Sandy. "Yes or no?"

"That's a yes," says EJ, and before I can protest or even ask what Hillside is, I'm herded out of the room, down the hallway, outside and across campus. Soon I'm passing under the PACA arch as my roommates and Sandy salute the guard. I follow along, mostly because I haven't any choice, buffered by waves of incessant chatter.

But I take comfort in that, actually.

I may be the most socially unprepared human being to have ever landed at PACA, but with these girls around, I at least have a chance of surviving in silence while I devise my escape.

3. THE UNFORTUNATE TRUTH

Torundi, for all that it means to me, simply can not compete with Penang in terms of cuisine. I'm speaking specifically about the *roti canai* and iced coffee I have at Hillside – which, turns out, is a wonderland of food stalls located, aptly, on a hill about a kilometer from our school. The whole experience of that meal kind of blows my mind.

Now, I realize that may sound flippant.

I am sure most people in my situation would be so depressed that they wouldn't care about a thing like food. They'd pine away for their estranged homeland and waste into a pitiable sag of flesh until the threat of self-annihilation proves their savior and sends them home, *tout de suite*.

But I can't do that.

I like food too much. So, I've got another idea for my PACA release that does not involve starvation.

You must understand, after sixteen years and eleven months of eating nothing but sticky rice, yams, boiled fern-tips, the occasional coconut (we've got to haul those from upriver, you know), fish, papaya, bananas and wild boar, discovering that cuisine can have actual *spices* and *flavor* is like finding the Holy Grail. While it is not a salve to my Torundi banishment, it does at least provide a distraction. And, after tasting what's on offer here, I want to sample as much as I can before I effect my jailbreak. There is one obstacle to both my escape plan and my culinary voyage, however:

Money.

Or, more specifically, the lack thereof.

Happily, when we reach the cafeteria at noon the next day, I notice a bulletin board with a single sheet tacked to it. It advertises five vacancies for dinner wait staff at PACA's going rate. I sign up immediately. I'm just putting away my pen when a thin man with dark, liquid eyes and greying hair pops up from behind the cafeteria line. He's in a white uniform.

"You are the very first!" he exclaims. "You must be …."

"Sam." I can't help but smile; I don't know why.

"The girl from Torundi, I assume? Excuse me, I suppose that is rude; I am excessively nervous – it is my first time to hire student wait staff and I did not think anyone would sign up. I like you, Sam, yes; I can see that straight off. You must call me Gajendra!" He says all of this very quickly, and then he throws a glance at the students filing through the line before turning back to me, his face thoughtful, assessing. He must have made up his mind about something because he gives a quick nod and then leans closer. "And to commemorate this occasion, I will tell you a secret. After a long day of travel," he whispers, "one might find the Hotel Chung Fatt Tze Mansion in the heart of Chinatown to be like a blue beacon from the past!"

I blink and say, "Um ...."

"Hotel Chung Fatt Tze Mansion. Blue Beacon. Heart of Chinatown." He nods. "In time, you will understand. Five o'clock? That's when kitchen duties begin!" He sails off before I can reply, by all indications delighted with our exchange.

I watch after him for a moment, still processing our encounter, but the smell of whatever is being served distracts me. I grab a tray and scoop a ladle of rice and some yellow-orange chicken concoction onto it – I think it is chicken curry, similar to what Sandy ordered last night at Hillside – and then I follow my roommates through the double doors leading to the seawall outside. I'm still pondering Gajendra's odd introduction when I realize Tess and EJ are speaking to me.

"Sam, are you listening?"

"What?"

"She's not listening."

"I *said,*" Tess whispers, raising her eyebrows in the direction of a rapidly approaching male student, "stay away from him. He's like a shark trolling for chum."

We're standing with our backs to the cafeteria, our trays resting on the seawall. In front of us, on the other side of the wall, the tide splashes over granite jetties that stretch into the water every twenty or so feet. Far to the left, a new hotel still under construction gleams white in the sunlight and, far to the right, enormous boulders loom over the water, creating a divider between thc sea and the wild swath of jungle gobbling up the sandy shore.

My gaze lingers on the jungle, the only familiar thing to me here. Green and tangled and deep. I fight back the urge to jump over the seawall and escape to that world. Soon, I promise myself. And in the meantime, I should just enjoy the chicken curry I'm eating because, honestly, it's amazing.

"Don't even think about it," says a voice. It sounds British.

I look up and discover the boy Tess just warned me about. He smiles, following my gaze. Something about the *way* he does this makes me feel as if he were doing me some sort of favor. I hear Tess mutter something behind me. EJ is grinning like a monkey.

"You're not allowed across the seawall," he continues, flashing super-white teeth. "Not during the school week, at least, and never without permission. They like to torture us by making us look out over the sea without actually allowing us to enjoy it."

"Off limits, like everything else," I acknowledge happily.

"Zach Perkins," he continues as if I'd asked. "Day student."

"Oh, leave her alone," says Tess.

"They can't stand each other," chirps another voice. I turn, grateful for the interruption, and observe a short, brown-haired girl standing on my other side. "I'm Julie, by the way, Julie Wagner. I'm two rooms down from you in our dorm – I was on your bus. This is Tommy and Caleb." Julie waves a hand at two boys beside her.

"Tommy Johnson," greets one.

"Caleb Reynolds," says the other, and I notice his accent. Australian, I think. Caleb looks like he's about to say something else when Zach steps between us, violating every law of personal space. I stumble backward. From the clatter followed by Tess's wail behind me, I gather I've somehow managed to flip her tray off the seawall and onto the cement patio. But I'm too busy wedging my own tray between Zach and me to risk helping her.

"I'm sure you've picked up on the fact that you're quite the celebrity," Zach Perkins resumes, ignoring the disaster, "but what we all *really* want to know is … *why* are you *here?*"

I freeze mid-wedge and stare down at my food. I should have known. Up until now, everything has been going far too smoothly. And while it may be an innocuous enough question to ask the new girl at a private boarding school where students are kept on such short leashes that anything new becomes riveting entertainment, what makes Zach's question so unnerving is that it's the *same* one I've been asking myself.

"The rest of us have a reason to be here," he continues coolly, and I think at least twenty people have stopped eating and are now gathered around Zach and me. "But you've grown up in Torundi your whole life. So why now?

And why *here?*" He grins slyly. "No one gets sent here from so far away, especially not just for senior year. So what was it? We've all be wondering. What did you *do?*"

A wave of nausea washes over me. I swallow hard – that last bite of curry rice just won't go down – and turn my face so I look back at the sea. It doesn't make any sense to me, either, no matter how many times I mull it over. In fact, the only conclusion I've arrived at is too depressing to admit to.

"Were you reared by goats, Zachary?" barks Tess. She's got her tray under control again, but she's definitely mad. I guess I can't blame her. That lunch was awesome and now all she's got to show for it are the sticky clumps of rice in her hair. "What kind of question is that?"

Just then the bell rings, indicating the end of lunch hour.

"Ugh. Let's go, Sam," Tess snarls, grabbing my arm. She throws a nasty look Zach's way as we return our trays to the cafeteria. "I told you he was awful."

I mutter something incoherent, too wretched to comment. Because all I can think of is Zach's question, and the answer to it stings so deeply that my eyes blur. But I have to face it. In a way, Zach is right. My crime isn't the juicy stuff he'd hoped for, but the truth is, I *have* done something, and it isn't just encountering that foreigner in the jungle a little over three weeks ago. I've been using that idea as a crutch; a way to hide from the truth, I think. Because the real crime I've committed is as simple as it is painful to accept:

I've grown up.

That's it, I'm pretty sure.

I'm not a cute kid anymore. I'm a burden and it's time for me to take care of myself. Or at least, that's what Dr. Jean must be thinking. Break me in slowly: boarding school and then college, so long as it means getting me off their backs and away from GMS. He probably thinks it will force me to adjust more quickly if we don't communicate. Total immersion. I feel sick again.

Thankfully, EJ is soliloquizing on how cute Zach's hair is and how Tommy should try doing something with his own because he wouldn't be bad looking if he just made the effort. She doesn't ask my opinion about that – already she knows I'm a lost cause – so all I have to do is follow my roommates to English class. Our teacher dives straight into a collection of Edgar Allen Poe, which, all things considered, aligns perfectly with my present mood.

After English, I have Foreign Language. My roommates are taking Spanish, so they point me to the French room and part ways.

"See you in Environmental Science," calls Tess.

I arrive a few minutes early to French and find my teacher lying on her back across two desks, gazing into a compact mirror as she applies a redundant layer of fuchsia lipstick.

"Ms. Reeds is cool," Sandy whispers, joining me at the door. "Strange, but cool. Wait until she talks about growing up in the Ozarks. She does a chapel lecture on it every year."

I nod and say, "Of course she does."

After French class, Sandy leads me to the science

building, which is located away from most of the other classrooms. "I want the scoop after class," she says with a grin before leaving me at the door.

"Scoop about what?" I say, frowning after her. Science is probably my favorite subject, but even I don't find it that interesting. Excepting, of course, the hilarity when Trudy's experiments are involved ....

But no. I'm not going to think about GMS. I'm going to go in there and get this day over with.

I open the metal door and peek inside. Long tables with chairs fill up the cramped room while, at the front, a wide desk faces the class. An old-fashioned chalkboard adorns the wall behind it. At the other end of the room, a wall of bookshelves divides the classroom from what must be the science lab beyond, but as that room is unlit, it is difficult to tell for sure.

I do my best to avoid eye contact with Zachary, who sits by the door, and wave at my roommates instead. They don't seem to notice. I head to their table anyway and wonder how it is possible that I am late – I came straight from French and never even heard the bell ring – but roll is already being called. The tables are long enough to seat four people each, so I scoot into the third seat next to EJ.

"Mr. Krikorian's running late from another class," she murmurs without turning. "He asked *him* to start on the attendance."

The classroom door opens again and the Australian boy I remember named Caleb appears. Good. So I'm not the only one who's late. Caleb is remarkably tan, I notice this time, and thin, with shaggy, sun-streaked hair. He catches me watching him and I look away. In the next moment, he's taking the last seat at our table.

"Don't worry, I'm much less obnoxious than Zach," he whispers, his blue eyes crinkling at the sides.

"Samuel Clemens," calls an unfamiliar voice.

My head snaps up. I glance toward the front of the room and see "Gabe Jones, Lab Assistant" scrawled across the chalkboard. I look from the writing to the individual currently facing away from us, evidently referencing an attendance schedule on his desk.

"Samuel?" he calls again. His voice is fluid and calm. Deep-ish.

But what really catches my attention is his accent. I'm pretty good at picking them out – I used to practice on Dr. Jean's lecture tapes that he gleaned from all over the place – but this one stumps me. Maybe for that reason, I fail to grasp the full misfortune of my circumstance.

"Okay," the voice continues. "Apparently, even on the first day of class, Mr. Clemens has tired of us. On to Naomi Douglas then. Ms. Douglas?"

"Wait!" I call before thinking things through.

The roll-call guy pauses, turning from the board to me. And then I suddenly realize the source of my roommates' distraction. Because Gabe Jones, Lab Assistant, is very ... striking; at least in this lamentable existence that is PACA. He is young – not many years older than us, I'd guess – but tall and definitely more filled out. Like an athlete. He has brown hair, olive skin and unusual eyes, although I can't meet them to decide their color because, even from where I sit, they feel like ice.

"Do you have something to say?" I suddenly realize he's addressing me. "Or are we to spend the entire next hour in breathless anticipation?"

Someone giggles.

"Say something before he goes away!" EJ whispers.

"Yes," I gulp in reply, which only brings me back to my present affliction. How is it that all the other class rolls but *this* one got the memo on my name? I feel every eyeball in the room on me. I've actually had stress dreams about this exact situation.

My pulse picks up. I hear the dreaded pounding in my ears. I try to swallow, but my throat resists the action. "I mean, that is to say, I am present …." I'm practically wheezing now. Of all the things to panic over, I do not know why this is my trigger. I don't know why my name should bother me more than my unholy family history, my refugee wardrobe options or even my current status as a deported orphan, but it does, it does, it so, *so* does. "I'm Sam Clemens," I finish.

Gabe Jones looks from the roll to me, taking entirely too much time for such a simple process. He's enjoying this, I can tell. "But it says *Samuel,"* he points out a little too earnestly.

I take a deep breath, battling the thing that threatens. It is an affliction of mine triggered by excessive anxiety: the verbal vomit of over-share that inevitably occurs at the most inappropriate of times. I should just go along with it; claim that Samuel is a typo or something, or better yet, just not care. I know I shouldn't care.

"I prefer Sam … for obvious reasons," I hear myself say instead, but Jones and the rest of the room are clearly waiting for more. I try to shrug it off; I tell myself it is none of his business and it isn't really that big of a deal. *I'm* the one who makes it a big deal. And I know that if I open my mouth again, I will most definitely regret it.

Too late.

"I know it says Samuel," I blurt, and it is like I'm watching a cartoon character run over a cliff in slow motion; "*I* can't help it if a geriatric nurse suffered a lapse in judgment all those years ago when she recorded my name. It was late at night! And I was dressed up like a boy when she found me, okay?" I take another deep breath. "I mean, it's never been an issue until now, but at any rate, just *pretend* it's short for Samantha!"

"Oh, wow," someone murmurs. I think it's Tess.

"Short for Samantha …."

"But I prefer Sam," I repeat shrilly, and then I press my mouth shut. I've got to control this.

"*Clemens* …." stresses Jones.

I nod, still clamping my lips.

Awkward silence. And my forehead is sweating.

Jones raises his brows. "Did anyone else know we'd have a literary icon in our midst today?" He surveys the room. Nobody answers that, probably because they don't catch the reference. I was counting on that, actually. "You look remarkably well for someone who's been dead for a century. And how's Tom Sawyer? Or Huckleberry Finn?"

I feel my eyes narrow. I hate him. Still, I know that I've walked right into this. Note to self: always think things through, especially before publicly claiming ownership to the moniker of a long-deceased, famous writer. And extra, *extra* especially when that name is also, to my everlasting chagrin, of the wrong freaking gender. Yes, that's right. I am named after none other than the almighty Mark Twain … if said Twain had actually gone by his birth name of Samuel Clemens instead of a pen name he dreamed up from his days working on river boats. It is a misfortune that will haunt me until I cease to be of this world, which at the moment, I kind of wish would happen immediately.

"Look, it is a long story involving a case of mistaken identity and an overworked mission nurse with an obsession for American literature …." I cringe, glancing at the faces floating before me. My face is flaming hot. And Caleb is trying way too hard not to laugh, which only reminds me that this would never have happened if I'd stayed in Torundi. "And although I find your wit *hilarious*, I am another Sam Clemens altogether. A living one. So can we move on with the roll now?"

Jones gazes back at me, utterly unfazed. My hands are shaking. And just then, the front door opens and a middle-aged man with curly, salt-and-pepper hair walks in. He plucks a pen from the pocket of his short-sleeved shirt.

"Mr. Krikorian, we were just on Naomi Douglas," Jones says with a smile, handing the roll to him. And with that, he gives a quick nod, strolls down the room and disappears into the back without another word.

As soon as Jones leaves, EJ whips around to face me. Her eyes are huge.

"Are you really a *Samuel?*" she whispers.

"Oh, good grief, EJ, I'm NOT a boy!"

"Agreed!" says Mr. Krikorian, but he looks confused. He consults the attendance sheet, frowning slightly. Another pause as he does a one-two from the sheet to me. "Now, Ms. Douglas," he resumes after some deliberation, "are you present?"

Well it could have been worse, I suppose, but I'm not sure how. In these situations, it really does feel like the only solution is to disappear. But there is no disappearing for me … or the regrettable name that is Samuel Clemens. I'm stuck with it, just as I'm stuck in this horrid place that is proving to be a force field of mortification. My original escape plan: desperately important. I don't belong here, I belong in Torundi.

I take a deep breath, calmed by just the thought. I even lift my head and notice the diagram Mr. Krikorian is drawing on the board. As I open my notebook and pretend to take notes, my mind races over my loosely made plan thus far.

I'll wait until Trudy gets back from furlough – she already said she'll help. And her furlough will give me just the right amount of time to arrange things so my return doesn't look deliberate. Otherwise Dr. Jean will just send me back. No, it has to be subtle: a hundred little misdeeds until PACA declares me recalcitrant and gives me the boot, orphan or no.

And then, I promise myself, feeling the tension leave my chest ….

And then I'll finally be home.

4. SCAVENGER

By the time Friday rolls around, I find myself mildly surprised to have endured an entire school week with little more humiliation. Zach Perkins lost interest in my presence after failing to obtain another audience at lunch hour and the lab assistant stays, for the most part, in the lab.

Even better, thanks to EJ's not-so-subtle inquiries, we learn that Jones will only be here for a short time. According to Mr. Krikorian, he's a graduate student in marine biology who is working on a thesis that has something to do with Southeast Asia. Mr. Krikorian met him over the summer, fell bedazzled by his references and – since Jones needed a lab for a few weeks and Mr. Krikorian needed an assistant – considered their meeting nothing short of divine providence. So long as that providence doesn't last much longer, I figure I can stick it out.

It is now Friday evening and I'm all set to celebrate my survival with the first night at PACA where I might actually be able to decompress. No study halls, no chapel services, no nothing but a novel and blissful solitude. I've already found the perfect little nook.

Alas, disillusionment is a hard master, and mine arrives after dinner, just as I'm heading up the stairs with my roommates and feigning digestive issues for the sake of my book night. But the cozy spot I've had my eye on all week is now obscured by the line of school buses ominously waiting.

Tess groans. "Right. First Friday," she says, shuffling toward the buses already filled with PACA's elementary, middle school and high school students.

"Wait! First what?" I clutch my stomach.

"Friday," repeats EJ, tugging me with her. "It's a PACA thing. Mandatory. Every semester on the first Friday back. Last time, we had a beach bonfire at a resort somewhere; come on, there's no use resisting."

We herd into the buses like the cattle we are. The buses roll in a line down the campus drive, now turning left on Tanjung Bungah Road. My fellow captives conclude that we must be headed to Georgetown.

I share a seat with EJ while Tess sits behind us with Sandy. They're discussing a canoe trip for Sandy's Canadian History class that's scheduled to take place after the rainy season. Apparently an eccentric philanthropist has donated an enormous canoe to the school and Sandy's Canadian

History teacher is planning its maiden expedition. I stifle a sigh, realizing that it is now official: I've been marooned on a campus where all the weirdness of the world awaits.

"That's Gurney Drive," EJ interrupts, pointing out the window. A swath of outdoor stalls, bedecked with twinkling lights, follows a promenade along the waterfront. "We'll have to go there sometime – they have the best food!"

The bus rumbles on. Condos and ancient merchant shops, chain restaurants and cart-pushers, stray animals and expensive vehicles flash by in various unlikely sequences. I feel overwhelmed with it all. Everything is so busy and crammed together, sharing spaces and streets and sidewalks, smells and noise, until the roads and the buildings and even the bus in which I sit blend into a chaotic soup.

The bus finally pulls over at a side street near a tall, round shopping center and the students begin filing out. So this is Georgetown. I look around at the crowds scuffling by. The air smells like incense and a mix of something sour, but I see now that's a trash bin five feet over.

And then I realize that the staff members from PACA are waiting on the street in front of us, all clothed in solid, bright colors. Everyone starts talking at once. Mr. King steps forward and asks for our attention.

"Welcome back to Penang," he begins, just as a public bus puffs past us. "We've got a special event planned for you tonight and almost all of our staff members have graciously agreed to participate." He coughs, waving a hand through the cloud of exhaust.

"On with it!" shouts one of the dorm parents – I'm pretty sure his name is Uncle Bob – and he's dressed from head to toe in purple.

"Okay then," Mr. King says with a grin. "Tonight's activity is … a scavenger hunt, with all of Georgetown as your playing field! You'll be divided into teams of six, identified by color. Each team will have a PACA staff member to ensure you remain safe … and no cheating occurs."

"What's a fun-filled Friday evening without a little chaperoning thrown in?" mutters Tess.

"Beside you, you will note the line of rickshaws waiting." Mr. King gestures to the open, two-seater carriages, each with a bicycle attached behind its carriage body.

The drivers smile and wave good-naturedly, even though I am sure they must think we're all ridiculous.

Or at least I do.

I can't believe I've been shipped across the Pacific for this. A month ago, I was researching anti-inflammatory properties of Torundi's Heila'a bush, for goodness' sake. Fine. Maybe I do sound like a nun, but at least I was doing something that actually *mattered.* Now look at me.

Suddenly I'm beyond homesick for one of those still, velvet nights by the Mokanan. Air so clean you could wash your face with it. Not a car or a shopping mall or even a street light to be seen. Just watching the stars, listening to the rustle of the rain trees ….

Mr. King's voice brings me back to the present.

"We have rented their passage for the next two-and-a-half hours," he's explaining. "Each team will have three rickshaws apiece to take you around Georgetown as you find your clues. After two-and-a-half hours, you must return to this point, regardless of whether or not you have finished your hunt. And remember, no cheating!"

Five minutes later, I stand with the Turquoise Group, headed by Ms. Janet Hobbs, a young teacher of fifth-grade English. My other teammates include Julie from my grade and a girl named Ruthie from third grade, a sixth-grade boy named Mark and a tenth-grade boy named Henry. We huddle together as Ms. Hobbs hands us our first clue. Henry unfolds the paper.

"It says, 'The Light of Penang showered blessings into the wilderness, and by this device, a city was born.'" He shrugs, passing the note around. Julie grabs it at once.

"See, the L's capitalized!" she beams, and at first I think she's being sarcastic. But no, she's really into this. "Our history class had a field trip last year to Fort Cornwallis! Captain Francis Light was sent to Penang to establish a trading post back in the 1700s. The island was totally forested when he arrived, so he stuffed coins into a cannon and shot them into the jungle. The locals cleared out the forest to collect the silver and that's how Georgetown was established!"

"Fort Cornwallis it is," someone says, and then everything shifts to fast-forward.

Before Ruthie and I can settle completely into our

rickshaw, we're off, careening the wrong way down one-way streets where taxis weave between vendors pushing carts filled with blocks of ice, sloshing soups and elaborate fried crackers. Cars honk their horns at nothing in particular. Wails of music and television and mosques collide in the air.

Throughout it all, Yanto, our driver, blithely dodges animals and automobiles while promising to get us there first. It's no idle promise, either. We reach Fort Cornwallis ahead of the rest and tumble into the golden lights that bathe the open, grassy area of the fort. Ancient stone walls surround the fort's edge, interspersed with cannons facing out to the sea. The tide laps along the walls, keeping time with the palm trees rustling overhead, and it is magical. I want to stay here all night.

Just then, the rest of the rickshaws arrive. As Julie, Henry and Mark charge toward the nearest cannon, I'm surprised to see a figure rise from the shadows along the wall. The stranger's back is to us, draped in an old, hooded cape. Then the hood falls away and the stranger turns, revealing a grinning, well-lipsticked Ms. Reeds.

"Bonsoir, mes amis," she trills, holding out the next clue. Ruthie jumps up and down in delight.

Our scavenger hunt continues in this manner, sending us off to St. George's Church and then to the Penang Museum and then the Hainan Chinese Temple. It seems the crafters of our game made each clue so at least one member of our party would know from last year's lessons where to go.

At some point, due to an errant clue, we're lost, but eventually we find our sixth destination outside the Bengali Mosque. Just one more riddle to go now, and Mark reads it out loud:

"In the heart of Chinatown, a blue beacon from the past beckons to weary travelers of the present with promises of good fortune." He crumples the note in disgust. "Excellent. As if *that* makes any sense!"

I stare at the wadded paper in Mark's fist.

Blue beacon. Heart of Chinatown.

"It's like they're making them harder and harder," grumbles Henry.

"Oh, it's a conundrum, to be sure," titters Ms. Hobbs. "But I can not help you."

Everyone exchanges glances. Tensions are rising. And I, for one, would very much like to salvage what's left of my Friday evening.

"I think I might know this one," I offer.

"How could you possibly know this one?" Julie demands with a scowl. "You weren't even here last year!"

"But isn't there some kind of famous mansion?" I persist, trying to figure out how to discuss Gajendra's waitress-commemoration-tip without giving him away. Working in my favor, however, is the fact that I don't remember it exactly. "It's just that I've ... heard about it. Guidebook, I think. Something about Chinatown and blue and a hotel with the name 'Fat' in it. Something Fat Mansion."

Ms. Hobbs regards me in astonishment.

"'Beckons weary travelers,'" repeats Julie.

"A hotel would make sense," agrees Henry.

"I think you mean the Hotel Chung Fatt Tze Mansion," says Yanto. "I know where this is. It is just north of here."

Well, that settles it.

My team shrugs and climbs into their respective rickshaws.

Yanto leads our procession as the two other rickshaws follow with their flickering headlights. Carriage wheels splosh in a puddle as we turn off Lebuh Chulia Street and onto Lebuh Leith, the small street signs barely lit by occasional overhead lights.

As our party passes a grand, old whitewashed building to our right, Julie screeches, "Stop! This is it!"

Pak Yanto mutters his disagreement, but stops anyway. The other rickshaws follow suit as Julie points at the white building. Just above the doorway, a large blue sign spells out, "Cathay Hotel."

"Don't you see?" Julie is saying. "Hotel? Blue sign? Chinatown? And most of all, there's Gabe Jones!"

My stomach squeezes. Julie, Mark, Henry and Ruthie dash across the street toward the gate of the Cathay Hotel, followed by Ms. Hobbs, who seems pleased by this particular turn of events. For some reason, I can't move from my rickshaw.

"Mr. Jones! Mr. Jones!" Julie shouts from the middle of the road.

Jones is standing by the fountain just outside the main door of the hotel, speaking with some men. I can just hear his voice, which surprises me because what I hear isn't English.

No, in fact, the language he's speaking sounds a lot like the Chinese I've heard the guards at school use.

Julie's still calling his name when he looks up. His gaze flicks from my team to the line of rickshaws on the other side of the street where I sit, cringing.

"Oh, Mr. Jones," Ms. Hobbs announces with a laugh, "we're on the school scavenger hunt, you see, and our little group seems to think you might have a clue for—"

Before Ms. Hobbs can finish her sentence, Jones mutters something to the group of men he's with and then stalks straight into the hotel without so much as acknowledging her presence.

She stops short, the look of indignation on her face priceless. My teammates halt beside her, equally perplexed.

"Well, I never!" huffs Ms. Hobbs.

"Should we try the Fatt Mansion?" I call, eager to get away. "Yanto says it's just down the street …."

Ms. Hobbs marches toward the men who still stand by the fountain. My teammates straggle behind her.

"Why did he walk off like that?" she demands, pointing after Jones. "And what's he here for?"

The men look at each other and then look back at her.

"Well?"

But the response they give is as enigmatic as Gabe Jones's. Without a word, they file away from the fountain, climb into a car parked by the side of the hotel and drive off. The only thing that keeps me from laughing is the bitter wish I could do the same thing.

"Well, there are some people who have not been educated on manners!" Ms. Hobbs declares, glancing from the vanished automobile to the Cathay Hotel. With a self-righteous swish of her skirt, she marches back toward the rickshaws.

My team trails after her, Julie casting one more hopeful glance at the hotel. Yanto turns to me while we wait for them.

"It is said that this hotel was used in the movie, *Beyond Rangoon,*" he offers, speaking in Malay, and I pick out enough to understand his meaning. We discovered the similarities between our languages about half an hour ago, as soon I told him where I was from. Since then, we've exchanged various phrases en route to our destinations, surprising each other with the words we hold in common.

"I'll have to see that sometime," I answer in Torundi. Just then, a movement in one of the hotel windows catches my attention.

Though no lights shine from the interior of the window's room, I can make out the flutter of a curtain drawing away from the lower right corner of the glass pane as the hotel's fountain lights glance off it.

The hairs on my arms prick up at once as I stare at the face watching me from the glass up above. Had it not been for the fountain lights catching the remarkable color of his eyes, I wouldn't have noticed it. But they had and I did. Something clicks in my brain, like pieces of a mechanical puzzle falling into place.

Suddenly, I know:

Those strange, teal-flecked eyes belong to none other than Gabe Jones. That much is obvious. But what makes my fingers dig into the plastic lining of my seat is the realization of something so unlikely, something so inexplicable that I have not considered it, not until the shadows and the light hit his face at just that angle, and I know now that I have seen him before. And he has seen *me* before. Because a month ago, far away on my island of Torundi, that same man rescued me from the fangs of a clouded leopard.

"Chung Fatt Tze Mansion," I hear Ms. Hobbs bark. Her voice sounds far away as the wheels under my carriage begin to move.

Ba-doom-doom-boom pounds my heart.

The rickshaw scoots onward until I find myself blinking into the darkness. All I can see are those eyes and all I can think of is that they belong to Gabe Jones, Lab Assistant. Nothing about that makes sense. Nothing about that seems *possible*. No one visits Torundi; maybe a wealthy tourist or two each year, tops. How could the same guy who saved my life there show up a month later *here* to use the science lab facilities of *my* school? Things like that just don't happen.

A thousand questions ping inside my head, and I am too full of them to chase any one down. Nothing matches up. I blink again, trying to focus, to make sense of it all. Ruthie is shaking me.

"We're here!"

I look up. And there, grinning in front of the doorway of the Hotel Chung Fatt Tze Mansion, waving a manila folder inscribed with "First Place" across the front, stands Gajendra.

5. DEATH BY PARASAIL

That night, I experience something I have never before experienced:

Insomnia.

Hours twist by as my roommates snore contentedly below my top bunk. I go through my stash of origami paper that I keep under the mattress, making all sorts of things: a boar, a water buffalo – I even attempt a reticulated windmill – but none of it distracts me.

I am haunted by what I saw in that window of the Cathay Hotel. Why was Jones in Torundi? Why is he here now? And why does he pretend to not recognize me?

Should I tell Dr. Jean?

No.

Dr. Jean does not want to hear from me; he's made that clear enough. No emails, no letters, no phone calls … nothing until I return for Christmas. I'll have to sort this out on my own, but that is the extent of my conviction. So I toss and I turn, flipping through theories that prove more ridiculous as the night creeps on.

When morning finally arrives, my roommates crawl from their beds and head straight for their swimsuits. EJ barks at me to hurry, saying something about catching the Hin bus to Batu Ferringhi.

I stumble down the ladder of my bunk, dazed from my night of sleeplessness, and rummage around in my drawer for my hideous swimsuit. EJ's eyes bulge in alarm.

"Are you serious? You're wearing *that?*"

"Leave her alone," yawns Tess. "She can't help it."

A week ago, this might have embarrassed me, but six days of social misfortune does wonderful things for a girl's indifference. Besides, I have bigger things to worry about now.

I barely have time to brush my teeth before EJ runs out of the room with her cute beach bag. "Signing us out," she calls. "Meet me outside."

I stuff my towel and book into my own beach bag, a canvas U.S. Postal Service sack. I really do need to speak with Trudy about our donation situation when I get back.

"Don't forget your prize," says Tess, grabbing the coupon I won last night from the scavenger hunt, and then we're out the door.

"Coffee," I plead.

"No time, you'll get it at the bus stop."

We pass under the arch and trudge toward the bus stop that will take us to the fabled Batu Ferringhi – a resort area of

Penang that Tess and EJ have been discussing all week. "PACA staff hardly ever go there," they'd explained, "so it's the one place we can actually have some fun!"

When we reach the bus stop, I head straight for the closest food stall.

"Kopi-Es-To-Go, please."

The man nods and begins the ritual of making Penang iced coffee – a beverage that, in the short time I've been here, has unequivocally become my favorite. I watch him pour the hot water through a filter stuffed with finely ground coffee beans, drain the espresso into a cup and spoon in a generous portion of sweetened condensed milk, then mix them together until the concoction looks more like chocolate milk than coffee. Finally he takes a plastic bag, fills it with ice, and pours the hot mixture into it. With his free hand, he wraps a plastic string around the lip and pokes a straw through the closure. Just as he's handing my drink to me, EJ yells that the Hin bus has arrived. I quickly pay, shuffle through the crowd and step beside Tess onto the bus, sipping my drink the whole way.

"Addict," she scoffs. "That stuff's poison."

"Nectar of the gods, you mean – ach!" I stumble from a push behind me and then stagger to the back of the bus. It's standing room only, so I clutch one of the straps dangling from the ceiling and brace for take-off. It's a nuanced business, riding these buses, but I got the hang of it while running an errand for Aunt Janie with EJ a few days ago.

Soon we're swaying along the narrow road that hugs the cliffside. Steep hills tangled with vegetation stretch down to the shore and, beyond that, waves crash over hunks of granite before thinning into arcs of foam.

The bus rattles along the winding road, making it impossible to hold a conversation. I take advantage of the noise to sort out my thoughts. There is so much I can't make sense of, so I start with what I know:

Jones is hiding something, that much is obvious.

He doesn't want me to recognize him, just as he didn't want to be found that evening in the rain forest after he saved me. Hadn't Dr. Jean and the Dyeens gone looking for him? Hadn't they returned without a trace of him, or of the leopard? Hiding from Dyeen hunters takes no small measure of skill ....

I exhale, suddenly realizing I've been holding my breath.

Who is this guy?

The bus groans around a sharp corner and I nearly fall into the lap of an elderly woman. Good thing I don't because she's already holding a chicken. I clutch my hand strap tighter and shift my weight.

Still, now that I'm reviewing things in the light of day, a small part of me has to wonder if I have it all wrong. How can I be so certain that Jones is the same man from Torundi? I was in a near-catatonic condition when all that happened. And it was dusk – nearly dark, really – and he'd been covered in some sort of camouflage ....

But I recognize those eyes.

I am ninety-nine percent sure.

"Earth to Sam!" EJ announces.

"We're here," clarifies Tess.

The bus screeches to a stop.

"Just follow us," instructs EJ, raising her voice over the jostle of the crowd, and soon we're tumbling out of the bus and sailing across the street, now working through a maze of stalls selling everything from coconut carvings and beach wraps to fried rice.

"Hello, girls!" calls an extremely fit male from one of the food stalls. He sits with a group of guys, all of whom look a year or two older than us, all athletic and all wearing swim shorts, flip-flops and nothing else. "You're back from the holidays, I see."

"Hey, Rami," Tess says with a smile.

They wave to the rest of the guys, calling out various greetings until resuming their march toward the sand.

"Rami," EJ tells me, "is what everyone calls a Beach Boy – they do all of the water sports here. Rami's sweet, but don't let him charm you. He has a new girlfriend practically every weekend."

It takes a while for EJ and Tess to agree where to set up camp. EJ proves very particular about location; it has something to do with the day, the time and which hotels have the most tourists. She eventually stakes our claim by a huge oak tree towering halfway between the cement promenade and the water. I'm grateful for the choice and, while my roommates position their towels under the blazing sun, settle in under the shade. I'm just arranging my flip-flops at two corners of my towel when I realize Tess is pointing at my left arm.

"Cool tattoo," she says. "That swirly thing you've got there – I noticed that before. What's it mean?"

I cringe instinctively and turn away. I don't know how to explain it; I'd hoped no one would notice … but luckily it doesn't matter now because both Tess and EJ are gaping toward the water. I follow their gaze. And then, just as quickly, I look down again.

"It's not fair," EJ moans. "Why can't he be a senior?"

"Because if he were a senior," answers Tess, "he wouldn't look like *that.*"

I watch my roommates and then peek back at Jones. He's strolling down the beach, wearing swim trunks and a light-grey T-shirt, his brown hair ruffling in the breeze. Every single female on the beach is staring at him. I bet he knows it, too.

Well, anyone could get an ego trip here. So far, the only Western men I've seen at Batu are variants of the pot-bellied, chicken-legged, overly tan sort. Of course Jones grabs attention. And besides, his nose is a little too big. He's not so much handsome as he is … well, it's the way he carries himself, I think. Paolo, for instance, is objectively much better looking. Why am I thinking about this?

I pull out the book we've been assigned for English, determined to ignore Jones until I've a better handle on the mystery that is his existence. But I'm shaken; I hadn't expected to see him again so soon, especially not here. And it seems incredibly narcissistic to consider the possibility – I'm embarrassed to even admit that I'm considering it – but here is the unavoidable question:

Is he following me?

Ridiculous. Unless Jones has a penchant for spying on awkward girls in eighteenth-century swimwear, there is no sane reason to assume such a thing, other than the unflattering realization that I'm being incredibly self-absorbed. Of course he is here. Why wouldn't he be? Just like us, he probably wants to get away from PACA and enjoy his Saturday. There.

And with that, I open my book.

I'm a quarter through *A Tale of Two Cities* when I realize I'm alone. I glance behind me, toward the cement promenade, and then just beyond that to one of the fancy beach hotels. A free-form pool landscaped with tropical plants curls out from the hotel and serves as a buffer between the public beach and the resort grounds. A tiki bar lined with patrons adorns one side of the pool and everyone's drinking colorful things pierced with pineapple chunks. I wonder what those drinks taste like.

I hear my name and turn to see Tess and EJ skipping toward me. Sandy and Julie Wagner are with them.

"I've scored a boat ride!" announces EJ. "The guy said I could take all of my friends."

"Australian tourist," Sandy says with a grin. "You've got to come!"

It really is the last thing in the world I want to do. This is the first chance I've had to be completely alone since arriving at PACA, and it feels good.

"You know, I have my coupon prize to use," I answer,

which is true. "Since it's only good for one person, I'll cash it in while you're all away. What do you recommend?"

"Jet skis, definitely," says EJ. "It's the most expensive – well, after parasailing, but that's off limits."

Tess nods her agreement. "Ever since the coconut tree incident last year, the hotels call Mr. King right away if they spot anyone under twenty-one in the air."

That sounds like an interesting tangent, but more importantly, it spawns a genius idea.

"What about boat rides with strangers?" I ask, weighing my options.

"We'd be totally screwed, but no one here pays any attention to that. Just the parasails," replies EJ. "You sure you won't come?"

I brandish my coupon.

"Watch and weep," Sandy says, which makes absolutely no sense to me, but I smile and wave as they scamper toward an older, bronzed gentleman in a Speedo.

I look down at my book. The water sports coupon had been my bookmark and now I've lost my place. I close the book and focus on the coupon. I've been at PACA for nearly a week now and, during that time, made little progress on my escape plan. I never sign out before meeting Gajendra in the cafeteria at five, true, and I walk around at night after curfew sometimes, but these infractions hardly count. Aunt Janie gets annoyed, but not much more than that.

I need to step it up.

I glance toward my friends again. I can hear them screeching as the speedboat takes off. It's now or never. Besides, parasailing sounds fun. I'm not sure what exactly it entails, but Trudy did it once while visiting her family in Florida and said she loved it.

So I slip on my shorts and march toward a forlorn-looking vendor who clearly could use some business. He's delighted to accept my coupon. Within minutes I'm standing on the beach, harnessed to a powerboat with a train of deflated parachute lying on the sand behind me. It is being explained that the boat will take off and that I must run toward it. Before I hit the water, I should be airborne. All I have to do is hold on to the harness.

It occurs to me that all of this is relayed in theoretical terms. The vendor guy, whose name is Ali, keeps using words like "supposed to" or "should."

"When it is time to land," Ali explains, "the boat will angle you back toward the beach. You should land on your feet and it helps to run forward a bit to keep from falling. It may hurt on your arches and shins a little," he adds conscientiously. "Do not worry, I have only seen two people actually break any bones."

I wonder if that has anything to do with the coconut tree reference.

"*Sam?*" someone calls. "Sam, what are you *doing?*"

I turn to see Caleb Reynolds trot toward me from the direction of one of the hotels. This confuses me at first until I remember that he's a day student. His parents probably have some sort of membership for the facilities here, a hypothesis supported by the pool towel slung over his shoulder.

"Hey, Caleb," I say.

"That's not the right kind of parasail!" He waves his arms. "The licensed guys actually put you on a boat and let you out with a winch. This thing must be, like, thirty years old!"

Before I can answer, I feel a tug coming from my midsection. I look down and realize that I am being pulled. The boat is moving. Ali looks slightly panicked.

"Run!" he shouts, though I am doing my best under the circumstances. "Did you not hear my instructions, lady? *Run!*"

My midsection tugs again and now my feet are in the air. I think I'm laughing – more out of shock, probably, and then I look around; everyone on the beach looks so silly … and there is water under my feet. From my angle, it looks like I am standing on water.

I glance up again, trying to smile reassuringly at a horrified Caleb when my gaze locks instead on someone else. Gabe Jones. He's standing on the beach, glaring straight at me. Well, good. Now I have two witnesses. Mr. King will have a fit. Torundi, here I come.

"Hellooo!" I call giddily. "Look, I'm flying!"

But my euphoria is short lived.

After a few moments of floating peacefully across the sky, I hear a disconcerting ripping sound. This is followed by the distinct sensation of falling, only in a slower, steadier fashion.

And then, I feel sure that what I see above me is a parachute that does not look at all healthy. In fact, it doesn't look like *a* parachute. It looks like *three* – ripped, tattered and rapidly deflating – parachutes. I wonder if I'd been dragged across razor blades when taking off on the beach.

No matter, for what grabs my immediate attention is the fact that I am sinking lower and lower toward the water. I'm still moving through the air, just at a significantly lower altitude that is becoming precariously close to sea level. My feet skim the water. It stings a little. I hover, waiting for the boat to pick up speed or something, but my feet are actually now *in* the water. The current rushes over them as my ankles feel warm and heavy, then my calves, my knees ....

Colorful nylon floats over me and I can no longer see the sky. Sun filters through reds and greens. I kick to tread water, but the cords about my harness tangle with my appendages as the boat continues to pull me under. I'm choking and I can't see. I can't breathe.

Down, down.

My chest is exploding. Something knocks me over and darkness washes everywhere. I'm not sure what happens next; I do not know if seconds or minutes pass until I realize that I am coughing. Hot, salty water sprays from my nose and mouth. It is so bright.

And then, I calm down enough to notice that I am lying on a hard, white surface – a boat deck, I think, but on a different boat than the one that took me out. I blink into the sunlight. I must be hallucinating because I see Gabe

Jones crouching over me, dripping with seawater. I erupt into more coughing.

"What happened?" I finally croak, but it feels like my esophagus is shredded.

"What do you *think* happened?" he snaps. "I had to dive in after you and cut you loose!"

I can only cough in response.

"Let's hope that pacifies the owner of this boat," he says as he pushes himself up. "And in the future, Ms. Clemens, *I* hope you make better use of your coupons."

I still can't speak, so I flop my head to the side and keep track of him as he walks toward the boat controls. I want to say something, but I don't know what. My throat throbs like crazy. He shifts into the driver's seat, his shirt sticking to his skin in the process. Through its current transparency, I can see the rise of a barely healed wound running from the bottom of his spine, across his back and ending at his left shoulder.

"How did you get that?" I gasp.

He doesn't turn around. The boat rumbles to life. It takes a tremendous amount of effort, but somehow I manage to push myself up. I'm shaking uncontrollably. Wind whips into my bones as we scoot across the water and I clench my teeth, willing myself to get up to the front of that boat. I make it to the passenger seat and grab a towel bunched up on the floor.

"How did you get that?" I repeat, but that's a mistake. Another fit of coughing ensues.

"I know this may be difficult," Jones replies without looking my way, "but you should really try not to speak."

I choose to ignore that. Also, the beach is rapidly approaching, so I know I don't have much time.

"I remember you." I try again, forcing the words through my throat. "In Torundi … the clouded leopard. And I can see your scar."

His gaze remains locked on the beach, his hands over the controls. "I think the saltwater has gone to your head, Ms. Clemens."

"*Who are you*, anyway?" I wheeze hoarsely, but then my throat has had enough. Tears streak down my cheeks from the pain as I gag on nothing but bloody lung. The engine howls over the water. I'm still coughing when the boat crashes onto shore and I vaguely recall some people huddled together on the beach. They look anxious. Caleb's there, too; he's saying something to a man in uniform and, before I can protest, I'm scooped up and handed off to another group of arms like a sack of slurpy seaweed.

"Get her to the hospital," snaps Jones. "And give her something to calm her down! She's delirious."

6. VOYAGE OF THE RED CANOE

My foray into parasailing definitely costs me. Everything backfires. Mr. King, instead of punishing me, blames my roommates for the whole thing. It was their duty to warn me, he says, and when I try to set the record straight, he only thinks I'm covering for them. Poor Tess and EJ are dorm confined for the next two weeks.

If that's how my actions will be interpreted, then I have no choice but to put my rule-breaking schemes on hold.

It takes ten days before I can breathe deeply without chest pains, which is the least of my problems because living in a tiny room with two disgruntled females proves a task I'd not wish on anyone. Even more irritating is the fact that I don't get any closer to solving the mystery behind a certain leopard-wrestling, hotel-liaison-ing, speedboat-absconding lab assistant, either.

September passes into October. Gabe Jones continues to show up on campus – a perfectly serendipitous turn of events for every female at PACA but me. I thought he would be gone by now. It wouldn't be so bad if we'd stayed in the classroom, but Mr. Krikorian shifts us into lab work – collecting sand and water samples, examining residue on shells, that kind of stuff – and puts Jones in charge while he works on his other classes. It gnaws at me to see Jones in the lab every day, knowing he holds a secret somehow tied to my home, somehow tied to *me*. But I never get a chance to confront him about it because he avoids me like I'm a septic tank. I'm beginning to wonder if I've imagined the whole thing.

And then, during the last week of October, preparations for Sandy's bizarre Canadian History canoe trip begin. Since it is intended to be a living history experience reflecting the lives of Canadian fur trappers and explorers from the 1700s, there is a strict rule that, while necessary toiletries and clothes are allowed, anything that runs on electricity or batteries is not. Well, except a camera. Her teacher, Mr. Windsor, concedes to that. Even the food has to be authentic. Every day after school for a whole week before the journey, I help Sandy make disgusting strips of hand-made beef jerky and odd globs of a baking-soda-batter substance that's supposed to be cooked on a stick or something.

The trouble is, Sandy's class only has ten students and the canoe needs at least fifteen. Somewhere along the line, Mr.

Krikorian decides our class should volunteer. And so, for the science students who agree to go, we are divided into teams of two and assigned an experiment tied to indigenous species. EJ and Tess choose jellyfish. Alistair Yip and Zachary are already collecting snakes, so they propose finding an extra garter or two at our various campsites. Caleb and I settle on plankton samples. I'm not sure how we arrived at that decision, but I guess it makes sense.

The day of our voyage finally arrives and my roommates and I lug our one-bag-each of clothes and toiletries down the stairs to lower campus. It is about six in the morning, and we are scheduled to take off in half an hour. Mr. Windsor wants to get as much paddling done in the cool of the morning as possible.

We throw our bags over the seawall and then hop over ourselves, following the narrow stretch of concrete walkway to the eastern side of the beach, just before the giant boulders and the patch of jungle beyond. From where we are, I can see that most of our crewmembers are already there, scurrying around the enormous canoe like ants.

I jump off the walkway ledge and land in the soft sand. Sandy, Caleb and Tommy Johnson, who are busy loading supplies, look up and wave. I wave back. Caleb looks disheartened.

I walk toward the canoe, swinging my postal bag and feeling strangely elated at the prospect of our adventure. But that quickly changes in the next moment. My bag falls from my hand. I turn to Caleb, as if he can offer some explanation, and instantly understand the expression on his face. He *is* disheartened. My roommates, on the other hand, are not. And the reason for this stands right in front of us, currently lifting boxes into the canoe.

"Why is *he* here?" I hiss. It takes a moment for me to realize I've just said that out loud, but Jones doesn't take notice. He continues with his cargo-loading, calmly giving instructions to the huddle of students nearby.

"He's the guide," gushes Sandy.

"B-but Mr. Windsor …."

Sandy shakes her head. "Didn't you hear? Mr. Windsor got really sick – flu or something like that. He didn't want us to delay things just for him, and Jones is the only one with experience who could make it on such short notice. Well, him and …."

"But he's not even qualified!" I argue. "We might as well just lead ourselves!"

"Oh no, he is totally qualified," cuts in EJ.

"But he's not even staff!"

"Covered," says Sandy. Just then, Ms. Hobbs crawls over the seawall behind us. She looks really excited as she jumps down to the sand and breezes past us. Jones looks up from the canoe.

"Group photo!" she gushes, waving a camera.

We're shuffled in front of the canoe and arranged at her direction. Great. In my haste, I forgot to brush my hair. Ms. Hobbs, of course, looks flawless. Jones looks like Jones.

The shutter clicks.

"It's evidence," she laughs, but we might as well have

been invisible because the only person she's looking at is him. "If any one of us is the worse for wear after this week, you'll be held accountable."

"Yes, ma'am," he says.

Ms. Hobbs beams at him like a mule on anesthesia. One thing's for sure: the Cathay Hotel incident has definitely been forgiven. And it occurs to me that Ms. Hobbs is quite attractive. Apparently I'm not the only one who's come to that conclusion.

"Guys?" Jones calls. "The bags are over here ...."

Caleb, Tommy, Zachary and Alistair tear their gaze from our female chaperone and get back to work. Before long, we are ready to launch. We take our positions.

"This is going to be epic!" Caleb says.

I try my best to match his enthusiasm as we push the behemoth into the warm, lapping tide. But I wonder if he realizes that in actual *epics* ... people tend to die.

Four days around the island feel like fourteen. It is hot and half of the crew gets seasick and throws up ...some *inside* the canoe. Plus, despite the fact that the rainy season is supposedly over, it rains torrents on us frequently. But I kind of like the adventure. For the first time in over two months, I feel as if I'm somewhat in my element.

We paddle from seven or so in the morning to about four in the afternoon, stopping in between for short breaks or lunch ... and when the rains force us to take cover.

By the fifth day, we are all exhausted, grumpy and disgusting. None of us has bathed in fresh water since leaving PACA, and the smell bears witness to this fact. When we reach our destination for the day, an island off the southeast coast of Penang that appears to be uninhabited, we crawl out of the canoe like galley rats.

Jones looks uneasy as he scans the skies. He keeps checking the notes left for him by Mr. Windsor.

We haul our provisions from the canoe and clear a space on the hill just beyond the beach. The area is buffered from the sea by large boulders, and pine trees grow around it in near-perfect formation, creating an ideal place to fasten our tents and tarps for the campsite.

After we set up, Jones heads off to collect firewood while Caleb and Alistair volunteer to go fishing. They trudge toward the beach, armed with a spear, a hand-made fishing pole and a long knife. I stare forlornly after them, certain we'll be eating fur trapper provisions for the fifth night in a row. Sandy, Tess, EJ and another girl from the Canadian History class named Annie head toward the water for a swim. I set off to collect coconuts, leaving Ms. Hobbs by the tents where she is unpacking her hammock.

I wander for a while along the beach, collecting felled coconuts and placing them in the sack that I drag behind me. At this point, anything is better than beef jerky and charred dough-on-a-stick. After a while, I return to camp and put my bag by the tree stump that serves as a makeshift table. I start shucking the husks using a sharp stick strategically angled in the sand. Technically, I suppose this is against the rules. I've never been to Canada, but I am pretty sure those fur trappers never encountered coconuts.

"Hey, Sam," calls Sandy, trotting in from the water. "Have you seen Tess and EJ?"

I pause mid-shuck. "They aren't with you?"

Sandy shakes her head and says, "They went off to find some fresh water; they thought there might be a stream or something in the woods."

I glance over at our tarps, where Ms. Hobbs is now napping. "Have you asked any of the guys?"

Sandy shrugs. "Only Caleb and Alistair, but they're still fishing. Oh, and Zach, who's passed out over there." She jerks her thumb toward a cluster of palm trees. "They haven't seen them. I don't know where everyone else is."

"I'll go look."

"You sure? I'd come with you, except . . .," she glances uneasily at the jungle, ". . . I'm more of an open-spaces kind of girl."

But I'm already headed for the trees. "Don't worry about it; I'll be back in a bit," I call behind me. And soon I'm under their canopy.

The smell of dirt and wet leaves hits me. I blink, adjusting to the shade. When my pupils acclimate, I spot a footpath winding through the bush. So maybe the island is inhabited after all. And if it is, then somewhere, there's fresh water.

I walk on, following the footpath as it slopes uphill. The shade is a welcomed change and the jungle comfortingly familiar; I almost feel like I am back home in Torundi.

Funny.

It has been weeks since I've thought of it. I've pushed the memory down for so long; I suppose it just hurts too much. And here I am now, treading the soft ground under eaves similar to those back home, and it isn't until this moment that it dawns on me:

In just over two months, I've gone from the flip-flop-wearing girl who researches plants and practices her *sumpit* aim with Pak Siaosi; who swims in the river with Trudy's students and eats yellow rice in the long house every Saturday night with the Dyeens; who spends her free time in the stillness of velvet evenings with no distractions, no lights, no care or interest in things like hairstyles and sports teams and clothing labels … I've gone from all of that to *this*.

Whatever "this" is; I can't quite capture it, even after two months of living in their world. But I've been a good Darwinian: I've adapted and survived.

The sound of falling water brings me back to my search. I continue up the path until I'm standing on a bluff and, for a moment, wonder if I'm seeing a mirage. From this viewpoint, I can see that the island is much larger than I'd assumed, and that the jungle goes on and on. But mostly, my surprise comes from a spring that bubbles from the ground not three feet away. It flows to the edge of the bluff and then tumbles into a little picturesque pool below. The pool, in turn, opens up into a river that cuts through the jungle.

It is beautiful.

I crawl down the bluff, using the tiny cutouts already in the hill until I reach the pool's perimeter. Rocks surround the water to form a natural lip around the reservoir, separating it from the river. I can feel its cool on my feet as it laps over my sunburn and dry, salt-crusted skin. I hadn't realized until this moment how exhausted I am. And I need a bath like nobody's business. I turn away. Not until I've found my roommates.

"Tess! EJ!" I call, but all I can hear is the waterfall behind me. I notice some footprints along the riverbank; they look about the same size as theirs, so I head to the shallow side of the river, following the tracks as I continue calling their names. I'm beginning to worry. It isn't like them to go exploring like this. Tess, maybe a little bit, but definitely not EJ.

I keep walking. I don't know how far down the river I am when I hear a low rumble. I look up. The clouds expand overhead, threatening a torrent similar to those that have plagued our trip thus far. I turn around, realizing I'd better make my way back to camp. Maybe Tess and EJ are already there, but if they aren't, then we need to form a search party.

The rain starts to fall.

The bank is slippery so I slosh through the water, planning on taking the path from the waterfall to the bluff overlook. Soon rain falls in sheets with a force stronger than the previous storms combined. Visibility cuts in half and I know I'm in trouble.

The land rises in steep inclines on either side of the river, making it impossible to climb up from where I am. Worse still, I can barely even see at this point. I remember spotting mangrove trees that led to a muddy slope some distance off, just before I decided to turn around, so I turn around again and head in their direction.

Something jabs into my foot and I slip, landing on my hands. I stagger back to a standing position and move forward again, but the whole jungle is made of water now; water rising from below and water pushing forward, water crashing from above and water spraying from the sides.

My surroundings instantly darken. All around me, water rushes and sprays and swirls. It is nearly up to my waist and still rising. A log darts by as I push through the river, squinting through the pounding rain. And then I barely make out the mangrove trees maybe one hundred feet off to my left. It takes everything I have to pull out of that current, but I do it; I don't think I've ever been so exhausted.

A muddy beach rises from the mangroves a few feet away. As soon as I reach it I limp out of the shallows and collapse on the ground, my panting inaudible against the roar of rain. I flop on my back, partially shielded by the ledge overhead, too fatigued to appreciate the magnitude of my escape. I know that I need to get up and climb to the rocks above me but I can't help it, I am so tired. Just two minutes. Two minutes and then I'll go ....

But I don't.

Instead, I hear my name and awake with a start. It takes a few seconds to catch up – it is confusing when moments ago, I was standing by the Mokanan under the shade of the rain trees – and then I see that the storm has subsided. The clouds still rumble as if threatening anew but, at least for the time being, the skies are dry. The river, though still somewhat swollen, flows sluggishly.

"Clemens! Sam *CLEMENS!*"

Then I see him; he is on the other side of the river, walking down the bank that has emerged from the water. I am not prepared for that. Part of me is tempted to hide until he has left, but then I remember my roommates.

"I'm here!" I call half-heartedly. "Where's Tess and EJ?"

He freezes in his tracks.

"Tess and EJ!" he roars, and in the next moment he's sloshing through the appeased river, stumbling slightly in the increasing darkness, but walking through it all the same, with no indication that a life-threatening current ever existed a while ago. "Tess and EJ are at camp, where *YOU* should be!"

He's already on my side of the river now, glaring down at me. I am positive I have never resented anyone more. And there is no point explaining myself because the expression on his face just makes me want to scream.

So I improvise.

"Stop following me!" I say, but Jones looks like he just swallowed a mouthful of charred dough-on-a-stick.

"This isn't a joke!" he shouts. "What is the matter with you?"

"Nothing! Well, surprisingly little," I amend, glancing away. I can't do it. I can't hold eye contact.

"You shouldn't wander off like that!" He's still shouting. "I didn't know where to look! If it hadn't been for Sandy—"

"I just got caught in a freaking *flash flood!*" I shout back, but my voice comes out way too screechy to sound defiant. I feel my neck rush with heat. "That's hardly my fault! And as for wandering off, what do you think you just did?"

"That's different."

"Why? Because you've inexplicably been assigned as our expedition guide? I don't get it. *YOU'RE* no more familiar with these waters than *WE* are!"

He looks away, his gaze resting on the shadows of the river bank, and I can't believe it, but I think my reply actually amuses him.

"Maybe it's because of something else," I keep on, furious now though I don't even know why. "Maybe it's got something to do with why you were in *Torundi!*"

The sky rumbles overhead. It couldn't be worse timing.

He looks up and says, "Let's get out of here. It's about to let loose again."

"*You* get out of here. I-I've got a place to wait it out!" With that, I slosh over the muddy slope and make my way to the rocky cliff overhead. It takes me a moment before I realize he's following.

"What?" I wheeze, struggling up the cliff, my legs feeling like jelly. "Don't … have any light to … find your way back?" I fling a foot over the ledge, flailing for a grip. I cannot fall in front of him; I just can't. "Should … have come … prepared, Group Leader."

I make it to the cliff top but barely, and as soon as I've got my legs back under me I turn, gasping in triumph. Jones appears at the ledge. He lets himself up with ease, his shoulders and arms flexing as he swings to his feet. Like he's a freaking gymnast or something. It's too much.

"You okay?" he asks, looking around.

He's not even out of breath.

I hear my brain howling inside my ears … or at least that's what it feels like. I say something really dignified like "Argh!" and then stomp into the recess of the cliff where a shallow cave opens up over the bluffs. It is darker in here but drier, too.

Just in time.

The rain roars down, permeating the air with a chill as the night closes around me.

7. FLOODS AND ARCHANGELS

There is something about the dark that changes how you consider things. It heightens your perceptions, certainly, but it's more than that, too. There is something about the dark that makes you face all those things inside that you don't want to face, makes you realize those things are real – maybe more real than everything else – and that they're not going away.

In my case, the darkness brings me back to Torundi; to the mystery of my banishment and why I am even here in the first place. And then, of course, there is the impending reunion at Christmas. What is that, anyway? A couple of weeks to pat me on the head, to act as though everything is just how it used to be – and then send me off once more, without another word from anyone? I am tired of that, tired of feeling that way. Like some dimwitted pet, too stupid to know when she is no longer wanted.

In fact, I am beginning to wish I wouldn't have to go back at all. I'm not that girl anymore.

But who am I?

"You're sniffling, Clemens."

I jerk my palms across my eyes, under my nose. For once, I am glad of the night – I'd completely forgotten myself.

We've been sitting in silence for hours. It feels more like a challenge, really. It is one thing to bicker in the daylight, but I have my pride, and when stuck all night in a cave with a surly stalker, being accused of excessive chattiness is where I draw the line. I can out-silence the best of them.

Clearly, I have won.

But the sound of his voice cuts a channel in the darkness, and all the anger that the night has brought on, all the hurt and betrayal I've felt since that day in Torundi, comes rushing through it. Wasn't he the instigator, after all? Wasn't it the evening of the clouded leopard when Dr. Jean started acting strangely? And the next day when Dr. Jean announced my exile?

Or maybe all of that is arbitrary; maybe Jones's appearance in Torundi really was a coincidence.

Maybe.

But it doesn't change the resentment I feel. And here he is now, dredging up memories I want to push away while simultaneously tormenting me with his secret. Knowing I know. And yet smugly denying.

So, no.

I guess I haven't won.

I cross my legs in front of me and try to ignore the pain in my joints. Everything aches. I am hungry. I am tired. I am really, really grumpy. And for reasons that make perfect sense to me at the moment, all of this is his fault.

"Why are you here?" I demand, and the steadiness of my voice pleases me.

"That is … profoundly uninteresting," he says with a sigh. "Not to mention obvious, but I'm trying not to point fingers. Surely there is something better to talk about?"

I shake my head, staring at the spot where his voice floats from the darkness. I want to punch it. And I've had hours – no, weeks – to think this over. There is nothing better on this planet to talk about.

"You're kind of like an insect, you know?" I say, determined to see it through this time. "I've thought about it and it's like you've got these four stages. They aren't cut and dry – sometimes the stages bleed into each other, so to speak – so try to be flexible in the interpretation. But generally speaking, there's the initial stage where you show up – and it doesn't matter where or how unlikely the scenario. Torundi, Batu Ferringhi, here, wherever. Just like an egg. An egg of something really annoying, I think … perhaps a fly."

No comment.

"Then there's the second stage where you do something completely out of character, which for some reason typically inures to my benefit," I continue. "This happens before you've really developed into your true identity: larva."

"Clemens, I don't think—"

"This is quickly tempered," I push on, "by the third stage where you act like a jerk – that's your pupa stage, of course, followed by the fourth stage of adulthood where you avoid me until the pattern begins anew. It must be exhausting though. Even insects stop after one metamorphosis."

More silence. Then he says, "I had no idea you were such an expert on bugs."

"Entomology," I say before I can stop myself. "And I study cicadas, mostly."

"Of course. And it's no *wonder* you're so widely popular."

I feel my eyes burn hot. I know what he's trying to do. So I grit my teeth and say, "*Why* are you *here,* Gabe Jones? PACA doesn't just entrust an unknown lab assistant with a canoe full of high school seniors! How did you do that? And why? Who *are* you, *really?*"

"You want to know the truth?"

"No, I'm just doing this for fun. Of course I want to know the truth!"

I hear him shifting. And just outside, a sliver of the moon peaks from the clouds. I adjust so that my face is turned from it. I do not want him to see me.

"All right, I didn't see the point in engaging, but I give up. Here's the truth: If I had the means, I'd be out of PACA in an instant. But Krikorian's offer is the best solution at my disposal. I have a thesis due in six months' time and to complete it, I need a lab located near the Malacca Strait. It's bad enough tolerating that pious little campus without being plagued by a student who insists I'm some person from

Torundi! I have no idea what you've been going on about, but to be honest, I'm embarrassed for you."

"You're lying!" I hiss into the darkness. "I *know* it was you! And if you think insulting me is going to shut me up, you're in for a disappointment. I'm practically immune!" I squeeze my eyes shut. It is maddening, yelling at something you can't even see. And that's just what he wants, for me to look crazy. "Listen, I recognize you. I know I'm right—"

"Let it go!"

My eyes fly open, and I see his gleaming before me.

"Just like that," I say, but my pulse swells into my throat, pinching words into whispers. "In Torundi. They glowed just like *that.*"

He says nothing. But he doesn't say I'm wrong.

"I don't think you're really a graduate student," I add, speaking slowly now. Careful. My pulse pounds in my ears, pounds everywhere. "There's another reason why you're here, and it has something to do with Torundi. I'll leave you alone if you just tell me what it is."

He says nothing. The moon draws back, leaving us again in the darkness.

"You're not really Gabe Jones, either, are you?" I continue, and the words are tumbling out quickly now, things I've mulled over for weeks, months, with no one to talk to. And now here he is, held hostage by the night around us, with no option but to sit here and face it. To face *me.* "That night, outside the Cathay Hotel, Ms. Hobbs and Julie called your name. You never even looked up until they were practically at the gate. They kept calling it and you never even responded, as if you didn't recognize—"

"That is enough." His voice is tight. "You don't know what you're talking about."

"I know you're not who you pretend to be."

A full minute ticks by in silence.

"That's your response?" I demand. "You've got nothing to say to that?"

I can sense him shaking his head, and there is something in that simple act that gives me pause. It seems genuine. But maybe that's just the dark; it makes a person feel weird things.

"Gabriel," he finally says. "My name *is* Gabriel."

I roll my eyes. "You really don't strike me as the archangel type."

"That's why I prefer Gabe," he says.

I stare into the darkness, lost. That was an unexpectedly easy reply on his part. Friendly, even.

"Speaking of names," he continues, "do you know that, where I am from, Mark Twain is a bit of a town hero?"

"Mark Twain …."

"Your namesake," he reminds.

"You're trying to distract me," I say.

"Is it working?"

"No! I mean, where …," I fumble, "are you from?"

But he doesn't respond. I feel my teeth grit against each other. We both sit in silence.

"Sam," he finally says, and the sound of him saying my name hits me like an electric current. I don't think he's called me by just my first name before; it's always Clemens, isn't it? I cross my arms in front of me. I don't know why. "If I told you that you were right – about Torundi, I mean – would you be able to let it go? Would you stop trying to talk to me about it – to anyone about it?"

The current buzzes in my ears. I say, "What do you mean?"

"I mean you and I should not be speaking of it. It isn't safe."

"Not *safe?*" I whisper. "That makes no sense."

More silence. He is shifting position, I think, and then he says, very slowly, "You are right. I'm not what I pretend to be. Are you? Are you really that girl who goes to classes and hangs out at the beach and, for the most part, acts like your world is no different than theirs?" I catch my breath and blink into the gloom, trying to discern where he is. "We all put on facades, Clemens. Anyone who claims to the contrary is lying – to themselves or to everyone else."

"But you won't tell me who you really are …," I say, ignoring the rest. He doesn't get to do that, to prospect what's in my head. That's mine.

"No."

"Because?"

"Because I can't."

"You *can't?*" I repeat, feeling my anger resurge. I am so fed up with this. Fed up with feeling like an idiot for daring to attempt any sense of things. Like I'm not to be taken seriously; like my existence is so insignificant that I'm not deserving of honesty – not from this guy or Dr. Jean or anyone else for that matter. "Not even when you appear in Torundi, to then arrive later at *my* school, which is located on an *entirely different continental group—*"

"Technically, Torundi is between Asia and Oceania," he corrects, but I'm too upset to concede it.

"Only to show up in my class with a … disposition to annoy *me* in particular and—"

"I don't mean to annoy you," he says.

This stops me mid-sentence. Is it the words or just the way he says them? Like a bucket of sand thrown over my fire. It is no use; any effort to understand only makes me look more ridiculous, I can see that now. I sound … petulant. Or worse, bratty. So I huddle closer against the wall, fighting the swell of frustration. We are both silent for a long time.

And then, slowly, our cave loses its darkness, warming slate into amber. Through the filtering light, I can see him leaning against the other side of the cave, his head tilted back, eyes to the ceiling. I hadn't really noticed until now, but he's changed since that day at Batu Ferringhi. His face is thinner, his eyes lined with shadow. But it is more than that.

"You don't look so good," I mutter.

He looks at me, then to the light outside. "You should talk," he says, pushing to his feet.

I glance down as he passes me, for the first time appreciating my condition. I am covered in patches of muck – like one of those spa treatments I've seen in magazines, only much less appealing – and the left side of my T-shirt is ripped and dried into a crusty mangle. It doesn't really matter. I have so much mud on me that I could pass for a two-legged hippo.

"Here, take it – you can't go back to camp like that," he says.

I look up and realize he's already standing on the ledge outside. He holds out his shirt, his back to me, and for just a second, I'm staring.

"For God's sake, Clemens. Like you haven't seen skin before."

I scramble to my feet and grab his shirt from him. I want to tell him that, in fact, I've seen lots of skin before. That the Dyeens wear less than that on a daily basis. That I've helped Dr. Jean examine more backs and chests and other body parts to last a lifetime.

But somehow, this is different.

"Skin, yes, but your scar looks horrible," I snap back, tugging his shirt over my head. The smell of him suddenly hits me: earthy and something like pine, I think, but also the sharp residue of a canoe trip's worth of dried sweat. I feel my whole body warm with embarrassment. It is too personal.

I yank his shirt down so that it falls mid-thigh, just above the hem of my cut-off army fatigues. Then I breathe in the morning that smells of rain, clear and clean. That's better. I turn and scoot over the ledge, equally relieved to get away as I am to discover that the descent proves much easier than the climb up. Soon I'm back on my feet, picking my way down the rocks.

"Sam," he calls. I cross my arms in front of me and keep walking.

"Yep?"

"When we get back, I know your friends will have questions . . . ."

"Don't worry," I say, landing on the beach. "I'll just tell them I waited it out until morning and then you found me by the overlook. There's nothing much more to tell anyway."

He stops somewhere behind me.

I do not turn around. I hobble into the river instead, scooping water over my face and neck. Then I hear him splashing in after me.

"We'll head for the waterfall," he says.

I'm still washing the mud from my face as he walks away from me, but my eyes wander after him. The sun catches his back, glowing over the movement of muscle on bone, glowing against the olive of his skin. The long, jagged pucker that runs up his back looks almost silver by contrast. I look away and quickly splash my arms.

We walk through the shallows in silence. The river bubbles merrily over my gashed-up feet, wholly unaccountable for the terror it caused the day before. If it weren't for my cuts and bruises – and for the wide swaths of bank littered with debris – I might just wonder if that storm really happened. I look around, surprised by how far I was swept away. All I can see from here is river and jungle, with no signs of that friendly little pool I'd found.

Something jabs into my foot and I stifle a yelp; Gabe turns around.

"Lost my shoes in the storm," I mumble, trying out another spot.

He shakes his head and sloshes toward me. "For a girl from Torundi …."

"Well, I'm used to rain forests, not sharp … *NO!* Put me *DOWN!*"

But I'm already slung over his shoulder, my head bobbing in the air like a pumpkin. "If we're going to get back before everyone awakes," he says, "then we need to pick up the pace."

"Then I'll pick up the pace!" I practically scream. He is too close. His skin is too close. And I can't push away without touching him. "Put me down! I mean it!"

"Fine." He lowers me to the river, but I miscalculate and stumble backward into the water. I scramble to my feet, ignoring the muddy rush of river from my shorts. He just stands there, hands in pockets, eyebrows raised. "Better?" he says.

"Ach!" I glare at him, and then turn down the river.

We continue on. I try to hide my limp as I walk as quickly as I can toward the waterfall.

"I've been meaning to tell you," he calls after a while. His voice has laughter in it.

"What's that?" I say without turning.

"Happy belated birthday."

I keep walking. I will not turn around.

"Wasn't it your birthday a while ago? I haven't had a chance to speak to you since …."

"The parasail debacle," I offer, still stomping through the water. "And I wouldn't say you haven't had a *chance* to speak to me. More like purposefully *not* speaking."

"You could be right."

I grit my teeth. It takes two to be toyed with, and I know the best way to handle this is to not respond at all. But I can't help it. I have to ask. "And how did you know about my birthday?"

"Oh, Krikorian's records, I suppose. He must have left them on the desk."

"Must have," I say, turning to catch his reaction. "There couldn't possibly be any other reason."

He smiles. "Can't think of one."

I try to hide my frustration and continue on with my march.

"Did you get anything?" he resumes politely. I hear his steps just behind me, and it occurs to me that I'm actually being herded, the threat of his presence goading me into a faster pace. Like a cow. "Anything from the mission?"

"That's not really ... the arrangement," I mumble, pausing mid-step. Then I lunge forward again. "And how do you know about the mission?"

He is walking beside me now, glancing down at the river. Sunlight grazes over his temple, hitting his dark lashes, and then his eyes slide up, catching mine. His irises glow lighter in the sunlight. I mean to look away. But it is almost as if they change color as we speak, shifting from teal to sea green. Alive and yet, at the same time, there is something about them that seems still. Like they are waiting for something. Oh, my God. I'm totally staring. I glare down at my feet.

"I know about the mission just like everyone else knows about it," he answers – a little too easily, I think. "You were famous at PACA before you ever got there, didn't you know? You should have heard Krikorian when he found out you were coming. He's read all about Dr. Jean's work there; from what I gather, it's been featured a few times in various magazines. *National Geographic,* even."

"Fifteen years ago," I say, peering up at him. But he is impossible to read. "Not exactly recent news. And he's still researching the medicinal properties of the Tuafi tree, so it's anticlimactic by now; everyone's lost interest. But I'm glad you brought Dr. Jean up. I've been meaning to ask: that day in Torundi … where did you go after I left?"

Gabe keeps walking. "I suppose I made my way back to my campsite. Why?"

"Because Dr. Jean and the Dyeens couldn't find any trace of you. No footprints, no leopard, no anything. Definitely no campsite. Now why would you have gone to all that trouble?"

He stops. The friendly smile vanishes. "This isn't a game, Sam. I've admitted to being there, just like you asked. But if you love your home as much as I think you do, you and I can not speak of this; we can't speak *like* this, ever again. Do you understand?"

I step back a little, stunned by the chill that feels more like a slap. My eyes narrow. "So why are you speaking to me now?"

His lips tighten. And then he resumes his walk through the river, quickening his stride. Soon he is a good ten or so feet away.

"Fine," I call, splashing after him. I wrack my head for something to ask, something to keep him talking. Any information at all is better than what I have right now. "But since you know about my birthday, then I should know about yours. That's only fair, right? So how old are you?"

"Then you'll let it drop?" He pauses, his eyes locked on mine. I am not sure if I nod or not. He smirks and resumes his stroll. "Better pick it up, Clemens."

My face is hot again and it isn't from the sun. "You owe me one answer at least!" I sputter after him.

"Nineteen."

I blink, now sloshing up to his side. "What?"

"My age. I'm nineteen."

"That's … that's way too young to be a graduate student!"

"I'm an overachiever," he shrugs, still walking.

I glare down at the river. "In *marine biology*."

"Exactly. It also helps that I told Krikorian I was twenty-four."

"But your references! I thought you—"

"Oh, look, what a pity. Time's up."

I raise my head. The waterfall is before us.

"I'll wait for you up there," he says, gesturing to the bluff above. "You'll want to rinse off the rest of that mud. You can return the shirt later today. Or toss it, whatever suits you."

He moves so easily; he's up the hill in a few, lazy strides.

I only realize I'm staring again when he glances back at me, impatient. I quickly look away, catching my reflection in the little pool instead. I look terrible. My neck, arms and legs are still crusted with muck. And my hair looks like electrocuted peanut butter.

I slip into the pool and let the water wash over me. I sink below its surface, face down, stretching out my arms and legs so that I suspend in its medium. The coolness is soothing. I feel calmer here, safe even. And I suddenly wish the water could fill up whatever it is that twists inside me; I wish it could numb that void and that ache, that sense of not belonging. But, technically, aren't those contradictory feelings? I mean, can you have an ache and a void at the same time? Shouldn't one negate the other? I suppose so. But I feel them all anyway. Always. And I wish I could flood it all out with this cool, calm stillness; wash it away so that I will not care, so that things might be simple. Maybe then I would be free.

I open my eyes and sink deeper and deeper. The morning sun dapples blues and greens, waving beams of light inside that watery world, flicking here and there between the shadows. *We all put on facades, Clemens …* weren't those his words? Yes, I think in reply. The mud dissolves into faint clouds as I move my arms and legs. My hair bends like seaweed before my eyes.

Even with myself. I know that now.

I shove back to the surface and crawl onto the rocky lip, wringing the water from me in the process. I look down at the hem of his shirt in my hands.

"Ready," I say. And then I make my way to the bluff.

8. VICHYSSOISE

The rest of our trip finishes as it began; the skies punish us with sun or pound us with rain. The waters slurp and jostle against our canoe, rocking it back and forth to the moans of my crew members.

On the sixth day, we pass under Penang Bridge, floating by garbage and carcasses of bloated rats, and the stench combined with the awful rocking makes almost everyone throw up. The smell sickens me, too, but I clamp my lips shut. I won't do it. I look ahead, always to the horizon, focusing on the flat, still line where sky touches sea.

The whole way home, I sit with my back to Gabe, unable to see him. I think again of that day in Torundi, when I first met him without knowing it. After all this time, it is strange to finally have his acknowledgement. But it doesn't make me feel how I expected; instead, more questions erupt in that place where only one used to be. I am grateful for the exhaustion, for the constant pull and drag of my paddle; it seems that the rhythm helps still my mind, helps me pull through the *why's* and the *what's* and the *how's* until I can sort out the ones I should keep.

On the seventh day, we pass Rat Island – a tiny, rocky piece of land that holds a lighthouse and not much else – before heading toward the seawall of PACA. Thoughts of showers, warm food and clean, soft beds propel us onward. Half a kilometer from shore, Sandy breaks into song. It is the Canadian anthem, and soon everyone is singing.

We stumble out of our canoe and splash into the tide. With one last effort, we heave our vessel onto dry ground. Tommy starts kissing the sand. Annie dances about in the shallows. Someone else shouts "Ahoy!" and another person answers, "Hark!"

Everyone is laughing.

I am untying the plankton samples when Caleb grabs the back of my shirt and pulls me to the ground. "We made it!" he croons jubilantly.

"Yeah."

It is all I can think to say. I sit back up and shuffle sand from my hair.

"What's the point?" laughs Tess, throwing my postal sack at me. "It's like shaking dirt out of a mud puddle. We're all disgusting."

"Group photo!" calls Ms. Hobbs.

I watch her as she organizes us once more around the canoe, considering her in a new light. She is young – no older than twenty-two or twenty-three, I'd guess – and she is pretty. Not beautiful, but pretty. Pretty in a way that men seem to like, with a nice figure and nice features and nothing too unusual. And she's always so upbeat, so sure in her role, whatever that is. Not like me.

I clasp my bag of plankton to my chest.

The shutter clicks.

We disband and I grab my sack of stinky clothes for the last time. I climb up to the seawall and make my way to the dorm, leaving my canoe-mates still reveling on the shore. Somehow, I don't feel like celebrating. And I can't look at him.

Two more weeks pass.

Gajendra keeps me busy with his preparations for Thanksgiving. As for Tess and EJ, a lot has happened since our canoe trip.

To begin with, EJ and Tommy are now dating; I totally missed it, but the romance apparently bloomed over the course of the canoe trip. It started after he asked her to the Christmas Ball, which is, from everything I've been told, the biggest event of the year. And then Tess is seeing someone named Aaron, an Australian traveling around Asia with his friends. They'd met last weekend at Batu, but since dorm students are strictly forbidden from socializing with anyone outside PACA, their relationship has to be kept a secret.

Between the two of them, it is a miracle I get any sleep at night. But at least their boyfriends keep them distracted, leaving me to ruminate in solitude the mystery that is only becoming more entangled with time.

I don't know what to do.

A part of me wants to break my silence and contact the mission. I have a right to, don't I? Maybe even an obligation. There is something important about Torundi that Gabriel-faux-Jones is hiding, and whatever it is, it isn't good. He more or less said so himself.

And he also knows about Dr. Jean's work, which indicates an interest in the mission. So is that it? Could it be something tied to Dr. Jean's research? It wouldn't be such a far-fetched idea after all. GMS is one of the most remote pharmaceutical research facilities in the world – purposefully so, because of the indigenous flora there. Plants like the Tuafi tree and the Heila'a bush have unique applications unidentified elsewhere, properties we're still discovering ourselves.

I twist paper in my hands. Why hadn't I asked more insistently about that before? I wish I could go back to that day in the river. I want nothing more than to be able to confront him properly this time.

But Jones ensures that will never happen. I never see him now except during science class, and in that hour he stays as far away from me as possible. There's no way I can approach him without drawing attention to myself, and besides, his warning still rings in my ears:

If you love your home as much as I think you do, you and I can not speak of this ….

I don't contact the mission, either. Instead I lie awake each night and fold paper objects for our ceiling fan mobile.

It used to help calm me.

I've made so many shapes at this point that my mobile sags from the menagerie. Tonight, I've just finished a crescent moon and I pin it up as my roommates chatter below, the sound of their voices blurring with the hum of the ceiling fan, the whimsical shapes flying in circles above me: frogs, beetles, birds, orchids … all of them swirling questions. And the biggest question of all is one I haven't asked – one I don't even know yet – but I sense it there, like a splinter under skin. Every day, it grows and festers.

I stare up at my mobile, my mind racing with the flying shapes that turn to dreams if sleep will ever come. I may be going crazy. I do not know what to believe anymore. Sometimes I wonder if Torundi really exists, or how it could be that I once lived there. It is too far away from this life here, a universe away; it seems unnatural for one human to have existed in both realities. Unnatural that I should be capable of it.

My eyes search the darkness for something to hold on to, something that is real. But all I see is a mad blur of shapes spinning chants in my head – like my paper boar and water buffalo, spinning and spinning. And a badly made windmill, because the world turns too fast. Next comes an egret, a swordfish and a frog, and I wonder how they fit together … three rhinoceros beetles glinting in the gloom. But then a bat flies by with a dragonfly, flitting in their secrets … while a clouded leopard crouches in wait . . . under a banyan tree, in a rickshaw, orchids everywhere, zoom, zoom, zoom.

A parachute floats by.

But the questions keep spinning and the blur does not stop. The speedboat does not stop, nor does the canoe. Churning and turning, the *why's* will not stop, the *how's* will not stop, the darkness can not stop.

Not for my paper moon.

The morning of our Thanksgiving feast arrives with perfect weather. Technically, it isn't actually Thanksgiving because it is Sunday, but since Sunday works best for such a big event, PACA always pushes the holiday back.

Gajendra takes the occasion very seriously. It is the one time every year, he has explained to me, when the campus opens its gates to anyone who wishes to participate. Locals, tourists, students and staff are all invited to join in the celebration. He needs all the hands available, so I get permission from Aunt Janie to help him in the kitchen during church service.

In honor of the holiday, I pull out the one piece of clothing I have that isn't from a pile of donations: a sleeveless, blue linen dress Nurse Kathy made for me as a parting gift. It's a bit lopsided, but a valiant achievement nonetheless. There's a reason why we all subsist off donated clothes.

I slip the material over my head and the smell of our mission's soap hits me: a mixture of candlenut and coconut oils, lye, fern leaf extract and a hint of frangipani.

I blink, feeling silly.

I've never thought about our soap until now.

I used to complain about it because we use it for everything: showers, laundry – we even dissolve it with a little lime juice for our dishes. I remember the day Trudy taught me how to make it. She wore rubber gloves up to her elbows and stood among containers arranged around the burner in the common room while Wagner played on the mission's record player in the background. She called it our soap opera day. I didn't get it.

"We use candlenut and coconut oil for their moisturizing properties," she explained, patting the vats beside her. I remember the swell of *Parsifal* drowning out her voice for a moment, but she didn't turn the music down. She just grinned and spoke more loudly. "They also provide natural UV protection, like our fern leaf. And the one over here is lye. We'll mix it with water and then add the solution to our oils. It reacts with the fats to help form the soap – but be careful or it will burn your skin." She wiggled her gloved fingers in the air then and pointed to a sealed bottle. "Fern leaf extract over there for its chemophotoprotective elements – Dr. Jean's little addition …."

"And frangipani because it's your favorite," I finished, grabbing the small vial.

She smiled at that and said, "Yes. Also, it contains anti-inflammatory qualities, which help with Nurse Kathy's rosacea …."

I blink into the mirror. That was almost eight years ago.

But the smell of the mission soap makes that day feel so recent that my eyes ache from the memory. Strange how a scent can do that.

And I wonder if Trudy's back from New York yet. Surely she'd write to tell me. My eyes water more and the ache swells up, sending quivers to my lower lip. I glare at the girl in the mirror.

No. Stop it. Gajendra's waiting.

It's around ten in the morning when I reach the kitchen. Gajendra's busy explaining something in exasperated tones to a new cook named Saul while the rest of the kitchen staff run between bubbling pots. Everyone's shouting in different languages – mostly a combination of English, Malay and Hindi. The ceiling fans shudder overhead and the windows are flung open to the sea, but neither helps dissipate the heat. I run a hand over my hair. I already know it's no use.

I walk over to the cupboard and grab a white apron, sliding the neckpiece over my head and wrapping the ties about my waist. I hate it – it's too big for me, but Gajendra insists we wear them. And I know that between my frizzed head and this mop of an apron, I must look like the world's most unfortunate Q-tip.

Within an hour and a half, most of the preparations are simmering on the back burners. There are ten huge turkeys in the oven, two vats stuffed with mashed potatoes, a ten-gallon cauldron steaming with corn bread stuffing, three gigantic pans of sweet potato casserole, cranberry sauce galore, baskets of fresh baked rolls, a broccoli and cauliflower medley with a thick delicious cheese sauce, boats and boats of piping hot gravy and a chilled potato-leek soup called *vichyssoise* that Gajendra claims is haute cuisine.

At five till twelve, church lets out and the remaining student wait-staff filter through the various cafeteria doors. I scurry about with last-minute preparations as Gajendra screams orders in the kitchen. From what I can pick out, a chilled salad has gone awry. I shudder, thankful I'm only responsible for the dining area.

And then, the Thanksgiving feast begins. The entire hall buzzes with chatter and I've never seen so many people gathered together in one place. I feel a little nervous, but that is probably because I am now staggering through the cafeteria, balancing an enormous tray of turkey over my shoulder.

I make it safely to my first table, pleasantly surprised to see Sandy and my roommates there. I am even more surprised when I notice that, sitting beside them as if they are all meeting each other for the very first time, are Aaron and his friends Guy and Pete. I thought they were supposed to be away this weekend – to Karachi or something. But Tess looks delighted they're here and that's all that really matters. I stab turkey onto all the plates at the table and then scurry to the next one, my head still swimming with Gajendra's pre-feast orders.

Julie sits at the second table with Zach, Alistair and another girl I don't know; I think her name is Maggie. I lower my tray toward her as I take count of my other patrons. And then I almost dump Gajendra's tray of beautifully braised bird on the floor when I spot Jones five seats over. Suddenly I feel like I've just swallowed an annual supply of cotton balls.

After two weeks and two days of completely ignoring me, acting as though our encounter in the river never happened, never even having the courtesy to nod or smile or otherwise acknowledge my existence in the lab ... after all of that, and out of all the tables in this huge dining room, *why* must he land at one of *mine?*

Stage One.

My pulse picks up at the thought. And what catastrophe does this imply? No, no, it is just coincidence. It means nothing. I straighten up and serve Julie. I won't let him get to me. He *can't* get to me.

Besides, I'm not even sure if he's aware that he is, in fact, sitting at my table. He's dressed in slacks and a white button-down shirt rolled up to mid forearm and is smiling over at an exceptionally pleased fifth-grade English teacher. Clearly they are here together. Of course they are. I force my attention back to the turkey platter and begin my round of humiliation.

"What a darling little waitress we have!" coos Ms. Hobbs as I place two slices on her plate. I blink between her plate and her perfectly groomed head. Ms. Hobbs: all big eyes and curved lips.

Darling little waitress.

With my frizzy hair, misshapen dress and ridiculous, over-sized apron, holding a prong of turkey meat. Such a comment wouldn't sting so much coming from someone older, but from a female only a few years older than me it feels ....

Well it doesn't matter. This is Gajendra's big day and I'm going to do him proud. So I smile back at her and then turn to Gabe.

"Three slices, please," he says.

I flick the turkey to his plate. I can ignore people, too.

I turn to the person next to him and am relieved to see Uncle Bob dressed in a tight polyester shirt and a clip-on tie that makes even my wardrobe look trendy. I plunk a generous portion of turkey onto his plate and move on.

As the banquet proceeds, I make it a point to avoid looking at Jones. I unload casserole, stuffing, cranberry sauce, fruit salad and vegetables without casting a single glance in his direction. I have just transferred the mashed potatoes to the table and am reaching for the gravy boat when I hear muttering.

"...could she be any slower?" Jones is saying, and I realize everyone at the table except Uncle Bob, Zach and Julie are trying not to laugh. But that's just because Zach and Julie are already sniggering and Uncle Bob is too engrossed in his cranberry sauce to notice anything else. "My turkey's developing staph over here and we're just now getting the sides!"

"Don't be so rude – she's doing a great job," whispers Ms. Hobbs, but it's hard to take her seriously when she's grinning at him like that.

It takes some doing, but I calmly place the gravy on the table. I refuse to react. Besides, I know I'm serving just as quickly as everyone else – I'd like to see *him* haul all this food out any faster. But Jones has other ideas.

"If it isn't too much trouble," he continues, and that sneering tone is in it, "would you bring Ms. Hobbs some more iced tea?"

"Oh … me, too, please," chimes Julie. At least she's polite about it.

"I don't know how they serve tables where *she* comes from," Jones adds loudly as I turn away to locate a pitcher, "but here, it is generally considered rude to dehydrate one's patrons."

The table titters with laughter.

That does it.

He is behaving exactly as I'd described to him that night in the cave. Only this time, he's skipped a stage – the one where he does something nice before turning into a jerk. I grab a tea pitcher, fill everyone's glasses and place it on the table.

"Stage Three," I hiss, glaring at him.

"Good," he smiles, popping a cauliflower into his mouth, "because Stage Four is my favorite."

I don't know what happens next, not exactly. I am aware of being back in the kitchen, where I scan Gajendra's menu by the prep line. One item left to go. I recall lugging the tureen out to the cafeteria and ladling soup into bowls. I recall hearing Sandy ask me something. I think she is wondering if I am okay. I hear Guy mumble something to me, too, but I'm not sure what, if anything, I say in response because I am already at the next table. I ladle out a portion into Julie's bowl, and then into Zachary's. I serve Alistair and the girl I don't know.

I move on to Janet Hobbs and scoop a portion into her bowl. She murmurs a dreamy thanks, her gaze never straying from its current fixation.

I scoop up another portion.

"Vichyssoise?" I offer.

Jones glances at me for a moment and then returns his attention back to Hobbs, as though indicating that I have interrupted their turkey dinner romance.

That is all the incentive I need.

A steady emulsion of leek and potato flows from my ladle – like one of those fondue fountains I've seen advertised – oozing soup over his head, now dripping down his face and ending in the lap of his pants.

"And *that's* how we serve things where *I* come from!"

I am dimly aware of Ms. Hobbs's wail. I move toward Uncle Bob, but he tells me he doesn't want any soup. Neither does his wife, Aunt Anne. I shrug and wander back to the kitchen, now listening to the hubbub coming from the dining room.

I hear Gajendra behind me. He's asking me what has happened; I think he thinks I might be ill. When I turn and look up at him, his concern vanishes.

"That is bad, Sam," he says with a gasp, his eyes narrowing. "That is very, very bad!"

He grabs a bundle of linens and dashes out of the kitchen, scurrying toward my second table, apologizing the whole way, insisting Gabe come with him to the kitchen to get cleaned up. At first Gabe protests, saying it is nothing to make such a fuss over, but between Hobbs's wails and Gajendra's dabbing, he finally agrees to accept help.

I slip behind the kitchen door as he is tugged through it and led straight to the industrial sink. He's already got his face more or less wiped down, but potato chunks fall from his clothes as he passes.

"Um, Jones," I say with a smirk, grabbing a giant leek from the counter, "I think you forgot this?"

He doesn't react.

Gajendra, on the other hand, whips around. His expression freezes the grin on my face.

"You!" he roars, marching toward me. "You have just single-handedly destroyed the whole festivity. What were you thinking? Dousing a man with chilled soup!"

"I … don't know what came over me," I say, dropping the leek, but Gajendra looks like he just might cry. "I'll make it up to you, okay?" I add. "Besides, it's just Mr. Jones. Everyone else is having a great time—"

"Just Mr. Jones!" Gajendra wails, throwing up his hands. "He is one of the few people who did not have to dine here today, and yet he chose *my* kitchen instead of all the restaurants of Penang to celebrate his Thanksgiving dinner!"

"Thank you, Gajendra," Gabe says.

"I don't think he's even American," I say.

"And what do we do in return?" Gajendra continues, his arms waving in the air. "We spill *vichyssoise* right down his articles of clothing!"

"I'll deal with this," says Gabe, taking the wad of linens from Gajendra's hand. "Don't let it spoil your banquet. I'll take her outside before she soup bombs the rest of them. She can rinse out the towels for me."

"Yes, and give her a good talking to!" cries Gajendra.

Gabe glances down at his slacks.

"Certainly."

This pacifies Gajendra somewhat, but it does nothing for me. I start to protest and then notice that all of the cooks are standing around, wide-eyed. Gajendra stomps off.

"You'd better go," one of the cooks says. "I've never seen Gaj so angry before."

Faux-Jones murmurs, "You heard the man," and then he takes my elbow. His hold is firm, his fingers wrapping all the way around my arm, and I know that if I try to twist away, I'll fail. So I walk with him as he escorts me out of the kitchen's side door and toward the far left of the seawall, where a small gate used by the cooks is open. He walks through it, pulling me along. Sand catches in my sandals.

We pass an old fisherman who sits on the beach, repairing a net. His gaze rests for a moment on Gabe's clothing before he politely looks away. We keep walking past scrubby oaks and palm trees, toward a rain tank that stands in the lot adjacent to the lower campus.

When we reach it, he finally lets go of my arm. I march over to a tree stump and sit down. He leans against the tank and says nothing for a good sixty seconds, but I enjoy that actually. The evidence of my retaliation is still wonderfully apparent.

He turns on the tap at the base of the tank and wets the dishtowels in his hand.

Then he says, "That wasn't very mature."

I snort. "How do you think *you've* been acting?"

"I know. I think I was …." He pauses and looks around again. He shakes his head. And then he adds, very slowly, "Do you remember our conversation that day in the river, just before we returned to camp?"

My head snaps up. What a question.

He glances toward the beach. "Remember when I told you that I couldn't tell you the truth?"

As if I'd ever forget – as if my sleep-deprived brain and circled eyes and cranky disposition evidence I've thought of much else.

"Do you still want to know?"

I nearly fall right off my tree stump. I recover and say, "What do you think?"

He dabs uselessly at his clothes.

"Tonight then," he says, and those two words hit me like a lightning bolt. "Can you get past the campus gate without being seen?"

"I … think so."

He splashes water over his hair and face.

"Good. Six-thirty, by the new hotel, the Nuevostar. I'll have a taxi there for you – you'll know it by the hibiscus hanging from the mirror."

"And … you'll tell me why you were in Torundi?" I manage, my voice barely a whisper.

"Yes." He turns off the water. "We need to go now. The staff are probably wandering what's happened to us."

He walks off, still dabbing at his clothes. I stumble after him, barely able to keep up. My legs feel like rubber. I am suspicious of this entire conversation.

We reach the gate.

He pauses and, when he looks at me, his expression assumes its earlier composure. I wish I could do that. Like masks thrown off and on.

"One more thing," he says, his voice still. It is so quiet I must turn my head and lean in to hear him. "Please don't mention any of this to your roommates, for any reason."

I frown up at him. "I wouldn't do that. You can trust me, you know."

"Not to serve me soup," he mutters, pushing the linens into my hands. I roll my eyes. "But what I mean is, you're being listened to. Your room is bugged, Sam."

He walks away before I can find my voice. I'm still standing there when he disappears into the cafeteria. Gajendra stalks outside and flips a dish towel over his shoulder, glancing from my face to the wad of linens in my hands.

"I can see that there was a good talking to!" he concludes, and then marches back to his kitchen.

9. REVELATIONS

That evening can not come soon enough.

By 6:15, I make my way southwest, toward the old fire pool. I slip through the narrow gate to the pool while the watchman chats with someone entering campus.

I scurry over to the bushes.

The concrete wall is a bit lower here and there is a ledge just behind a clump of gardenias, making it possible to climb from it to the top of the wall. I'd found it by accident a month ago when Sandy was trying to teach me disc golf.

In a matter of seconds, I am on the other side. I hug the shadowy edge of grass that follows the wall and then dart west toward the new hotel. When I reach it, I try to appear as inconspicuous as a high school girl wandering alone on a Sunday night outside a fancy hotel can possibly look.

I scan the area for taxis.

I've never noticed until now how popular flowers are with taxi drivers. I see three or four drivers trolling the circular drive in front of the hotel – all of them with pretty little wreaths dangling from their windows.

One of the taxis slows to a stop; it has a Lat sticker, a common enough cartoon here, on the left side of its bumper, but then I notice the single red hibiscus tucked neatly behind the rearview mirror. My pulse roars in my ears.

I stare at the taxi.

The driver stares at me.

I do not know this man, of course. And I also do not know Gabe, not really. I have no idea who he *really* is, and even less of an idea of what I am getting myself into. I know that what I am doing is foolish and irresponsible. But my gut says to go.

I open the door and slide in.

My pulse pounds harder.

We rumble down Tanjung Bungah Road in the general direction of Gurney Drive and Georgetown. About five minutes after passing Hillside, the taxi slows and I see a bus stop to my right with a large apartment complex behind it. The driver then veers left, bumping down a small, dirt road headed to nowhere.

The road begins to open and, minutes later, I notice with some surprise that we're passing an outdoor amphitheater festooned with red Chinese lanterns and paper-mache dragons. I can hear the sounds of an opera revving up for a show. A player comes out in an elaborate costume, bathed in golden light, but we rumble on before I can observe anything else.

Soon the taxi stops. We are in a wide, open space.

Banyan trees circle around us and, to one side, an outdoor eating area is set up. Various stalls burn kerosene lamps and waft out delicious aromas of fried noodles and char-grilled seafood.

To the far right of the clearing, about halfway between our taxi and the beach, a round cement tower rises from the ground. It is clearly unoccupied and partially open to the elements – perhaps another vestige from World War Two. Beyond the tower, the beach curves down to the sea. The sea is dark and can not be seen from where we are, but I can hear the steady sound of waves against shore.

I turn my gaze back to the banyans.

A little gibbon sporting a red and gold vest hops under one of the trees, tugging at his leash. A vendor, presumably the gibbon's owner, is tying the leash to one of the banyan's enormous roots, and he turns at the sound of the taxi, regarding us in silence for several seconds. I look away.

The taxi driver clears his throat and then points toward the beach. "That way," he says.

My heartbeat swells into my throat, into my ears, into my head.

What am I … boom, doom … doing?

I am opening the door. I am leaving the taxi. I am walking past the vendor and the little gibbon, past the circle of kiosks, past the cluster of tables and chairs ….

Boom, boom, boom.

The sound of ocean waves grows dominant. My pulse calms. I blink into the darkness. It is difficult to see now that the lights are behind me.

Gradually, things come into focus. The beach is empty, but I can see another fort-like structure farther down the way. This one is a good bit smaller and square, with a wide, terrace-like landing overlooking the waves below.

I walk toward it. Sand flicks from my flip-flops, sticking to the soles of my feet as, in the distance, the sharp cries of the Chinese opera wail into the night. The opera keeps a strange rhythm with the steady, lapping tide. And everywhere, the smell of salt and seaweed wafts in the breeze. It is pleasant, comforting even. I breathe it in and keep walking.

I follow the crumbling steps that lead into the fort. It is even darker here; the thick, cement walls and ceiling close around me. I look toward the open terrace on the opposite side of the room, where the walls end but the roof continues to project from above, and I can see the moonlight breaking from the clouds.

"You came," floats his voice. It makes me jump. I look around, but I can not see him. "I had begun to hope that you wouldn't."

"And you're not from Missouri," I blurt nervously into the black. I frown and hold my breath for a moment, trying to control the pounding. "Mark Twain was from Missouri," I explain. I can make out his frame now. He moves away from the far wall, toward the terrace. The moonlight falls over the left side of his face so I can at least catch some expression.

That helps. "You said he was a hero in your hometown. I assumed you must be from where he was from or something. But you are definitely *not* from Missouri."

He turns to face the ocean.

I walk to the terrace and stop beside him. Waves crash against the foundation below and, as the water churns, tiny pinpoints of blue shimmer for a moment and then are gone. *Bioluminescence*, I remember Dr. Jean teaching me. *"No one ever thinks about it in the sea,"* he'd said. *"It is always the fireflies that captivate ...."*

My eyes follow up the fort wall and come to rest on Gabe's hands. He stands so still, so easy, but his fingers grip into concrete so that the tendons pop like spokes.

We are here for the truth.

And I have two hours and one minute before curfew to get it.

"So I'm here, my room's bugged and you're not from Missouri," I say as calmly as I can. "You're not a Mr. Jones and not really a science student. You do have some other reason for being here, and you also happen to speak at least two other languages. So far, I've counted Torundi and what I think was Cantonese, but maybe it was Mandarin – I really wouldn't know. That's about all I've got."

He shifts so the moonlight falls away, leaving him once again in darkness. His silence annoys me.

"What's your *real* name?" I say.

"Gabriel Degen," he replies without pause, and the sound of his voice saying his real name goes through me. Focus.

"German?"

"Swiss," he corrects. "At least, that is where my boyhood home was."

"Swiss," I echo. I hadn't thought of that.

"I am going to explain this only once, Sam, so please keep up," he says, and his words are now measured – clean and flat. Like a machine stamping metal. It sounds so cold next to the storm in my veins.

"I am here because I work for an international company called UnMonde," he continues. I hold my breath again, forcing the pounding to quiet. "It is an extremely prestigious organization that remains unknown to most. This is intentional. Their business ranges from offshore investing to political strategy services to energy production. Whatever UnMonde chooses to undertake, it is always done with such immense discretion that no one would notice their mark on any affair, much less be aware of their existence …." He pauses. "As you can imagine, they are extremely selective in choosing their clients."

I blink for a moment, stunned. I hadn't imagined anything of the sort. And I am not sure I believe him.

"UnMonde has a foundation that serves as its nonprofit arm," he resumes. "It also provides a convenient venue to engage in activities that might otherwise be called into question. Since I was very young I've been trained by this company – I was brought in as one of their youngest recruits. They saw promise in me and, in return, I received the best education, the best training, and all the comforts any person from my humble beginnings could ever hope for. I went from having nothing to having whatever money could buy, whatever education could give."

He turns somewhere in the shadows. I wait, my mind racing with questions.

"It was not until several months ago – ten, to be exact – that I was included in their current plan. Or at least brought closer to it. At that time, it was revealed to me that a certain project they'd been working on for years had finally come to fruition. It involved an amazing discovery and a mechanism that was so elegant, it would change the world as we know it. All they needed was an obscure resource no one had ever heard of and then ...." I can hear the grimace in his voice. "And then, the sky's the limit. For UnMonde, that is."

My arms prickle at those words. I hear him move, and now the moonlight glances off his forehead. He looks over the water as he speaks.

"Four of us were assigned to obtain this resource. We were sent to a remote little spot in the Pacific, a place UnMonde's charitable arm has been managing for nearly twenty years. It was my first real mission."

The goose bumps spread everywhere.

"Apparently, our location just happened to have the largest deposit of this substance known in the world. It had been discovered years before, quite by accident, during a site visit for a medical research client. It was during this expedition that a local guide led UnMonde's representative to an ancient crater deep in the jungle – most likely a meteor site, but the people there consider it to be holy." His gaze flicks to me, his jaw set. The words come out calm and direct, straight as a fold in origami, when he says, "Do you know it?"

I take a step backward. Of course. I know Torundi's holy site so well that my memory of it is as clear as a photograph. Dr. Jean and I used to go there all the time when we'd visit the outer villages ….

"The Tanah Yatim," I whisper, calling the site by its local name. His eyes stay on mine as I speak. "How … how do you know the Tanah Yatim has what you're looking for?"

"Because UnMonde's representative brought a sample back all those years ago," answers Gabe, returning his gaze to the sea. "When they realized what it contained, UnMonde's focus, their projects, everything they engaged in changed."

"What …?" I clear my throat, trying to keep my voice from squeaking. "What was in the sample?"

"The most expensive and rarest substance known on earth," he says. "Concentrated levels of the isomer Tantalum-180m, to be more specific. Currently valued at seventeen million for a *single gram*. But it is the rarity that is truly astounding. The entire world's supply – up until now – has only been a few *milligrams*."

I have no idea how to respond to that.

"But here's where things get interesting," Gabe continues. "Tantalum's potential has only been calculated assuming its limited supply coupled with its unstable nature. Even with that, it is believed that one kilogram stores 900 mega joules of energy – an impressive sum. But if that output could be increased and controlled, its power is so complete that, in theory, its uses are limitless. There is *nothing* matched to its possibilities."

I let this sink in for a moment.

"And the way to control the release of this energy . . .," I say.

"Is what UnMonde has been working on for nearly two decades," Gabe finishes for me.

"And now they've figured it out?"

"And now they have. But the story is not finished just yet."

I swallow hard and turn to the ledge, listening for a moment to the rhythmic lapping of waves. The air is cooler now, and it is silly to suppose, but it feels as though I am somehow touched by the moon – that its fingers are reaching in, chilling my blood to silver. I take another breath and then face him. He too, looks changed, the tan of his skin turned to marble. Just like his expression. Just like the tone of his voice.

"Okay," I say.

He nods.

"Our story returns to nineteen years ago, when UnMonde first discovered the tantalum. As soon as they understood the resource at their disposal, it became their priority, as I said. UnMonde's first course of action was to grow their presence in Torundi without its motivation for doing so becoming known. They knew that, if they ever hoped to gain total control over the island's resource, then Sultan Djadrani, or anyone else for that matter, could never learn the truth. It should have been easy enough; UnMonde – or rather, one of its NGO subsidiaries – was already in the process of establishing a medical research project there …."

"GMS," I whisper, stunned by the revelation.

Gabe nods again. "It was a different time in Torundi then. The queen had just passed away; the king had been deceased for twelve years. In the absence of an heir, Djadrani had come into power. He was eager to reap the rewards of Torundi's unique resources, and medical research presented the potential for creating great wealth. It couldn't have been more perfect. The proposed objective from UnMonde's subsidiary was, of course, conclusive research regarding medicinal applications of select endemic plants, such as your Tuafi tree."

I nod slowly.

"Djadrani, despite his eagerness to exploit Torundi's resources, was notoriously suspicious of any foreign presence," Gabe continues. "Yet his vice outweighed his xenophobia. He was also a shrewd leader. He allowed UnMonde to develop a long-term presence in the kingdom on two conditions: First, that all property tied to the research facility become the possession of the Torundi government. And second, that a mission be established as well, offering medical care for the people … and himself, of course."

"So … UnMonde recruited Dr. Jean and Nurse Kathy."

"Yes. Kathy was already retired when she applied for the post. She was looking for meaning in her life, a little adventure where she could incorporate her skills. In exchange for room and board, she agreed to be the caretaker, more or less, and helped set up the clinic. And Dupuy was the perfect fit for UnMonde's purpose: a young, idealistic doctor – with a background in biochemistry – fresh out of residency, who thought he was only doing a two-year loan payback program."

"*Two* years!"

Gabe shrugs. "UnMonde had plans for recruiting similar professionals on a rotational basis, luring them with scholarships in exchange for a few years of indentured servitude at their idyllic little mission tucked away on a tropical island. They didn't anticipate having much difficulty filling the post."

"But …."

"But after two years, Dr. Jean Dupuy simply chose to stay," Gabe says. "Of course, this made things easier for UnMonde. From what I've been able to gather, when Torundi fell under Djadrani's administration, the sultan made it almost impossible for Westerners to enter the kingdom. And then, of course, the purge that occurred a few years later didn't exactly make the mission appealing to potential recruits. Dupuy's decision and his friendship with Djadrani – whether genuine or merely a political ploy – could not have been more fortuitous. More years went by. Dupuy's mission became a fixture in Torundi, the only permanent Western presence tolerated by Djadrani. And then, UnMonde made its first attempt."

I am staring at the ground, trying to focus on his words without any distraction, but at this last part, I glance up.

"Attempt … at what?"

"Dr. Dupuy was approached by the representative of his sponsoring company. He had – and has – no idea that GMS is tied to UnMonde, of course. He and anyone else familiar with GMS believe your little island mission was formed as a special program sponsored by a charitable collective. And the representative of this sponsoring "collective" has always been Marcus – an operative of UnMonde. At any rate, Marcus asked Dupuy to use his connections to help … facilitate an agreement."

"For the Tanah Yatim?" I ask, incredulous.

"It was a bit more subtle than that," replies Gabe. "Marcus wanted Dupuy to use his friendship with the sultan to gain a charter that would essentially convey all rights of Torundi's holy site to a sister NGO involved in environmental conservation. Of course, environmental conservation wasn't exactly what UnMonde had in mind."

I think about that for a moment, feeling more than just a little bewildered. "What happened?"

"Dupuy refused," replies Gabe. "He stated that the sponsor's involvement of him was unethical; that he could not use his relationship with Djadrani to persuade or manipulate for outside interests."

"And … UnMonde just accepted that?"

Gabe leans back, dissolving once again into the darkness. "Remember, this was many years ago – they hadn't even discovered the means to effectively control the tantalum yet. So UnMonde decided to bide its time. Dr. Dupuy went on with his research, the mission went on with its mission, and all was well with the world. And then, not twelve months ago, UnMonde perfected their discovery. There was no longer any doubt: Tantalum-180m could be used in ways that, until that moment, had been beyond even their aspirations. Marcus was assigned the task of trying again with Dupuy, and again Dupuy refused. This time, they did not respond so casually. They even cut off funding, but he wouldn't waiver."

"But," I say, shaking my head, "we never stopped operations."

"At that point, the fixtures of your mission belonged to Djadrani anyway as a condition of the contract," Gabe reminds me. "So Dupuy knew that the mission and the assets therein were more or less out of his sponsors' reach. What he needed was money. He actually went to such lengths as to solicit other support to defray expenses while the mission reorganized. I can imagine that, in his remote circumstance, this took no small amount of effort. But somehow, the mission continued on." He pauses. "Are you still following?"

I realize I'm shaking my head when he asks that. I stop and nod instead.

"It was after this last attempt that my team was sent," Gabe continues. "UnMonde desperately needed insight into how to gain control over the Tanah Yatim while keeping our presence covert. We were to reconnaissance the situation there – political unrest, dynamics between groups such as the Dyeens or the Tagolis, issues with your mission, anything – and report back. It was at this time that I first became aware of you."

"The clouded leopard," I whisper.

He raises his brow in acknowledgement. "I was on my way back to our camp when I heard someone approaching that day," he says. "I slipped out of sight, and as soon as you came into view, I knew who you were. I couldn't use any weapons without giving my presence away. To be honest, I shouldn't have done anything. I'm not sure what propelled me to do what I did; the smart choice would have been to stay invisible."

I don't say anything to that. He's right.

Gabe looks over the water.

"After that – after you went back with news of a foreigner in the rain forest – Dupuy reacted like a man who knows he's watched. Maybe Marcus had approached him already while we were there, maybe he'd insinuated threats I was not privy to … I don't know. But I do know that Dupuy was prepared."

I squeeze my eyes shut for a moment. That helps a little. "How do you mean?"

"I mean Dupuy had planned the PACA contingency months before," says Gabe, "with the help of a friend from his medical school days, I gather, who has a connection there. But that night, after he and the Dyeens returned empty-handed from their search, he finalized your enrollment. It took us a few days to sleuth out where you were being sent."

This last bit smacks me out of my daze.

"So … that's why …," I sputter, struggling to control the emotions exploding inside me. I can't quite believe it. My original presumption that my banishment to PACA was directly tied to the foreigner in the rain forest that day – the same presumption I later accepted as a ruse to hide the unflattering truth that I was simply no longer wanted, that I was little more than a burden to the mission – *that* presumption, incredibly, had been correct after all, despite the fact that I'd had no grasp whatsoever of the actual motive behind it ... until now.

"I mean," I finally say, "the whole reason for sending me away, and the embargo on communicating with the mission … it's because of this! Dr. Jean is trying to *protect* me?"

Gabe's grimace returns. "He thinks he's sent you out of harm's way. What person in his situation would ever dream UnMonde would go as far as this? He realized we were after the Tanah Yatim, just not *why*. He probably thought the reason had something to do with his research."

"And then you were sent here?"

"It was a babysitting mission, really," he says with a shrug. "No one wanted to do it. So I volunteered, knowing it was my chance to prove myself, to show that I was ready. Besides, my age gave me a leg up."

"Babysitting ...."

"To keep track of you, yes. To report any information you may receive from the mission, to ensure your safety, to trace your whereabouts, to go where you go."

I feel my forehead tug together. "That seems like a lot of trouble to go to when I have nothing to do with any of this."

"That's where you're wrong," he replies. "A company like UnMonde takes no chances. The expense of sending me here is nothing to them – a drop in the bucket. But Dupuy's reaction when you reported a foreigner in the jungle that day wasn't. Now, they know what he's afraid of losing, what he wants to protect. You've become their shiny new pawn. They'll do whatever it takes to get what they want. And I'm here to help them get it, to make sure you stay in one piece … until they're ready to use you."

It is so casual, the way he says that.

"So." I clear my throat, instantly sobered. "So, if UnMonde wants to kidnap me or torture me or chop me up into little pieces …."

"I'm here to see it through."

I blink, barely able to take in what he is saying. "And my bugged dorm room …."

"Overkill, if you ask me, but it wasn't my decision. Just another way to keep tabs on you."

I'm gripping the edge of the veranda. "Is anything else wired?" I gulp, not caring that this should probably be the least of my concerns. "The science lab? My whole dorm? The cafeteria?"

"At your school? No."

I shake my head. This is too ridiculous to believe.

"And the night outside the Cathay Hotel …." I begin again, trying to make sense of it all, but it feels like the ground is warping under my feet, and the walls of the fort are warping with it. And I don't know if the rushing in my ears is from the waves or the wind or just the sound of shock flooding my brain.

"Contractors," he says. "We were discussing support needs that I might have, but after that evening . . . ." He trails off with another shrug. "Under the circumstances, it was better to offend your scavenger team than to invite their litany of questions."

My forehead tugs tighter and I shake my head, my mind chasing after a question I haven't asked. One that I *need* to ask because nothing about this conversation makes sense.

I turn to him. He continues to gaze out over the water, his hands once again on the veranda ledge.

"Why are you telling me all of this?" I say.

"Because you have under three weeks before you leave for Christmas vacation," he replies quietly. But he doesn't turn my way. In fact, he speaks as though he is reporting for duty, as though I'm a total stranger to be briefed on a subject.

"In the meantime, I may be here, I may be instructed to leave tomorrow. I have no way of knowing. So when you get back to Torundi, I want you to find a place away from the mission, a place no one else would know about, no one else would go to, and tell Dupuy what I've just told you. If he wants to save his mission – if he wants to save Torundi, for that matter – he needs to act now. I know my organization has been making other plans in the interim; I know time is running out for all of us, and I know that if UnMonde doesn't get what they want from Dupuy, they'll soon have another solution. One that will not require his presence in Torundi any longer."

I swallow. "Not *require?*"

"They'll stop at nothing, Sam. Do you understand that?" His voice is hard when he says it. "Your life, Dr. Jean's, even Djadrani's … they are all expendable. As is anyone else who gets in their way. They'll do whatever it takes to obtain what they want. And now that Dupuy knows what they want, UnMonde won't just allow him to carry on. He – and every other person involved – has become a liability."

That last word sinks in, slippery and smooth.

We both stand there, looking out at the sea. Neither of us speaks for several moments – for different reasons, I suspect. I'm trying to still the spinning in my head. I need to know what his reason is. "But why … why are *you* doing *this?*" I gesture limply around me, my mind racing with too many questions, but that one – that one of all – is the one I most need to know.

He straightens his tall frame, the light falling over him, and then he turns. "You need to go," he says.

"I don't—"

"You need to go," he says again. "Time's up, I'm afraid. The taxi's waiting for you."

I look around, confused.

"Tick, tock, Clemens."

"You just …." I try again, but his complete lack of emotion or empathy or anything resembling a normal human response unglues me. "You can't just dump a bomb like that and then tell me to *go away!* You just told me our lives are in danger! That Torundi is in danger! You just told me that *I* have to save the mission, Gabe! That the Tanah

Yatim and who knows what else might be destroyed if I don't somehow communicate all of this … this *craziness* to Dr. Jean! And you're just standing there like … like … *ACH!*" I throw my hands up, furious. He doesn't even have the courtesy to blink. "What's *wrong* with you?"

"Look, I know this has been quite a shock. I had hoped you'd be able to handle it. Regardless of how you may feel at the moment, Clemens, the fact remains that we've been too long as it is. The taxi will take you back to the Nuevostar. Please make sure you are careful returning to campus."

My face is flaming hot – I can feel it getting worse, too – and my ears are pounding again. I am too indignant to think straight, too confused to even respond, and the worst thing of all is that I feel the burning tingle under my eyes and at the sides of my nose, and I know that at any minute, I am actually going to cry.

"Fine!" I say, and then I stomp out of there before he can notice.

My eyes are full-on watery now.

The slope of the beach warps before me.

So I practically run toward those merry, twinkling kiosk lights, never looking back. I wipe my eyes just outside the circle of trees. I compose myself as best I can.

And then I get into the taxi.

10. ON THE ROCKS

Here is another *if:*

If I could have dreamed up the scenario I now find myself in, I would gladly accept that as an explanation. But I am not that creative. I think I peaked at origami.

I've never felt such a mixture of panic and confusion and anger. And I can not completely absorb the idea that a *company* could hold so much power. That they've gone to all this trouble for a resource my little kingdom has to offer. That, if Dr. Jean can not convince Djadrani to hand over the Tanah Yatim willingly, they'll find another way to get it – even at the cost of lives. It is all too bizarre for my head to put together just yet.

And then there's the other quandary chewing up my insides: Gabriel-faux-Jones-turned-Degen. It doesn't make sense. If he's telling the truth, then he just risked his career – possibly his life – to help a person he may end up having to kidnap or torture or maybe even kill. Why would he do that?

I trip through the next day in a haze.

As my classes progress, so does my agitation. I feel desperate to talk to him, to demand an explanation. He just unloaded the most improbable scenario known to man – one that threatens my home, my friends, everything I hold dear – only to shoo me off before I can even process it.

By French class, I am in a near frenzy. The closer I get to Environmental Science, the harder it is for me to concentrate. Ms. Reeds devotes an entire period to the history of *foie gras*.

I glance at the clock on the classroom wall.

Tick … tock.

And then, it is finally time for science.

EJ and Tess meet me at the door. We walk into the classroom while EJ says something about the Christmas Ball. At least I think she does, I'm not sure. I peek toward the lab, my heart pounding in my ears, but the lights are too dim to see anything. All I can think of is: *He is in there. Somewhere. Right now.*

"Are you even listening?"

I scoot into my chair. "Sorry, EJ, I … what was that?"

"Never mind," she says with a scowl. She opens her notebook, glaring at nothing in particular. Mr. Krikorian shuffles to the front and begins a lecture on ecosystem ecology. I barely hear a word of it. After thirty minutes, he glances at his watch.

"Your lab projects are due in a week," he says. "Please use the rest of this hour to complete your presentations; I'll be up front if you need me. Mr. Jones and I will be working on our research for the Penang Environmental Society."

We file into the laboratory as Gabe walks out of it. He carries an armload of supplies and two large folders marked "PES" in block letters.

I chew on my bottom lip as I take my seat at the counter, trying my best to act normal. My arms feel sweaty. So does the back of my neck. Caleb picks up our draft presentation and reviews the latest additions. I pick colored pencils from the drawer and resume my inept illustration of a dinoflagellate – probably the worst rendition of phytoplankton that science has ever seen. I don't know why Caleb makes me do this. I obviously can not draw. Across the room, Tess and EJ are arguing over their jellyfish population.

"They're down by thirty percent," Tess insists. "I just don't understand it; I've been following all the instructions … you *have* been feeding them, haven't you?"

"Of course I've been feeding them!" says EJ, a little too quickly. But then a commotion toward the back of the lab distracts all of us.

"Don't panic! Not poisonous!" Alistair cries, sprinting across the room.

I move out of the way just in time. Alistair lands on top of the lab counter, sending my microscope over the edge. I scramble to catch it and, when I look back up, see that he's holding a large, green snake in both his hands. I glance from

Alistair to the snake aquarium, where the lid looks decidedly *not* where it should be.

"Poisonous! Poisonous!" Zachary howls.

The lab explodes into screams.

Two cobras, a python and a few garters slither across the floor as a stampede of panicked science students and rogue snakes on the lam all race toward the nearest exit. Test tubes and papers fly everywhere. EJ wails for Mr. Krikorian. Naomi screams while kneeling on top of a lab stool. Zachary, Caleb and Alistair dash through the door, wielding sticks and nets.

Mr. Krikorian appears between the classroom and the lab, momentarily confused. Tess fills him in on the details. When she gets to the cobras, his face turns white.

"No bites," I put in quickly.

"So far!" says EJ.

"Jones!" Krikorian roars. Gabe strolls over. "Clean this up, will you? I have to go after these idiots." He stomps outside and bellows behind him, "Death by cobra is *not* an explanation I can send home to their parents!"

Gabe orders the few remaining students out of the area. He has to pry a petrified Naomi from the lab stool and carry her to the door. He mutters something under his breath as he grabs a long, wooden ruler and stalks into the laboratory. Here's my chance.

"Forgot my notebook – I'll catch up in a moment," I call to Tess and EJ, but they're already running out of there as quickly as they can, dragging Naomi between them. I dart into the lab and close the door behind me. Gabe turns around. I set my jaw. "I need to speak with you."

"Are you serious?" he snaps, turning his attention back to the floor. "Better join your friends, Clemens. Snake bites are not a recommended part of your curriculum."

"If you don't want me to blab about our chat last night," I say, "you'd better comply. *Dès que!*"

"I have no idea what you …."

"I MEAN it!"

He stands still for a good thirty seconds. He turns around. His mouth is clenched so tight I think it must hurt a little. "Four o'clock. By the rocks," he says, glaring at me.

"Don't be late!" I snap and dash out of there. I'm terrified of snakes.

By 3:50, I am over the seawall and scuttling toward the eastern side of the beach where the rocks lie waiting. I know Gajendra and his staff are the only ones on the lower campus right now, and I'm sure that if they see me, they won't say anything to Mr. King or Aunt Janie. Funny. Three months ago, I would have hoped for the opposite.

I reach the conglomeration of boulders and look around.

Another minute ticks by. Then two. My shirt sticks to my back and my arms are slick with sweat. It's so hot out. And the breeze is practically nonexistent today, making the humidity hang in the sky like a steamy blanket. It smells weird here, too, like something's rotting.

I hear a low voice. It comes from somewhere beyond the footpath that leads into the jungle. My skin bristles into bumps. I forget all about the smell and the heat as I dart into the trees. As soon as I'm under their shade, I see Gabe standing there.

"Did you get the snakes?" I say, but my voice sounds far away, choked by the pounding in my ears.

"Out with it, Clemens. What is it?"

I swallow, fighting the anger that instantly swells.

"*What is it?*" I repeat. "You can't just dump something like the fate of one's island on a person and then sneer them away!"

He rolls his eyes, impatient.

"Do you have any idea how confused I am right now?" I continue, too angry to care that he's mocking me. "No, you don't, I know, because you have no interest in things like that! So why did you bother telling me in the first place? That's what *it* is! I can't make sense of it – I don't know what to do with it!"

"And that," he says, "is not my problem."

"Are you serious? Do you have one of those social-disconnect personality issues or something?" I say, but he just stares back at me. "I can't make sense of you! Why do you act the way you do, only to risk everything to tell me? That's not the way things work; people don't *do* that, not without a reason! After everything you told me last night, how else am I supposed to believe you – let alone trust you – if you won't tell me *why?*"

"Aren't they the same thing?"

"What?" I say, glaring up at him, and I feel the tears gathering in my eyes. I look away.

"Trust and belief. I think they're the same thing."

"I – I think it depends on what you mean by belief," I sputter, still staring at the ground. What are we talking about?

"And it doesn't matter!" I rally, glaring at him. "I asked you a question and I deserve the answer. Why are you doing this? It doesn't add up and until it does, everything you told me might as well have been some elaborate story concocted for your … for your entertainment!" I struggle with this last bit because he is too calm. He should get angry, annoyed. Something.

"You want me to demonstrate my sincerity?"

"You make me sound like an idiot!" I practically roar. "Don't rephrase me like that!"

"How do you want me to put it, then? From what I gather, you feel you have no reason to trust me because I haven't convinced you of my earnestness."

"We're not in some nineteenth-century tea parlor, for God's sake!" I bellow. "Speak like a normal person! And what do you think? Would *you* believe *me* if the situation were reversed?"

"Probably not."

"Exactly! I don't know anything about you! And you supposedly know all about me, about my home, about the work we do there. Why should I believe that you're trying to help me – help us – when all I know about *you* is that you're some kind of spy?"

"That's a fair question. How do feel about heights, Sam?"

"Don't change the subject!"

"I'm not."

"Then answer my question!"

"I would if you'd let me."

I stop, realizing I've been following him through the woods, ranting the whole way.

We are now standing beside an enormous tree. The trunk is twisted with vines and stretches so far into the canopy above that its branches become indistinguishable from the rest of the jungle.

Gabe uncoils one of the vines and tugs at it. I see now that it isn't a vine at all, but a rope. The hue and width of the rope allow it to fit in perfectly with the rattan and other vegetation draping about. This is strange enough, but stranger still is the rope ladder that has just dropped down out of nowhere and now sways back and forth beside me.

"Like I was saying ...." He rocks back onto his heels, hands in pockets, and nods to the ladder. "A token of my earnestness. So, are you or are you not afraid of heights?"

I look from him to the tree.

It's really tall. So, so tall. And that flimsy rope concoction hardly looks sturdy enough.

"Not even a little," I say, grabbing the ladder.

It feels like I climb forever, but it is probably only a few minutes. I do not look down. I know I must be close to forty feet in the air before I stop, staring in amazement. A round platform with a roof nests in the branches, encircled by a low, bamboo wall only about four feet high. The platform must be camouflaged somehow from underneath, because I failed to see it until now. Facing the ladder is a small opening in the bamboo wall that's just wide enough for a person to squeeze through.

I scramble up the last few steps, pull myself through the opening and grab the nearest thing that is sturdy. Then I take a good look around.

Traditional woven bamboo mats, called *tikars*, cover the floor of the platform. To one side, a rattan shelf holds some books, a small box and a few bottles of water. Every three or so feet, bamboo pillars stretch up from the floor and attach to the thatched roof overhead, leaving a wide open space between the roof and the low wall. I turn and realize I can see the ocean – and most of PACA – from every angle of the little hideaway.

"So, what do you think?" asks Gabe, joining me on the platform.

Air pops through my front teeth, creating a funny "tuh" sound.

"Eloquently put," he says.

I ignore that and wipe my forehead. "Did you … did you *make* this?"

"Yes, Clemens," he says, pulling up the ladder. "I spend my free time building tree forts. And you?"

"I'm serious. Where did this come from then?"

He's coiling the ropes onto the floor just outside the entrance. I watch him. His T-shirt sticks to his shoulders as he moves.

"I think it must have been a look-out post back in the day," he says. "I found it over the summer. My company wasn't sure if they could get me into PACA or not, so when I found this, I did some repairs. The nearby hotel doesn't have a view of your school, and there isn't any other vantage point around here to use ...." He slides to the floor. "This was the most practical option."

I look away as soon as he's facing me. I take in the *tikars*, the low walls, the plastic tarps rolled up between the bamboo poles, presumably to protect the place from rain. Then I look down at him. He is sprawled across one of the woven mats, watching me. I can not make sense of him.

"Why didn't we just meet here last night?" I ask, feeling my eyebrows tug together.

He reaches over and grabs a bottle of water from the shelf. "With the guards patrolling the beach at night?" He tosses the water to me – I barely catch it, but I don't think he notices – and grabs another. "Besides, I didn't know how you would respond to what I had to say. I thought it would be best to break the news somewhere a bit more removed."

I twist the water bottle in my hands as I gaze toward the campus arch, where the guard booth stands in relatively clear view. And I can see my dorm from here, too. In fact, I can see EJ walking from the student center with a group of other people. Her long, blonde hair flashes in the sunlight. I turn away, disconcerted. I feel like I am living in two different worlds. And at this moment, I am lost somewhere in the void between them.

I lean against one of the bamboo poles and let my knees relax. Slowly I sink to the floor and put the water bottle beside me.

"They've never been here," Gabe is saying. "No one knows of it but me … and now you. So go ahead."

It takes a minute before I realize I should respond. "Go … where?" I ask vaguely.

"Ask me something." He says with a shrug. "That's why you're here, isn't it? To figure out if you can trust me? So go ahead. Ask me anything about myself."

"About yourself," I repeat.

He smiles in reply. It is mildly off-putting to sit here while he smiles like that. Especially when the first question that pops into my mind is something along the lines of *"Have you killed anyone before?"* But I decide against it. I'm not sure I want to know.

"Okay, um …." I pause, trying to think of something friendly to start with. Something simple. "How many languages do you speak?"

"I'm fluent in six, but I'm working on my Torundi and Malay," he answers.

I draw back a little. And here I am, proud of knowing English and Torundi and enough French to at least eat well.

"So, eight then … if we're going to be concise," I fumble.

"Yes." His eyes stay on my face. "But you can do better than that, Clemens. You didn't demand this meeting on account of my linguistic skills."

I look down at my hands and nod. He's right. I need to focus. On what, though? I almost feel paralyzed by the options. I think of Dr. Jean, of the days and nights we'd spend pouring over a single idea. What do we do when we don't know how to make sense of a subject? We reorganize and start at the beginning.

"That first day of class, during roll call …," I say, trying again. "Why did you call attention to me – to yourself – like that? I mean, if you didn't want me to know who you were, why did you act … that way?"

"Like a prick," he clarifies.

I feel my neck crawl with heat. "That's a charitable description, but yes."

He leans his head back so that his gaze flicks to the canopy above us. The sun filters through the green of his irises, and for a moment, I'm taken back to that day in the river.

The day everything changed.

"If you were confronted with a person whom you did not want anyone to know you had met before," he replies slowly, "what would *you* do?"

"I don't know, ignore them?"

He twists the cap off his bottle and lifts it to his mouth. "But if you *had* to acknowledge them," he says after swallowing half the water. "And if you only had one shot at how it played out, what then?"

I don't know what he's getting act, but I do feel sweat slipping down the side of my right temple. I wipe it away. Why do I sweat so much?

"Think about it, Clemens. If I'd been polite and civil and finished our roll … and later on, you'd shared with your friends that you recognized me, that would have put me in a compromising position, wouldn't it?"

"So … you attacked instead?"

"I humiliated you in front of your peers. Everyone saw what I did. Everyone saw how you responded. If you later claimed that you knew me from Torundi …."

"Then I'd look ridiculous," I finish the thought, stunned by the realization. "Like I was trying to drum up drama or something."

He smiles and puts his bottle on the floor. "What else have you got?"

I look from his bottle to my hands, suddenly too flummoxed to recall the arsenal of questions stored up inside. Because each time I'm with him, everything I thought I had a handle on slips away. And all my questions – all the *why's* that plague me – seem … misdirected. It is the truth that I'm after. Do the *why's* behind it really matter?

They do. To me, at least.

I reach for my water bottle, but my gaze stops at the dark, circular scar on my left arm – the vague shape of a new fern leaf unfolding. It helps to focus on it, on something tangible; it helps clear the muddle in my mind.

"Is that it?" floats his voice. From my peripheral vision, I see him gesture at my arm. "Is that where they ... marked you?"

I keep my eyes on the scar, not even surprised that he already knows about it. Of course he does.

"Do you remember?" he continues. "No, I suppose you wouldn't, would you? You were only an infant."

My throat tightens. I flick my gaze to his, defensive. But he didn't mean that to be cruel, I can see that. For a moment, I'm too confused to know how to respond, probably because I've never discussed it with anyone but Nurse Kathy before, and that was years ago. I was only seven at the time. She told me what she knew and then made me swear I would never speak of it again. But that was in another life, in Torundi, and I'm tired of obeying rules I don't understand. It is my scar.

"They marked my mother, too," I say. It is strange to hear the words from my voice. Silence does that. It makes it so that the thing no longer feels real. As if the silence can wipe it away, like chalk from a blackboard. Well, I'm tired of that, too. "The Tagolis don't take kindly to outside relationships," I continue, recalling Nurse Kathy's explanation in every detail. I've spent hours of my life reviewing it over and over in my mind. "If a man does not claim responsibility – especially if the relationship is outside the village – it brings great shame to them. The marking was to show that we are taboo." I frown, hating that word. But I don't know a better one to use. "To my birth tribe, it is as if I never existed. Even acknowledging my birth would be forbidden."

"But there have been others before you . . . ." Gabe begins.

"The Tagolis outcast for all sorts of reasons; they are not exactly known for their tolerance," I say. "And other villages use the same marking for punishment as well, so it is actually quite common. I've seen all kinds of methods used to erase the taboo mark, even to the point of actually cutting it out.

It's awful." I shudder at a particularly unhappy memory at the mission clinic, years ago. "I was lucky. Shortly after my mother brought me to the mission, my marking was changed. What I have now is the Dyeen symbol for rebirth – it hides the center spot that the Tagolis gave me. Anyway, I suppose my mother was on thin ice as it was. Nurse Kathy said my grandmother came to the Tagolis as an outsider, too – with no claim to another village. For some reason they accepted her, but when my mother committed the same offense, it was too ill of an omen for them to bear. They are superstitious about these things."

"They sound lovely," says Gabe, his lip curling with distaste. "I think you're really missing out."

I laugh a little. It surprises me.

"And ... your mother," he says after a moment, "she was exiled directly after you were born, correct?"

I swallow, forcing down the throb in my throat. He's just asking. It isn't his fault. It's probably healthy to talk about it.

"They just left her to die in the forest," I say. I look down at my scar again, wondering how I can feel so sad about losing a person I have never met, not with cognizance, at least. As if I had done the deed myself, done away with a central part of me, a part I've never even known. Or why I feel as though I failed her somehow.

"She wrapped me in a traditional *ta'omala*, the cloth used for males," I continue, hoping my voice sounds steady enough. "I suppose to protect me, I'm not sure. Or maybe it was the only choice she had." *But why?* rings the question. I've wondered over that for seventeen years, but I've never gotten any closer to the answer. "My mother had already lost so much blood; she'd walked for hours, carrying me the whole way until she made it to the mission. She found Nurse Kathy and told her what I've just told you. She said she wanted to be buried anonymously, so that no one would know it was she who had come there. She didn't want the Tagoli scorn to shadow my own life, I suppose. And then she asked Nurse Kathy to give me a name. She wanted a Western name, she said. Nurse Kathy was so distressed; she never even thought to question it, much less confirm my true gender. She just gave me the first thing that came to mind under the circumstance."

Gabe stares back at me, his eyes wide.

"That's why the mission never changed it, even after they realized the mistake," I explain with a shrug. "In our culture, the one who names you becomes responsible for you, like an adopted parent. My mother must have been holding on until she heard it, until she knew I was safe. So now, even though my name is ridiculously inconvenient, it's too solemn a thing to change …." I trail off, suddenly embarrassed. I've never shared that with anyone before.

"I had no right to ask about that … about her," he says after a pause.

"No, I'm glad you asked." I stand up and turn to stare at the forest below. I don't want him to see whatever it is that's going on with my face. "To speak of her with someone else. It … somehow makes her seem more real."

"*You* make her real, Sam."

It sends something through me, those words. Can I make her real? I wish I could. I glance back down at my arm.

"I know this sounds odd, but I kind of like it, my scar," I say, and I don't know why I am telling him this. It is completely insane. But now, I don't want to stop. "I guess it makes me feel connected to her, like she left something for me. Does that make sense?"

"I think so." His voice is low, like it always is, but it also sounds oddly controlled. I whip around. If he's making fun of me, I will summon up every lesson I've had with Trudy and jujitsu him right off this platform. But he looks serious. I think he's serious.

"And I like it, too," he continues. I relax a little. "It is part of who you are. I like that about scars."

I watch him closely. How he can do that? How does he switch from being the most caustic person I've ever known to the most genuine? I don't trust it.

"But somebody else said it best, I think," he adds after another moment. *"Out of suffering have emerged the strongest souls; the most massive characters are seared with scars."*

I lean against the bamboo pole. Okay. So he's not making fun of me. "Who said that?" I ask.

He's still watching me, his eyes never leaving my face. "Kahlil Gibran, I think."

I've never heard of him.

And I don't speak six languages fluently, either, I remind myself. For that matter, I don't rehabilitate post-war treetop vantage posts in the jungle, I don't work for a diabolical company on the cusp of global dominance and I am not a child prodigy, international spy. If that is actually who he *really* is. At this point, I have no idea because he keeps morphing every time I think I have a handle on things.

"Why do you talk to me this way?" I demand, forcing myself to meet his stare. "So familiar, when we don't really know each other?"

A faint smile flicks at his mouth. He leans his head back and says, "I suppose you could say that I believe in you."

I try to keep my face blank. I clear my throat. "You … *believe* in me."

"And besides," he continues as if I haven't spoken, "you and I hold quite a bit in common. So in some ways, Clemens, I do know you."

"What could we possibly have in common?"

"Unusual upbringings, to begin with," he says. "But our similarities run farther back than even that. In fact, it has to do with your namesake."

I think about this for a moment.

"Your hometown in Switzerland?" I guess.

"You remembered."

"So where is it?"

He doesn't answer at first. As he rests his head against the side of the low wall, his gaze falling away, I feel impatient to hear his story after all I've shared. I take another drink of water and then sink back down to the floor, determined to wait him out.

"It is a tiny town called Weggis, located on Lake Lucerne," he finally says after a while. "It is beautiful there, cobblestone streets and quaint shops, half-timber homes trimmed with flowers – just like a picture book – and the lake spreads all about with its crystal blue waters framed by mountains. In fact," and his eyes slide from faraway to straight at me, "Mark Twain called it the 'charmingest place' that he had ever vacationed in. But then again, he always had lavish praise for the towns he visited. Have you ever noticed? That, or he absolutely loathed a place, so his judgment may not be all that reliable."

I try to see it, not really listening to the rest. A pretty little town like he says, like you see in travel posts about Europe. But mostly, I see a young Gabe, shirtsleeves and pants rolled up, running along the shore of this lake, the sunlight filtering through his hair. Maybe it would have been lighter then, almost blond even ....

"Of course, I only lived there until I was six – until I was recruited by UnMonde," he adds, the tone of his voice no longer playful.

"And your family?"

"That," he says, and I can see his jaw tighten, "is where we are not so different."

I'm not sure what to make of that. And his demeanor is confusing – like he doesn't want to talk about it, but he's still offering it up. Why? "I don't see the parallel," I say, shifting my legs. I suddenly feel the urge to move them, to do something. "Could you be a bit more specific?"

"I mean I also grew up without family," he answers matter-of-factly. "Before UnMonde, I was raised by a couple who had taken on the burden of raising me. When UnMonde found me, it was the first time I was actually *wanted* somewhere."

"So your parents …." I pause, unsure how to ask it. He props himself into a sitting position, his broad shoulder leaning against one of the bamboo poles, directly opposite to where I sit. We now face each other. One posture mirrors the other. The thought strikes me as ridiculous.

"I was left at a hospital when I was a week old," he says. "The couple who agreed to take me received a modest fund, but whatever that amount was, it was less than what UnMonde must have offered six years later. My parents, whomever they might be, never sought me out. And I've never bothered to look for them."

"And … the couple who raised you?"

"They were eager to accept UnMonde's money. I was eager to leave."

There is a darkness in his voice, an edge that betrays a deeper meaning. For a moment, I forget to respond.

"I'm … sorry," I finally say. It sounds incredibly lame.

He shrugs.

"So now you know all about me. You know my name, where I'm from, who I work for. You know my sad, sad story." He smiles in that half-sarcastic, half-genuine way of his. That smile should be outlawed. "Do you trust me now?"

"That's not fair."

"I never said I was fair."

I shake my head, trying to shake out the muddle. There is so much to digest. Too much. And it doesn't help that he keeps his eyes locked on me. There are a thousand things in that stare, things that pull me in. My words. My thoughts. Me.

I grab my water bottle and twist off the cap. "I've, I've got to go," I say. I take a long gulp, spilling half of it down my T-shirt. Crap.

"So soon?"

"Yes!" I wobble to my feet, wringing my shirt in the process. "Gajendra's probably waiting for me."

"But, Sam …."

"What?"

"Please be careful."

"I … I am careful." I stumble past him. "I'm always careful. Super careful – I'm, I'm practically known for it!" I cringe. This is awful. And I don't even know what I'm saying. "I mean, I know how to sneak back without being seen."

"I don't doubt it."

"What then?" I ask, peeking back at him.

"I meant going down the ladder," he says, and his eyes are bright with laughter. "You look a little shaky."

11. CHRISTMAS BALL

When I was younger, my favorite evenings were, hands down, movie nights at the Dyeen village. My friends and I would string a bed sheet between the rain trees by the river while Dr. Jean lugged out his ancient "dream-maker."

As the night settled in and the stars twinkled above us, the generator would rev up and then, the bulky projector would sputter into life, flooding that white canvas between the trees with fantastical moving pictures, usually Buster Keaton and Charlie Chaplin films.

The entire village would gather on the grass to watch, transfixed by the flickering scenes, as the call of crickets, occasional *"oohs"* and *"ahs"* interspersed with titters and Dr. Jean's translations accompanied the steady, whirring sound of the projector.

As I grew older, I would marvel at the magic of those evenings. It didn't matter how many times Buster Keaton stuck his head into a cannon or stood, oblivious, while a house fell over him; the scenes were always met with gasps of dismay, not laughter. To the Dyeens, the wonder of those images was too profound to laugh at, to disrespect in such a manner, and if that sad, silly little man could not be more aware of his surroundings, then it was a pitiable thing and not something to find humorous.

But in *City Lights*, when the shop-girl sees Chaplin's homeless character for the first time since gaining her eyesight, and he is frayed and dirty and every bit the tramp he portrays; and when she hands him a flower, not knowing he's sacrificed everything for her, not knowing he is her benefactor, that he loves her more than anything in life; and he takes that flower, the hope dying in his eyes because she does not know who he really is … *this* scene is met with nervous sniggers.

The Dyeens think it strange that a man should behave in such a way. They don't know what to make of it, or why Miss Trudy and I sit, breathless, just before the shop-girl looks up at him and says: *"You?"*

And then the tramp says – with that light in his eyes sparking ever so slightly: "Yes. You can see me now?"

And then she says: "Yes, I can see you now."

Miss Trudy bawls her eyes out every single time, and the Dyeens look back, every single time, astonished by her lack of grace. Ibu Trudy should be happy for them, not sad! The girl can see him now! *Why* is Ibu Trudy *crying?*

I think that is how I feel tonight.

Like I just watched an old, foreign film – something in a language I can not decipher – and the things I see confuse me to the point where I don't know if I should be sad or happy or even ambivalent. I don't know if my reaction is closer to the Dyeens' or closer to Trudy's. I don't know anything except for this:

I can see him now.

And the Gabe I see is nothing like the one I've come to think of. He has shown me a quiet side; a side that, like my scar, is more real than all those loud, distracting things around us. It's the part of him that holds still, the part that waits for the occasional thread of truth; a gleam that shivers for a moment and, if not seized, is lost in shadow. I know I have seen this in him: the truth. And even though I can't tie it all together yet, I hold on to that thread, believing that if I do, it will lead me to the answer I still seek.

Science class fixes that.

I show up as I did the day before, giddy with some poorly thought-out expectation; that is to say, having no grounds whatsoever for believing I will encounter him on any meaningful basis, but delirium has convinced me otherwise.

Mr. Krikorian grumpily marches up to the front and, at first, I think he's still mad about the snake frenzy.

"I'll expect more responsible behavior from all of you," he barks, frowning around the room. "I don't have time for shenanigans or for chasing after cobras, especially not now!

I've got five classes, three labs, a commitment to PES, the after-school Super Snoops, a wife, five kids and NO lab assistant!"

My stomach lurches.

"What about Mr. Jones?" EJ asks.

"Mr. Jones has asked to be relieved of this class," Mr. Krikorian grumbles. "He'll still cover my Chemistry lab, thank goodness, but still, it couldn't have come at a worse time!"

I take a breath, but it feels like I'm breathing in water. Mr. Krikorian rambles on, saying something about final exams and our papers, but I don't follow. *"Jones ... relieved of this class ..."* rings in my ears like one of the Dyeen village gongs.

I blink, glancing down at my arm. Caleb's jabbing a folded paper at me.

I open it.

"Go to the XMas-B with me?" it says. I look from the words to Caleb. He grabs the paper back and scribbles something else on it:

"Please? You have to – there's no one left to ask."

Well, that helps. It is official. In under four months, I have managed to become the biggest reject at PACA.

EJ sees the note and beams. She snatches it. *"Of course she'll go!"* she scrawls in reply, and then pushes it directly to Caleb, narrowing her eyes at me in the process. I slump in my seat.

Caleb nods in satisfaction.

"Figured you could use the offer – try to find a decent dress," he whispers.

Before I can reply to that, Mr. Krikorian glares over at our table and demands to know what is so interesting that it should take our attention from his lecture. I mumble an apology and open my notebook, now scratching down random words. My head races with too many questions, too many possibilities.

He was here yesterday, so his absence has to be tied to our tree-top meeting. He's avoiding me. That's obvious, but *why?* I don't know how to find that out. This class was my only way to contact him.

And now?

The thought breathes the other question, the one that makes my stomach roll so that I truly feel sick: Without this class, how will I see him? No, it's even worse than that. It's so awful that my eyes burn with heat and I can hear the thumping in my ears, the swell of panic in my chest, in my neck, in my fingers. Because really the question is … *will* I see ever him *again?*

"Homeostasis …," Mr. Krikorian is saying. I write the word down, foggily recalling its meaning:

The property that regulates an organism's internal environment in order to maintain a stable and constant condition.

I stare at the word, turning the definition over in my mind. *Or in other words*, I think miserably, swallowing down the roar in my head, *to define it another way*:

Not me.

***

Two weeks and three days pass. During that time, I see Gabe only once, as he walks from the lab after third period toward the PACA arch. He doesn't notice me.

It is now Friday and Christmas vacation is upon us. Tonight, I must face the dubious celebration of PACA's Christmas Ball. And then tomorrow, we'll all fly home for our three-week holiday. The thought makes my throat dry. I know that when I get to Torundi, my life will change in ways I have no way of predicting. That part I can deal with. But the other?

I know it is selfish. I know I shouldn't care. I know I'll do whatever I can to help the mission, to help Torundi; that I'll do my duty. But still, that last meeting with Gabe plays over and over in my mind. I am obsessed with it. How he smiled. What he said. The way I left, just assuming I'd see him again when composure had returned to me. And now, he'll be gone. I'll be gone. *That* part ….

That part is an ache I can not put into words.

I look into the full-length mirror. The last thing I want to do right now is go to a stupid Christmas Ball. But Tess's home-ec teacher, Mrs. Perry, is standing before me, beaming with pride at the sight of me all decked out. I owe it to her to at least pretend. She helped me sew the dress I'm wearing, after all – two weeks of after-school labor and three years' worth of leftover fabric scraps. Mrs. Perry did most of it, really. She insisted after Tess relayed my wardrobe dilemma.

I look again. The gown is a pale chiffon and patched-silk concoction that I actually kind of like. But I do not feel like wearing it. I hug Mrs. Perry goodbye and thank her again.

"You just have fun tonight, okay, sweetie?" she says, smiling up at me. She's short – maybe five-three or so.

"Okay," I say.

She pats my arm and then leaves the room, reminding me to lock up. I watch after her for a moment. She's so nice. I wonder if I would ever go to all this trouble for someone I hardly know.

I slip off the dress, put my regular clothes back on, lock the classroom door and then carry my creation back to the dorm. When I reach it, Tess and EJ are already entrenched in the mayhem of Christmas Ball preparation. From outside, I can hear Tess gushing excitedly about Aaron. He flew in yesterday to see her before Christmas break, and somehow Tess has convinced Aunt Janie to allow him to go to the ball with her.

This concession is unprecedented at PACA, but it probably has something to do with Tess's explanation: an ingenious story involving her soccer trip to Kuala Lumpur a few months ago during which she supposedly first met Aaron at a church that she (never) went to where his dad (who has actually been deceased for two years) is the preacher.

It doesn't matter that the facts could be easily controvertible if actually checked into. All Aunt Janie hears is "pastor's kid" and "church."

Tess has cracked the code.

As soon as I walk through the door, my roommates stop talking. I barely have time to hang up my dress before I'm shoved toward the desk chair where EJ stands waiting, flat-iron brandished in the air.

"Sit!" Tess says.

"I've wanted to do this for months," EJ says with a grin, and then it is as if a tornado of makeup and nail polish and straightening irons hit me at the same time, like in one of those annoying movie montages. And all the while, Tess is rhapsodizing over Aaron as EJ complains about Tommy and I listen, stone-faced, wondering how I'm going to break the news to Dr. Jean when I get home. And will it make any difference? It may be too late. Is that why Gabe has been avoiding me?

I swallow down the ache in my throat.

It is more than that. It is an ocean more than that. A space so wide I've no hope of reaching him more than that.

By 6:30, I have on more makeup than I've ever worn in my life, but that's not saying much as I don't wear the stuff in the first place. But I don't think it's overdone. And my hair looks fantastic – not a strand out of place. It falls in a silky curtain around my shoulders, with loose sections pinned away from my face. I didn't know I could look like this.

I slip on my dress and then sneak another glance at the mirror, amazed by the transformation. Tess and EJ are geniuses.

"Wow, that's … not bad, actually," says EJ, turning to me.

"Geez, EJ!" Tess glares, flicking a straightening iron

through her own hair. "After all the grief you've given her, that's the best you can do? You look *hot*, Sam."

I stiffen a little, embarrassed. I don't know if I've ever been called "hot" before. Attractive, maybe at certain times, but I've always had an insufficiency of tribal tattoos for the Dyeen's taste. I grab my shoes as a cover.

"Well, you both look amazing!" I say, which is entirely true. It's also more or less a given. Next to my roommates, I always feel like I look years younger and decades out of date. Probably at least five pounds heavier, too, but I try not to fixate on that. They're both so skinny they could be models.

"Oh, my God, *NO!*"

I turn, mid-shoe, to see what's the matter. EJ's halfway into her long, blue dress. With her huge eyes, open mouth and frozen posture, she looks like a horrified anime character. "Please don't do it!"

"Do what?"

"Are you *kidding* me?"

She really does look distressed, so I follow her glare and arrive at, I have to say, the most splendid pair of leather hiking boots a girl could ever hope for. Trudy would be crushed.

"But they're from Italy," I protest, lacing up my strings.

"They're *BOOTS!*"

"No, we can make this work," I say, slogging on the other shoe. I am getting good at this. Four months of living with EJ has practically made me a PR expert on Torundi fashion. "It's like funky, bohemian-gown-meets-vintage ...

Alps climber." I glance over at Tess for help, but she looks almost as aghast as EJ. "Besides, I don't have anything else to wear. It's either these, sneakers, my ratty, slip-on sandals or flip-flops …."

A bus rumbles outside, distracting EJ from the monstrosity of my footwear. Perfect timing. My roommates scramble with last-minute touch-ups and I slip out, boots and all, to the common room where the boys are waiting.

I find Caleb sitting on the couch, one gangly leg thrown over the armrest, dressed in a black tux and bowtie. He's in the middle of a conversation with Tommy – something about rugby, I think – and when he sees me, he waves me over and then finishes whatever it is he was saying, giving me an unsubtle up-and-down in the process. Who says chivalry is dead? Fools.

"Ready?" I say with a grimace.

Caleb shoves a rose in my face – by way of an answer, I can only assume.

"If we hurry, we'll get the best seat on the bus," he says, getting up. And then he grabs my arm and pulls me out the door.

Twenty minutes later, we file into a swanky, five-star hotel located at Batu Ferringhi. The resort staff usher us into a ballroom shimmering with white Christmas lights. A giant Christmas tree, dripping with ornaments and more lights, looms in the center of the room, surrounded by a dance floor. Dining tables and chairs ring around it all and, at the back of the room, a brightly polished buffet steams with all sorts of aromas. It is incredibly lavish, but the most picturesque thing of all is the front of the room, where the glass wall looks out over the hotel's lagoon-style pool and the sunset beyond.

"Want to go outside?" Caleb asks, but I think it must be a rhetorical question because he's already escorting me through the doorway.

We stop by the pool. Lights flicker in the palm trees overhead and drape between flowering plants that curve along the poolside. The pool, in turn, is lit from its interior, lighting the turquoise water with its glow.

"Not bad," says Caleb, looking around. "But it's not as pretty as you."

I accidentally snort-laugh in reply. I try to hide it with a cough, but Caleb's not buying.

"What's so funny?"

"I just … nothing," I say with a shrug, fighting to keep my face straight.

"No, really. What?"

Well, I have to say *something*.

"It's just that you … catch a girl by surprise is all," I attempt, but Caleb's frown is going in the wrong direction. I try harder. "I mean, I didn't think you noticed I was even in a dress, Caleb! And then you just throw something like *that* at me and I … sorry. I mean, thank you. You look nice, too."

"You're horrible at taking a compliment."

"I know." I glare at the pool grout by my feet.

"Anyway, I was just trying to make you feel comfortable before," he says after a moment. "I know you didn't really want to come to this thing."

I glance up at him. "Really?"

"Yeah." He shrugs, stepping a little closer. "But you're not easy to read, Sam. I—"

"Mr. Reynolds, Ms. Clemens," floats a low voice, "aren't you supposed to be with the rest of the students?"

I spin around. He must have emerged from behind a palm tree. Even so, if he'd materialized from pool vapor, I doubt I could have been any more stupefied.

He stands just behind Caleb, dressed in a tux like everyone else. But he doesn't look like everyone else. He is only two years older than Caleb. Two years older than me. But on him, every line and muscle is defined, as if molded for a specific purpose. And standing there … well, poor Caleb looks like a well-dressed noodle in comparison. My pulse thumps so hard I am sure he can hear it. I glance from him back to Caleb.

He looks from Caleb to me. "Interesting."

"What's that?" Caleb snaps.

Gabe doesn't seem to hear him. "I would be remiss in my chaperone duties if I didn't escort you two back inside," he replies instead. His eyes float over my dress and pause for a moment at my feet. A twitch tugs at his mouth. "You're supposed to stay within the banquet hall."

I want to shove him into the pool. I want to scream at him. I want to grab a huge goblet of that red fruit punch I'd noticed on the way out and throw it at his impeccable tux – and where did he get that thing, anyway? Geez. I want to demand to know why he disappeared on me and why he is showing up *now*, like *this*. But I am too proud.

Caleb's grip on my arm tightens. I force my gaze toward the pool, struggling to get control over this. I don't think I can. It has been over two weeks since we've spoken. No, over two weeks since we've even passed within the same perimeter and now, right now, *this* may be the last time we ever see each other. Ever. He doesn't care. I know he doesn't care. Between this epiphany and my hiking boots, I'm pissed off enough to gain some semblance of dignity.

"C'mon Caleb," I choke out – eloquence personified – and turn to go.

But Caleb surprises me. Instead of slumping off as I'd expected, he leans forward and smooths a few stray strands of my hair from my face. He leans closer. I am momentarily paralyzed. I think he may actually try to kiss me, right in front of our fake chaperone. But he doesn't.

"I don't know about you," he murmurs into my ear, loud enough for Gabe to hear, "but I'd rather hang out where staff blatantly watch us than be spied on by this creep."

I nod quickly, not trusting myself to speak, and walk with Caleb toward the ballroom. I'm grateful for his hand on my arm now. I'm not sure I'd know where I was going otherwise.

***

The rest of the evening passes pleasantly enough. At least I assume it does. I struggle to concentrate on Caleb and my friends, but all I can think of is the fact that Gabe is somewhere in this room. Just a few feet away, maybe. A few feet away, but he may as well be a thousand.

Why did he do it? Why did he come here? I doubt very much he's attending for his personal enjoyment. And I know for a fact that PACA does not need additional chaperones; the room's already filled with staff members. *Real* ones.

And then there's the way he looked at me ....

I gulp back the awful swell in my throat. I blink my eyes and try to think of something stupid to fend off tears. I can not cry. I've got all this eye stuff on.

But why? repeats the question. It was bad enough before. I stare miserably at my plate. And for the first time in my life, I can not even eat a piece of chocolate lava cake.

By ten, the banquet is over. We are shuttled through the hotel lobby, decidedly out of place amongst the tourists stalking about in shorts and flip-flops. That's not the only thing out of place, I realize, because tonight marks the end of my banishment from Torundi; a period I thought I would never survive. Tomorrow, I'll finally be returning to my precious island.

Except here's the thing:

I don't want to go anymore.

I think about that the whole way home. I think about *him*. I don't even notice how quiet Caleb is until we reach my dorm. He politely escorts me to the door of the common area. I know I should say something.

"Thanks for the evening, Caleb," I manage. I try to smile and then wave my droopy rose. Caleb only grimaces in reply. Several of my dorm-mates file past us, waving bye to their dates and giggling excitedly.

"It's him, isn't it?" he demands after a moment.

"Who?"

Caleb rolls his eyes. "And here I was, thinking you weren't like the rest of them."

"Wait," I say, stunned. "What's *that* supposed to mean?"

A sarcastic smile replaces the grimace, and he says, "It's supposed to mean that I liked you because you're different, or at least I thought you were." He tilts his chin at me, as if examining a sack of sullied goods. I feel my face getting hot. I am so not in the mood to be judged by my lab partner, especially when this entire date has merely been one of convenience. *His* convenience. I set my jaw.

"First of all, Caleb," I say, trying to control the resentment in my voice, "I don't know what you're talking about, but whatever you like or don't like about me hasn't changed over the course of four hours. I thought we were friends! You don't just get to line me up like I'm some kind of cow at an auction and then dismiss me for bad teeth or something!"

Caleb's mouth puckers. "It's horses, Sam."

"What?"

"Horses have their teeth examined, not cows. If you grew up somewhere normal you'd know that."

"Whatever!" I snap. "The point is, I *made* a *dress* to go to this thing with you, all because you needed a date. A *dress!* What did you do?"

"You haven't answered my question."

"Why do you even care?" I say, even though I know I should just ignore it. I shouldn't take the bait. But my face is burning now and I can't seem to stop myself. "*I'm* the one you asked out as a last resort, remember?"

For a moment, Caleb is silent. "Yeah, so." He shrugs, and a chunk of blond hair falls over his eyes. "Like I said. It's him."

I open my mouth, but nothing comes out as Caleb turns and walks away. I watch after him, feeling as though I've been slapped in the face. It isn't fair. "And we do have water buffalos, by the way!" I call angrily.

"Oh, Sam, dear, is that you?" floats a voice from inside. It's Aunt Janie. "Come here for a moment, please."

I stand in the doorway, watching Caleb stroll toward the PACA arch. He doesn't turn around. I squeeze my eyes shut and press the palms of my hands to my burning cheeks. I don't want to talk to anyone right now. I want to crawl into bed and cry my eyes out.

"Yes, Aunt Janie?" I turn and shuffle across the common room to her apartment. She looks up at me from where she sits on the sofa.

"You look lovely, dear."

I try to smile. "Thanks, Aunt Janie."

"Well, you see," she says distractedly, "you missed an important visitor while you were away tonight."

My spine snaps into a rod. "Who?"

Aunt Janie takes a sip of something. It looks like apple cider, but I can't be sure.

"Miss Trudy, from your mission, is on her way to KL for some sort of convention and she stopped by to see you," she says, looking up at me with an uncharacteristically relaxed expression. "She was so disappointed to find out that you weren't here. She said she's leaving tomorrow and won't be back home over the holidays. She desperately wants to see you before then. Something important. She asked if you could meet her at her hotel and she promised me that she'd take you straight to the airport tomorrow. She had a meeting to attend tonight, otherwise she'd have waited for your return ...."

I stare at Aunt Janie in disbelief.

"Anyway, she was such a polite young woman. I told her it wouldn't be a problem, and as soon as I saw you return from the ball, I'd send you straight to see her."

"Y-you did?"

Aunt Janie gives me a peculiar, goofy smile. "I did," she answers, but it sounds more like, "Ideeaud."

Just then, a horn blares outside. Aunt Janie lifts her arm to her face and goggles at her bare wrist. "Right on time," she announces dreamily. "That must be your taxi. She said she'd be sending it for you."

12. SAILING

I stand at the edge of an expansive bay. Boats of every size dot the glossy surface, shimmering with colorful Christmas lights that reflect off the water.

Before me, a narrow pier leads to a sailboat. It is the only vessel that doesn't have lights strewn over the mast, but the moonlight spills across the bay and, overhead, stars pierce the sky, lighting up the boat enough for it to be seen. Behind me, the sound of the taxi's engine fades into the distance.

"Gabe?" I whisper, looking around.

There is no answer, nothing but water and boats bobbing placidly. I look again at the sailboat. A small ramp hovers between it and the pier. I step forward, leaving my suitcase at the pier, and soon the ramp shifts under my feet.

"Here," Gabe says, appearing over the sailboat's side. His eyes gleam in the shadows. He extends his arm. "Give me your hand."

I stare at his hand. I've never touched him before. Not on purpose, at least. There is something about the space between us that already feels too close, like I might forget who I am if I'm not more careful.

But I must have taken it.

I'm on the other side now, standing on the deck that moves under my weight. I grab a braided wire that runs up to the mast, trying to catch my balance, just as Gabe hops over the side and walks to my suitcase. I watch him. He's changed out of his tux and into a T-shirt and shorts, and he moves with an easy kind of freedom, as if the night has brought to him a lightness of being. He suddenly looks years younger.

He is back on the boat now, slipping my bag into the cabin. Then he lets loose the ropes that tie us to the pier. We drift over the water, the mainsail tugging us outward with the gentle wind. Within minutes, we are in the middle of the moonlit bay. He extends an anchor and cinches the rope to a metal stay. I do not offer to help, partly because I've no idea what to do, mostly because I don't think of it until seconds later.

He folds down the mainsail.

He turns to me. He stands perfectly still, watching me as if he'd asked a question and is waiting for the answer.

"I don't understand," I say, but it comes out as a whisper. I clear my throat to force the sound through it. "You just left, without even a word."

"Yes," he says.

I make myself match his gaze, ignoring the pulse drumming in my ears. "Why?"

"I think you already know why."

I suddenly feel as if I've been holding my breath underwater. I look around, exhaling slowly. Yes, I really am here. He really is there. And I'm gripping the wire so tightly that it cuts into my hand. I hold tighter and say, "I think I deserve a better answer."

"Because I had to get away. And then, because I couldn't." His voice is so still when he says this.

"Are you ... are you taking me to them? To UnMonde?" I ask, meeting his stare once more. His expression changes in that instant.

"You're a clever girl, Clemens. Is that what you really think?"

"No," I admit, looking away.

He does not respond to that, and I can not meet his gaze. We both stand in silence, the wire cutting my hand until it registers that I should let go. I lean unsteadily against the cabin instead, eyes to the floor. It feels as if the pressure from my heartbeat will explode out of me. There is nowhere left for it to go.

And then, slowly, the throb calms to match the rocking of the boat. His silence is like a vacuum. I feel the draw as I stand there, searching the white deck at my feet for an answer I know I am afraid to actually find, because I know that it is there, just six feet up, in that face that stands watching me, in those direct, unyielding eyes. And I know that if I meet them, they will pull me down somewhere liquid and endless.

He waits.

I raise my eyes to his.

I don't know how it happens, but the sea stops rocking under my feet. It feels as if a cord has flicked its ends into each of us, and I move from the cabin to where he remains at the bow, perfectly still. His eyes never leave mine.

When I stop a foot away from him, I am momentarily panicked by what is happening. When he leans into me, I worry my awkward self isn't up to the task. And when his hand brushes against my neck, I suddenly just don't care.

The Southern Cross can be seen nearly every night in the tropics. It is a fact that comforts me.

When I first arrived at PACA, I used to sneak out at night after curfew and stare into the sky until the red gleam of *Gacrux* made itself known. From there, I'd trace south to *Acrux* and then pick out the other three stars, just as Dr. Jean taught me. I often wondered if someone back home was doing the same thing. Maybe Leila or Pak Siaosi, staring into that velvet like we used to on those calm, cool nights by the Mokanan, at those diamonds that the Great Spirit had found.

The Southern Cross is the Western name given to this constellation – the constellation of Gabe's world, I guess. In Torundi, we call this same group of stars a name that translates to the Flying Fox. I learned later that in Penang, it is known as the *Buruj Pari*, which means the Stingray. The same suns in the same sky for millions of years. Perhaps the more constant a thing is, the more we see it differently.

Tonight, I see all three of them: His sky. My sky. Our sky.

I look from the stars to the boat deck, where we lie near the bow's railing. Then I look at our intertwined arms, still not quite believing. I follow the contours of his hand, running over tendons that stretch into fingers. What constellation would they form?

I feel him watching me as I do this. I have this silly feeling that, if I were to meet his gaze, it would see through me, go into me. I don't want it to.

"What are you thinking?" he murmurs.

Well, I'm not going to tell him *that.* It isn't as if I've never kissed a boy before, but I'm suddenly shy about this thing between us. I know I feel far more than I should, far more than is safe; I've known that for a while now. And I know that, even if he feels a fraction of what I do, his world and my world are not realities that mix. I know it, I know it, but my heart does not. So I keep my eyes on his hands and force my mind onto other things.

"What happens if Dr. Jean can get to the sultan?" I offer instead, and Gabe turns to me, raising an eyebrow in question. "And what if Djadrani comes up with a way to protect the Tanah Yatim? What if he can do this so that UnMonde wouldn't suspect the mission – or you? It still wouldn't solve the problem, because Djadrani would just exploit the resource himself."

He exhales a mock sigh. "You're a romantic, Clemens.

And here, I thought we'd be speaking of our feelings ... or of something really profound, like the universe. Or, for example, the curious fact that sharks are the only fish with eyelids, and what does it all really *mean?*"

I duck my head. I know he's joking, but it cuts too close. Because I know that, right now, if I were to actually talk about my feelings, it would cause a landslide that would carry me right down with it. "I'm serious," I say, focusing on the practical, on the things I may actually have the ability to sort through. "That's the best-case scenario, right? So, what then?"

He props onto an elbow.

"Then if we can wish for anything, it would be that Djadrani will realize the long-term potential," he answers. "Once he understands he's sitting on a crater worth more than a million diamond mines, perhaps he'll treat it exactly as that."

"You mean control the production." I frown, turning to see his expression. I don't like that idea. I don't like any idea of harvesting a resource from the Tanah Yatim, of ugly gouges in our perfect land, of machines and dust and greed.

Gabe looks back at me in silence. Then he says, "It's inevitable, you know. Torundi can't stay that way forever. And there are ways to mine that don't have to be so intrusive. It just costs more and takes longer, but your resource would be an ideal fit, actually."

"For whom?"

"That would be up to Djadrani, wouldn't it?" he replies. "But if Dupuy has any influence, perhaps he can convince him of a plan that would benefit all of Torundi. There certainly would be enough profit to go around. If Djadrani kept the supply miniscule, Torundi could reap unprecedented wealth without devastating its resource. UnMonde would have to bid and woo along with everyone else for whatever amount Djadrani allowed. And other companies would develop ways to use it as well; it would wrest the power from UnMonde's hands and Torundi just might become the most progressive and environmentally sustainable country on the planet. It's a bit overwhelming to consider. You could go from being an unknown dot on the map to the wealthiest on earth – the best infrastructure, healthcare, education ...." He stops. "What is it, Sam?"

"Where do I start!" I say, turning to face the sky. It isn't his fault, but just speaking of Djadrani as someone who is sane or remotely responsible makes me angry. And I don't understand how Dr. Jean has been friends with such a man for so long. Or if not friends, then somehow a confidant, someone who obviously has his ear. The ear of a monster, in my opinion.

"I'm sure you know enough of our sultan to realize he hasn't exactly shown his benevolence in the past," I remind Gabe. "Even leaving out what he did in the purge, there is a reason why he resides in a fancy palace while his people live in thatched huts. Why he has power boats and helicopters and who knows what else, and the rest of the kingdom doesn't even have electricity. Some say he isn't even the rightful ruler. They say there was once a half brother who shared his power, one whose lineage was linked closer to the king's, but Djadrani somehow ran him off. You probably know more about that than I do; information is just another example of what our sultan has suppressed. But I do know enough to recognize that Djadrani is selfish and corrupt … and that your idea of a future Torundi is highly unrealistic!" I squeeze my eyes shut for a second and take a breath. "Sorry. I guess it winds me up."

I hear him shifting again. He joins me in gazing at the sky, his arms crossed behind his head now. "You are right," he says. "And Torundi is completely unprepared. The thing is, companies like UnMonde won't wait much longer to be invited. Wars have been started for less. In fact …." He stops. "Well, there's nothing we can do about that right now. We have to find out what Dr. Jean is willing to do; until then, we'll have to wait."

We are both silent for a while, the slosh of low ripples the only sound, the moon and stars the only light. It feels as if we have been removed to another dimension – one to be lived in for a few fleeting hours, perhaps, but I know I will remember every single second of this for the rest of my life.

"And what about you?" I ask. The thought I've been agonizing over escapes me in a rush. "If the plan you've just told me succeeds, won't UnMonde suspect your hand in it? You'd lose everything. If they're willing to take such lengths with me …." I pause, unable to utter what comes next, not out loud. "You'd always be looking over your shoulder," I substitute. "They'd never stand for it …."

I hear him laugh in reply. It throws me off. I look up at

him, wondering how he can make light of such a thing. He slides down, turning on his elbow so that his face is just above mine. And then he leans closer. I close my eyes from the fear and exhilaration of whatever this is, and realize it doesn't matter. I've slipped in and there is no going back.

"That should've been mine," I say.

"What's that?" he asks softly.

I open my eyes and watch his face, maybe afraid of what I might find, but I watch anyway. I reach my hand up and trace my fingers down his back, trailing the jagged pucker of his scar. "That should've been on me, not you," I answer. "Your scar … I want it back. It's mine."

He doesn't laugh this time.

He is so close now.

I am mesmerized by the nearness of him, of pure energy that feels so good I think I might melt into it. I wiggle closer until there is nothing between us but breath, until even that is gone. When he kisses me, his mouth turns my stomach into shivers, into throbs that only want more ….

"Sam," he mumbles.

I feel like I'm swimming up to him. His eyebrows are knitted together when I look into his face. We stay that way for a while. Face to face. A tangle of arms and legs. Of wonderment and pulses and sneaky little fears.

Then, after a while, his mouth tugs up at the corners. "There it is," he says.

"What?"

"That look. The same as it was four months ago."

I clear my throat, trying to focus. "Four months ago you hated me," I remind him.

He laughs at this and then props himself back on his elbow. It isn't fair how easily he recovers, especially when my head is still spinning. He says, "Haven't you ever behaved in a way that's the exact opposite of how you really feel?"

"Like right now?"

"So there you have it."

Definitely not fair. And he is too close. "What is *'it,'* exactly?" I frown, leaning away.

He turns on his back, folding his hands behind his head so that he stares again at the stars. "Haven't you ever experienced something," he resumes slowly, and I watch his lips move as he says this, his teeth glinting white in the darkness. I want to touch them. "Some favorite place in Torundi, perhaps. Or a painting. Or read something, a single line or a whole story, and the truth of it speaks to you?"

"Of course," I answer distractedly. It would be weird to touch them … right?

"Only this time, it doesn't just speak. It reaches in so that it becomes a part of you, a part that *should* be there, something better than everything else. And it grows until there's nothing left to do but give whatever you have for it – even though a part of you warns not to – because it is the truest thing you'll ever know?"

I think I am supposed to reply. But his question hits too deep, and that ache comes over me, that joy and that terrible fear.

"It is selfish, really," he continues. "Selfish because you need this for yourself. And if you try and fail, then you'll at least know it exists, and that is better than nothing." He tilts his head so that his gaze captures mine, holding it so that I can't look away. I gulp back a hiccup as his words shudder over me, too wonderful to catch. Words like that don't belong to me; I can't trust them.

"Sam?"

"Well, I …." I fumble, breathless. "I mean that's not exactly how I see *it.*"

"What do you believe then?" His mouth does that twitch again, like he thinks I'm funny, but he's trying not to show it.

"It's stupid."

"Please tell me."

I glance over. He looks earnest. And he deserves an answer, even if that answer is embarrassing.

So I take a deep breath. "It's just that it's ... it's all so beautiful and terrifying," I attempt, searching for the right explanation. And I can't look at him while I say this; it's just too awkward. So I lean my head against him instead, hoping he can't see my face. "Like … like diving into the ocean with no land in sight, no boats, no boundaries. You dive in, hoping to find whatever it is that made you take the leap in the first place … and you may find it, but you don't know. You may find it or you may sink into the darkness, lost forever. You have no way to know which one it will be. You only have your belief."

"Yes," he says after a moment. "It's like that, too."

I nod, keeping my head against him. I feel like I'm high

or something, and now, I don't even care; I don't care how stupid I sound or how much I'll cringe at my words when the light of day burns off this magic. I don't care, I don't care because I've already said it and now I feel like I'm floating. "That's where I am right now," I murmur. "I'm swimming in that dark, deep ocean, and there's a light, a glow so beautiful it can't seem real, but I'm swimming toward it anyway."

"What color is it?"

"Hmm?"

"The light."

"Oh, it's . . . golden," I answer dreamily. He feels so good. He smells so good.

He shifts against me. "Then you're swimming the wrong way, Clemens. That light's up here."

I look up. It takes a second to realize I'm staring at a gold locket, shaped at slightly rounded angles, only turned so that it hangs from a corner, like a kite. Unusual scrolling loops from each corner, curling toward the center where a single opal shimmers.

"Like it?" he says, clasping the chain around my neck.

I look from the locket to his face, too stunned to respond at first.

"It's different than most. It slides open like this ...." He twists the locket between his fingers so the front and the back slide apart, like petals on a flower. Then I see that the bottom portion of the locket contains an empty frame, still perfectly intact, but instead of a picture, the space is filled with a glassy, dark surface. "Well?"

"What?"

"What do you think?"

"I, uh … I think … I think it looks really old," I stutter, suddenly panicked. Is this a gift? I'm not even sure. And I don't have anything for him. But maybe he's just showing it to me ... did I just say the wrong thing? I think I just insulted his gift. But is it a gift? "I mean – not old, like ugly. Not that I mean old things are by default ugly. I mean, old things are often beautiful …. This is beautiful. You're beautiful. I mean, I don't mean that you're old. I just—"

"The word is 'thanks,' Clemens," he says with a laugh, rolling his eyes. "Or not even that, but just take it. Please. For both of our sakes. It's only a locket."

"But I don't—"

He leans down, his lips barely brushing against mine. "You're hopeless, you know that?"

"I know."

"Do you like it?"

I take a gulp of air and nod.

"But you don't know how to reciprocate?"

I nod again, relieved that he understands.

"Then I'll help you out here by changing the subject," he continues, still grinning. "For instance, how did you find your Aunt Janie after the ball tonight? Enjoying herself?"

I study his face, still dazed. After everything that has happened this evening, I had almost forgotten that piece of subterfuge. I take another gulp and then try to match his mood. "How did you manage it?"

"Oh, it just takes the right tourist, really. You'd be surprised what people will do for a little extra cash. And the special cider?"

I try to forget about the super-fancy amulet hanging around my neck as he asks this. But how much did that thing cost, anyway? Actually, I don't want to know. God. And I didn't get anything for him; not even a card or something ....

Focus.

I attempt a disapproving glance and say, "Alcohol is illegal at PACA, you know. She could lose her job for that."

"I'm sure she's furious; probably poured it straight down the sink." He chuckles, and then he grows thoughtful once more. I watch him, following every expression that crosses his face, holding them in my mind for later, when days and oceans come between us. The thought makes me forget all about the necklace and Aunt Janie's inevitable hangover, but it reminds me of something else. Something I've been dying to ask, that I *need* to ask.

"What about Janet Hobbs?" I blurt out. Then I bite my lip, embarrassed. "I mean, you two looked pretty cozy at Thanksgiving. Aren't you two ... I mean, I don't want to—"

He shrugs. "Janet asked *me* to that banquet, Sam. Nothing ever happened between us. I think ...." He grimaces and looks away. "Well, we should go ahead and get this over with I suppose, and the truth is, I was a bit out of my head that day. I think I was hoping it would make you jealous. There. Happy?"

I press my mouth together, fighting off a smile. I feel strangely victorious. "Oh," I say. "Well, it worked."

"So did your date with Caleb."

I'm grinning now. "I think he's jealous of you."

"Caleb is jealous because he assumed you'd be there when and if he wanted," he answers briskly, and I draw back, surprised by the hardness in his voice. "I'm glad you had the opportunity to set him straight. You are no one's standby, Sam. Not even Paolo's."

I feel bumps wash up my arms. For a second, I'm too stunned to speak. "You know about that?" I manage to ask. "With Paolo, I mean. You know what happened?"

"I know about as much as I think I want to know," he says, looking away again. "Why Paolo would think you were obligated to betroth yourself to him is incredible, even considering the Dyeen custom."

I shake my head, amazed at the sudden turn in conversation. But also, in a way, I feel relieved. I wasn't sure how to bring the Paolo thing up with Gabe … or if I even should. How do you explain a childhood sweetheart to someone whom you've – comparatively speaking at least – just met? But somehow, talking about this feels right. I feel like I could talk to Gabe about anything.

"It was more than that," I say. "It was the whole male-shortage-thing, too. Paolo is three years older – he could have had anyone but he waited for me. When I broke it off with him last year, it wasn't just a personal rejection. It was a public one, too. Everyone thought …." I stop, because the way he leans in is positively distracting.

"I don't want to talk about Caleb," he murmurs. He reaches up and twists a finger around my hair, now tracing my lips. He smiles at something, I don't know what. "And I certainly don't want to talk about Paolo. I want to talk about your eyes. I think they haunt me."

I blink back at him for a moment. How does he jump from subject to subject like that? I'm barely able to keep up. And worse, I've suddenly got a serious case of the yawns.

"Well, that's fitting," I finally say, "because the Dyeens call me *Mata Hantu*."

He bites his lower lip. It's so distracting. "*Mata* is eye, right?"

I nod.

"What's *Hantu*?"

"Ghost ...." I stifle another yawn. "It means Ghost Eyes."

His hand drops away, but he keeps looking at me. "Of course," he says and then he pulls me to him. We fold into each other, my head resting between his chest and shoulder. "But it is late. You should get some sleep."

I don't want to sleep. I want to stay awake and live every second of what's left of our time together. But the feel of him is unbelievable. And the sound of his heartbeat so calming, the smell of him so warm, that now, I suddenly don't want to move at all.

"Sleep," he says again. "I'll wake you up in time."

I tilt my head, my gaze following the line of his jaw, out to the darkness beyond. The moon beams a silver path over the water and the stars shine in the great, velvet expanse above. I yawn again.

And then, my eyes flutter closed, into that perfect night.

13. THE TANAH YATIM

I return to Torundi with a bewilderment almost equal to what I'd experienced when I left it. Nothing here has changed; it is as if no more than a few hours have gone by, perhaps, but I have lived years in the interim.

I hadn't expected that.

We string colorful, old-fashioned lights in the rain trees that hover over the mission grounds, just like we do every year. And at night we sit under the eaves, telling stories and gazing into the glow that plays over the wide, twisted trunks curling up from the earth as the sound of the mission's generator hums in the darkness beyond.

We make sugar cookies from our stock of imported flour, and all the Dyeen children help decorate the Santa and snowman and star shapes with homemade frosting, just like always. Nurse Kathy plays steady streams of holiday music from her old record player. And Trudy is back from her furlough, complete with one *Breakfast at Tiffany's*-inspired photograph and no inkling whatsoever that an ocean away she'd arranged for the most magical night of my life with a bottle of spiked apple cider.

Three days into my vacation, an outbreak of dengue fever hits the village. The mission is a madhouse from that moment on, with no time for anything but boiling potable water and stringing up mosquito nets.

In a way, the chaos is a relief as it keeps me occupied … and away from Paolo's still-hostile glances. I have to admit, I miss having him as my friend. At least Leila is as good-natured as ever, and whenever I get the chance I sneak off to the village to spend an hour or so just hanging out with her and cooing over her adorable son.

But otherwise, the chaos is frustrating. I try a few times to get Dr. Jean away from the clinic so I can talk to him as Gabe has instructed, but he won't hear of it. Too busy, he says, and I don't know how to convince him otherwise without sounding suspicious.

Over a week passes.

We are in the thick of it, probably due to our proximity to the Mokanan, but when our patient population dwindles to a manageable trickle, Dr. Jean announces his plan to visit the outer villages over the next few days, just in case they need help.

I grab at the chance.

It is early afternoon, around lunch hour, but I don't think Dr. Jean has taken a break yet. I open the door to his clinic and find him sitting at his desk, eyeglasses perched on his nose. I place a bowl of food and utensils in front of him.

"Since when do you wear those?"

He looks up at me, distracted.

"Your spectacles," I say, pointing.

"Oh, yes." He fumbles with the rims. "I asked Trudy to bring them back for me … a casualty of life, I suppose. Funny how quickly they pile up."

"They suit you. You look distinguished."

"Really?"

"Yes!" I can't help but laugh; I'd forgotten how absent-minded he can be, or how surprised he always gets at a compliment. "Now you should eat," I say.

Dr. Jean looks down and takes a suspicious sniff. "What is it?"

"Fish curry with green papaya chutney, compliments of Gajendra's training," I announce, reaching for a piece of scrap paper from his desk. I am suddenly nervous. And if I don't keep my hands busy, I'll only fidget with my necklace, which is definitely not something I wish to bring to his attention. "We're terrible cooks here, did you know that? And you, a Cajun! You're getting too skinny, besides, so eat."

He harrumphs at that, but he obediently picks up his fork, glancing up at me in the process, his warm hazel eyes crinkling at the sides. "It is good to have you home, by the way. Have I told you that yet? We all missed you terribly. It just wasn't the same without you here."

I make a few quick folds of my paper and beam back at

him. This moment, I realize, has brought me full circle. Four months ago, I felt utterly betrayed, filled with a hurt and resentment I was sure I'd never overcome, and now here I am, and it is all I can do *not* to tell him how much I look up to him, how much I admire everything he has done for me, for all of us; to tell him that I understand. But that will have to wait.

"I've missed you, too," I answer instead, wondering if my voice might give me away, or if something in my demeanor might alert him to my apprehension, but Dr. Jean just studies his lunch for a moment longer before he finally takes a bite.

"Speaking of your absence," he resumes tentatively, "I've been making plans for you. After graduation."

I stop folding.

He looks up, eyebrows raised. "What? No fuss? No defensive statements before I've said my piece? What's happened to you?"

I try to laugh, pushing down the thump in my chest. I want to tell him he can stop the ruse now; that there's no point in going to all that trouble.

But sitting here in his office with the knowledge that everything being said is most likely being listened to … well, it is incentive enough to bide my time. And then I can't help but wonder where people put those things. How does one hide surveillance equipment in a remote clinic in the middle of a tropical island? Is it like the movies: little, black chips in lamps and behind switches?

"I think it's something PACA puts in the water," I joke, trying to change the conversation. "Oh, come on, Dr. Jean. Eat your lunch already. We'll talk plans later."

"Bossy, too," he mutters gloomily. "But I was just going to ask how you'd feel about attending my alma mater?"

I resume my folding, frustrated. So much for diversion.

"Tulane," he clarifies as he stabs at another bite. "New Orleans – this is delicious, by the way. I've got some friends there who've offered to help get you settled. They've agreed to look after you and make sure you have everything you need. And if you do well enough – and I know that you will – then you could attend medical school there, too. It is what you wanted, after all, to be a clinician. Well?" He pauses, mid-chew. "What do you think?"

I look down at my hands, busying them with the scrap of paper, and I know it is time to have our talk, *the* talk, the one I've been putting off because there never seems to be the right opportunity. But time is running out.

"Why don't we talk about it over a picnic?" I suggest – very smoothly, I think. I make a few final folds on my origami. "We haven't had one of our bike trips yet and I'll be gone again in a few days. How about tomorrow? Just you and me. We can stop on the way to one of your site visits."

"Tomorrow …." He looks confused.

"Perfect," I say, jumping from the chair. I place my paper cicada on his desk and lean over to kiss the top of his head, which I have just noticed is decidedly more grey now than brown. "I've got to scat. Trudy and I are meeting Leila in the village—"

"Trudy!" he exclaims, frowning. "Where's the 'Miss'?"

"She told me to lose it. I'll meet up with you in the morning." I leave before he can reply, glancing back for a moment as I close the door behind me.

Dr. Jean remains seated at his desk, his face a study of befuddlement, and I feel guilty and worried at the same time. He carries the weight of our world on his shoulders, I can see that. The last several months have not been kind to him; he looks five years older, at least, and I realize he is the one thing in Torundi that has changed. I wonder what it must be like for him, to bear this secret – one that even he doesn't understand. All he understands is that it looms there, threatening everything, and he doesn't know how to keep it back.

At least he won't have to feel that way much longer.

The next morning, we eat a quick breakfast of sticky rice topped with crushed peanuts, shredded coconut and dark palm syrup. It is my favorite. Dr. Jean throws rueful glances every now and then at our new art addition hanging prominently on the wall before us: a black-and-white of one Gertrude "Trudy" Wallace.

She wears a black, sleeveless gown and dress gloves, her hair in a high twist, a cigarette stem in hand and a puff of smoke in the air as she poses outside Tiffany's.

"That one," he mutters, shaking his head.

"It's herbal."

"So's tobacco! Does that make it healthy? And what's it

supposed to *mean?* I shudder to think what I'll be looking at when she finds out about Tulane!"

"I think she looks gorgeous," I say, scooping up a final bite of food, but Dr. Jean's brow puckers in protest.

I hold back a smile, glimpsing between him and Trudy's portrait. Dr. Jean catches my glance. He scowls and then stalks with his bowl to the kitchen. I follow after him, wondering about that. I'd never noticed such a dour expression on his face before ....

"Let me drive?" I call behind him.

He only snorts in reply.

Ten minutes later, we are bumping over the forest path on Dr. Jean's Yamaha. I sit directly behind him, the wind whipping over my face. I love it, this feeling of speed. Of freedom.

The motorcycle hums steadily as we thread through tall trees that diffuse the sunlight. We approach a familiar fork in the trail and I wait, hoping he'll choose the trail we used to take when I was younger, the one branching to the right. He does. After a while we ascend a hill, the trees falling from us until only grass sweeps the ground. We stop at the crest and take off our helmets.

"It's been a long time since we've been here," says Dr. Jean, walking to the spot where we used to have our picnics. The breeze rumples his thick hair. He looks over the arch of bending grass, then down at his watch. "Too early for lunch. Want to hit the Djurds first? I doubt they'll have much for us to do there. We can come back in a couple hours."

"What does your sixth sense tell you?" I say instead, glancing about us. It is all perfectly normal as far as I can tell. The wind rattles the dry grass and birds caw from the trees in the distance. Not too quiet, not too loud. "Think we're alone?"

Dr. Jean turns to me, eyes troubled. "Undoubtedly."

"And over here," I continue, walking to a recess in the hill, "the way the wind skirts around that, it's like a natural sound barrier. It would be difficult for voices to carry, wouldn't it?"

Dr. Jean follows me. "What are you getting at, Sam?"

I sit down. He sits down.

And then I tell him.

Dr. Jean sits perfectly still the whole time, his handsome face shifting from shock to astonishment to grim understanding. When I finish, he continues to stare at the ground. "These last four months … and they've always known where you were," he eventually murmurs.

"Can you get to the sultan?" I say.

Dr. Jean slowly nods. "Get to him, yes. But it's a bit more complicated than that. Djadrani is a patient of mine; you know that – it's the only reason we've been allowed to stay on here …." He pauses to shift his legs, scanning our surroundings as he does so.

I wait.

"Even assuming he'd choose a path that would benefit Torundi and not only himself," Dr. Jean soon continues, "there's the matter of his influence." His voice fills with unease. "The east side of the island is of particular concern. It started shortly before I sent you off, but civil unrest there has since escalated. And there are whispers of an heir who should have acceded to the throne."

"The half brother?"

Dr. Jean plucks a piece of grass and twists it between his fingers. "Harim. I always assumed he was dead. Perhaps not. I may have lived here for nearly twenty years, but I am still an outsider. No one dares speak of what happened during that time, especially to a foreigner. And Djadrani only tells me what he wants me to know."

"But you think this unrest … this business about a potential heir is somehow tied to UnMonde?" I ask.

"It fits," he says, tying a knot in the blade of grass. "I'd suspected it before; why else have they been so persistent? And the things that were said the last time …." He stops abruptly, his brows creasing all the more.

"What was said, Dr. Jean?"

He doesn't reply at first; he just sits there, twisting the blade between his fingers.

"They really will stop at nothing for this," he says after a while. "It's amazing. All of this," he tosses the frayed grass to the ground. "All of our studies, all of our work with the Dyeens. It was never real, was it? I wonder if they've even *looked* at my reports over the past three years. And here I was, assuming my new test results were just redundant; that someone else had already presented them. I never thought I could be so blind."

"You're not blind, Dr. Jean. You're an idealist."

"Same thing," he grumbles, pulling another blade from the ground. He looks at me for a moment, his face filled with a bitterness I've never seen in him before. "Well, it doesn't matter now, does it? And what of our plans for the Dyeens? What will we tell them? We're part of their fabric now. If the mission were to go away, so many things they've grown to rely upon would be taken from them."

I watch him, mystified by this unexpected moodiness – it is so uncharacteristic of him. Dr. Jean is pensive, certainly; distracted, almost always; but I'd never known him to allow self-pity.

"So, we're completely isolated," he resumes, lifting his head. Despite this unhappy forecast, I am relieved to hear that trademark logic return to his voice. "We're hardly even on the map. No one, except those with a vested interest, cares about our island. Most don't even know it exists. And the information we have isn't vetted to convince anyone who could make a difference anyway. UnMonde couldn't be more poised to get what they want. Even their presence is invisible. By all appearances, GMS is a nonprofit completely unrelated to any corporation and Marcus is the only contact I actually know by name. If they can grab control over the island, there will be little repercussion from the international community; nothing will stand in their way because no one will ever even know about it."

"But if we talked to Djadrani?"

"That's our only real option," agrees Dr. Jean. "Talk to him and hope he still has what it takes to stand up to them. But even then, it will be obvious how he discovered the truth.

I'd be putting everyone's safety at risk; Djadrani's a loose cannon. You're too young to appreciate the terror he caused all those years ago."

I think about that. It is the one piece of history I do know about. Everyone does. The horror of Djadrani's purge. I swallow down the bubble of guilt that always surfaces just from the thought that I and every female in Torundi survived that year … but 300 first-born males did not.

"I'm sorry, Sam." Dr. Jean flinches as he turns to me. "I shouldn't have brought that up – I know how it makes you feel. It's just the morose nature of this business that made me even think of it."

I nod, eager to change the subject.

"And this Gabe fellow …."

"I trust him."

"Yes, I can see that." He presses his mouth together, glaring down at the grass.

I sit beside him in silence. Something he said tugs at my mind. Gabe had mentioned it, too: about this man named Marcus. It sounds as if he has been visiting Torundi for years and years. Since before Dr. Jean's time, even. Since before I was born. Could it be possible ...?

I don't know how to broach the subject.

"The Tanah Yatim's pretty close to the Djurds," I say after a while. "You and I used to go all the time. So it wouldn't be unusual to pay a visit, would it?"

Dr. Jean glances up to the tree line, perhaps thinking that one over. "All right," he says slowly. "Why not?"

A visit to the Djurds and some two hours later, Dr. Jean and I pull to a stop at the ravine's edge. I look around, awestruck. I'll never get used to it.

Below us, the earth slices open in a long, narrow gash, ending in a pool of the brightest aquamarine water I have ever seen. It is so brilliant it looks fake. No wonder the place is considered holy. All along its sides, undergrowth climbs down the ravine, and halfway down the eastern edge, I can make out the familiar dark smudge marking the entrance to the cave of the Tanah Yatim.

I hook my helmet over the bike's handlebars and grab the flashlight from the storage space under the seat.

"I think I'll check out the cave for a minute," I say, following a barely perceptible footpath down the side. "You staying up here?"

"Oh …. I'll follow in a minute," Dr. Jean answers, fumbling for something.

I edge down the ravine trail until I reach the cave's entrance. It only takes about ten minutes. Wildflowers grow in spidery clusters about the threshold and vines drape from the opening, creating a natural curtain. The effect is picturesque and oddly appropriate – without these accoutrements, the opening would seem naked in some way.

I click on my flashlight and step through the tendrils of vine, into the darkness. The noise of the jungle instantly vanishes, the heat of the day becoming just as irrelevant. I pan my light over the walls, highlighting the ancient, whimsical shapes that float over cold stone. There is a story here, it is clear, but no one has ever deciphered it. My fingers trace along one of the reliefs; it is the figure of a man, but his head is that of a boar instead of a man's, and in his right hand, which is raised to his shoulder, he holds an object that looks as if it might be a lotus flower, but I can't be certain. Around the man, from the ground up to mid-torso, a snake coils with its jaws wide open, its mouth facing the viewer. The relief is definitely intriguing, and a little unsettling. But the biggest puzzle of all lies in the image of the snake: Torundi doesn't have them.

A noise distracts me and I flash my light toward the opening, expecting to see Dr. Jean, but find nothing there but the hazy glow of vegetation. Something about that makes my skin prickle. I shift uneasily and run my flashlight around the cavern, beaming it toward the far side of the room, where a small tunnel leads deeper into the ground. I stop. For a moment, I'm too shocked to register the reality that has just presented itself.

But no. *Someone* is there.

I blink, hearing the ringing in my ears, and I think I scream but can't be sure. I stare back at the man, unable to move. He is dressed in dark clothes in a fashion similar to the Djurds, but his face betrays the paleness of a foreigner. He stands as still as a statue, his eyes locked on mine, interested.

"Sam, are you okay?" shouts Dr. Jean from somewhere outside.

The man smiles, sending a chill through me. And before Dr. Jean's call is over, the man slides through the opening of the cave, disappearing into the glare of light. I scramble after him, my pulse still roaring. I pass through the curtain of vines and blink into the sunlight. I am too late.

Dr. Jean hurries down the path.

"What happened?" he asks, panting.

I scan the vast ravine before me, hoping for a movement somewhere within the tangle of undergrowth. Nothing. It is as if he's dissolved into the earth.

"Sam, talk to me! What happened?"

"There … was a man," I manage, jabbing my flashlight from the cave to the ravine below. It strikes me that the man's eyes were eerily similar to the blue of the waters there. "He just appeared …."

Dr. Jean's face goes white.

"Blue eyes," I add dazedly.

At this bit of information, Dr. Jean grabs my arm. "Let's go," he says, and without waiting, he pulls me up the path.

"It felt as if he knew me," I say, stumbling after him. "Do you … do you know him?"

Dr. Jean walks faster, tugging me in his wake.

"I think we can safely assume," he finally answers, his voice dark and tense, "that you have just met Marcus."

14. THAIPUSAM

The plane touches down and bumps over the runway, my pulse bumping right along with it. These three weeks have felt like an eternity, with no word and no way to know how Gabe is doing. I wonder where I will first see him, or when we'll have a chance to be alone. It is all I can think about.

I fidget with the seat pocket in front of me and pull out the shellacked, rectangular prayer card sandwiched between the airline magazine and the safety instructions pamphlet. I flip it over in my hands: It displays a Catholic prayer, Islamic prayer, Buddhist prayer, Protestant prayer and Hindu prayer, each written in three different languages, targeted, I can only suppose, toward the expected audience of each. "For use in emergency," it says.

The seat belt lights ding off and my fellow travelers

shuffle out of their seats in synchronicity, paying no heed to the attendant's request to remain seated until the doors are opened. And then we are in the airport, queuing in lines to proceed through Immigration. I look around, a part of me not quite trusting the idea that I am actually here. After the cave incident, I wasn't sure what to expect from Dr. Jean. He didn't want me to return to PACA – I could see that right away – but, thanks to our blue-eyed visitor, PACA won out as the lesser of two evils.

I am still fighting that dazed feeling when I run into Julie Wagner at the conveyor belt. And it feels incongruous, as if my world in Torundi couldn't exist at the same time as this: just two girls meeting up after their holiday and waiting for their bags.

Julie does most of the talking and, from the sounds of it, she's spent her vacation applying to schools. "Can you believe this is our last semester at PACA?"

"No," I say distractedly, glancing around the baggage claim area, but of course he wouldn't be here. I know that. I look again.

"So, where have you applied?"

"Oh, um, Tulane, I guess," I answer, not knowing what else to say. Technically, I suppose this is the correct response. *I* haven't applied anywhere, but it seems that, by proxy and despite her wishes, a Ms. Sam Clemens has applied nonetheless. The thought hangs uneasily in my mind, but then our bags bob down the belt, momentarily putting off the rest of that conversation.

We stumble with our suitcases toward the inspection

tables, where Customs officials riffle through our things. Julie giggles and whispers that she's packed her underwear at the top because it curtails the inspection process. "They get so embarrassed!" she says.

I have my doubts about that, but it probably does distract them from the chocolate bars she's hoarded at the bottom. A few bras and panties later, the officials nod for us to proceed. We head through the exit and toward the PACA bus that waits for us outside, Julie still rambling about Christmas break and college applications as we find a seat.

The bus rumbles to life and heads north up Jalan Sultan Azlan Shah, just as Julie switches from the subject of Christmas vacation to the Christmas Ball and, in particular, Zach Perkins. I try to comment and smile at appropriate times, but my mind is kilometers away.

"He's surprisingly old-fashioned," she says. "I mean, he even wrote me a few letters, like *handwritten* letters." I nod as she continues, barely able to think about anything other than a particular person who will hopefully be loitering somewhere about campus when we arrive.

"Hey, did you hear?" she asks.

"Hmm?"

"Caleb. He ... started dating Annie over the holiday," she says uneasily. "Zach told me. I thought you would want to know ...."

"Oh!" The implication yanks me back to the present. How odd. It seems that everyone but me had put the two of us together. "Well, that's great," I say, feeling unexpectedly relieved.

My response must have confused her because we sit in silence for the rest of our journey. When the bus finally rolls to a stop at the student center, Julie squeals and then quickly looks down at her lap while I peer gloomily out the window. No sign of Gabe but Zach is there, leaning against the soda machine, hands in pockets, hair disarrayed to perfection. Julie practically floats off the bus. I shuffle after her.

As soon as my feet hit the pavement, Tess and EJ bounce toward me, commandeering my luggage while never breaking stride with their prior conversation, which apparently had consisted of a dispute over talking points. Tess must have won because she grabs my arm and immediately relays minute details of her family vacation in Bali, where Aaron flew in to meet them for a week. That guy must be loaded.

We are halfway to our dorm when EJ stops. "I will throw up if I hear anything more about Aaron," she announces, glaring at Tess. "Even Sam is bored, and she just got here!"

"What?" I fumble. "That's not … I was just …. How's Tommy?"

But I gather from EJ's response that Tommy is no longer a contender. A tanned son of a businessman from Spain superseded him over the holiday, and EJ has the photos to prove it. I glance between the pictures on her phone and the campus arch, now searching the stairs leading from lower campus, now again the student center.

"So what do you think?" demands EJ, and it is clear I'd better respond. I force my gaze back to her phone.

"He's very handsome. Um. Is that a gun you're holding?"

EJ grins and then delves into a delightful story about spear fishing, snorkeling and other holiday-romance-related activities while I look around again.

But I never see Gabe on campus that day. Or the next. I don't see him for a week. Then two. No one knows what's happened. He wouldn't just disappear, not without a reason, I know that now. I've never felt so helpless. And all Mr. Krikorian can offer is that he'd seen Gabe over the holidays – they'd even worked on their PES project during the break -- so his absence is just as befuddling to him.

I get through another school week, the days blurring one into the other, my sense of desperation only growing worse. I feel stuck between two imploding worlds. I don't know what's happening in Torundi, and I don't know what's happening here. I also don't know what to *do.*

It is now the sacred Hindu holiday of Thaipusam. Most of the kitchen staff are off for the day, so my waitressing duties are, too. This does not help, actually. I prefer to stay busy.

I wander miserably toward my locker, bracing myself for another weekend with no word from Gabe, and I am just reaching for my French textbook when my hand freezes in the air. There is a ringing in my ears. I squeeze my eyes shut and then look again, but it is still there:

An envelope.

My name is scrawled across the top in a script that I know better than my own.

I tear it open.

Almost four hours later, I sit in the back of the taxi with the Lat bumper sticker. It pulls out of the Nuevostar and turns down Tanjung Bungah Road. A red hibiscus swings from a ribbon tied to the rearview mirror, keeping time with the thudding in my chest as the golden glow of dusk slowly fades to grey. I look from the waning light all around to my hands, which clutch the note tightly. So far, it is exactly as his instructions had said. I can hardly believe I am finally going to see him, to find out what has happened in the weeks we've been apart.

Before long the taxi veers left and heads down the familiar, narrow road that leads to the stalls under the banyan trees. We pass the outdoor amphitheater, now empty and without its golden lights. And then we finally stop.

I jump out of the taxi.

In my excitement, it takes me a moment to register that the place is filled with people. Music blares from loud speakers where the kiosks had been before, and smoke enshrouds the whole area. The grove under the trees swarms with Thaipusam observers moving toward some unseen event. I can hardly distinguish one body from the next, even under the throb of lights. From somewhere beyond the outer ring of bodies small, circular tents peak above the chaos.

I squeeze through the crowd, eager to make my way to the beach, now passing a man who walks bare-chested, his back threaded with silver hooks as he hauls a decorated chariot behind him. I recognize this at once as a ceremonial burden or a *kavadi,* just as Gajendra has explained it to me.

The weight from the *kavadi* pulls at the hooks in the man's back, tugging his flesh into triangles. He walks on, trance-like through the massive crowd, by all appearances completely pain-free.

I pass more devotees, some pierced through their cheeks with long needles, some touting colorful platforms on their shoulders, some with hooks in their chest and back that swing with little, metal pots. Then I'm in front of a crowd. To my left, a fire licks at bricks and charcoal. Before me, a path of glowing coals stretches over the ground. Several men are walking barefoot across it, their expressions utterly serene. I skirt around the smoking pathway, continuing on my route.

"Sam!"

I turn at the sound of my name. Gajendra stands before me and the light from the nearby fire flickers across his face, reflecting an eerie red.

"Sam, what on earth are you doing here?" he demands. "And all alone, at that!"

I'm jostled to the side. "Don't worry, Gajendra. I'm fine," I call, now grateful for the crowd. "Please don't tell anyone; I'll see you tomorrow!" And then I squeeze through the throngs before he can stop me.

When I finally reach the beach, the crowd has thinned to a trickle. I head straight for the fort, passing a few random people who don't take much notice of me. I run up the steps, my heart pounding with the deafening rhythm of the festival I've just left behind. I look around. No one is here.

"Gabe?"

I step to the edge of the terrace, now peering down at the water that crashes below. A white object catches my attention to the left of the fort. I lean forward and crane my head around the side of the veranda, where a narrow cove curves into the shore. A seaplane rocks back and forth in the shallows there.

"Gabe?" I call again.

"I see you have been admiring my plane," floats a voice behind me.

I spin around. I think I am too shocked to notice anything at first, but in the next moment, I recognize the pale face, the striking blue eyes. A chill rolls up my stomach. Instinctively, I back away. The veranda ledge presses against my lower back, but still I watch him, fascinated.

"We've met before," says the man.

My skin prickles at the memory. But not in the way I'd expect. I am not afraid. And I can see the rest of him now. Dark blond hair, a wide-ish nose, lips that stretch tight across his face. He looks around Dr. Jean's age, maybe a few years older. But the most distinguishing characteristic remain his eyes. I look back at him, my ghost eyes meeting his blue. And I wonder if he's wondering a similar thing.

"It would have been much easier then," he adds gently. "I'm sorry to cause such a shock, but I'm not the one who makes these decisions."

I want to ask him. It is right there, at the edge of my mouth, the question that has haunted me for seventeen years.

Instead, I say, "Who makes what decisions?"

He steps closer. Something glints in his hand.

"This," he says.

Pain explodes everywhere, springing me up and backward at the same time, and in the next instant, my knees collapse under my weight, sending me to the floor. The cramp rips through me. I can't speak. I don't even know if I am writhing in pain or if I am now somehow paralyzed.

And then just as suddenly, everything goes black.

I awake to the sound of voices.

Sunlight filters through bamboo cracks. I am lying on some sort of crisp, but soft, surface. It is too bright. Pain stabs at my temples, making it difficult to think. I can't remember anything after I spotted the glint of metal in Marcus's hands, so I quickly close my eyes, feigning sleep until I can sort out what has happened.

"Why are we all being held here?"

I stiffen, immediately recognizing Trudy's voice. Impossible.

"I think she is awake now," returns a calm tone.

"Leave her alone," growls another. It is Dr. Jean, I am positive. My eyes fly open.

"Ah, I knew it!" Marcus smiles warmly. "How are you feeling, Sam?"

I blink, looking about me. I am lying on the exam table of our mission's clinic, directly in front of Marcus. Trudy, Nurse

Kathy and Dr. Jean sit in a semicircle just behind him. There is something unnatural about their postures.

I roll my head back, the pain splitting my vision. I think I might throw up. And I'm so hot. I take deep breaths, trying to calm down. I look to the door, and only then do I notice two other men standing there. They are both tall – well over six feet. They both hold military rifles.

"What's going on?" I whisper, but it sends another wave of nausea through me. I press my lips tight, trying not to moan.

"We've just been waiting for you to recover," replies Marcus. "Dr. Dupuy will be off shortly, but I wanted to give you a chance to say goodbye first. It is the least I can do, considering …." He pauses, looking from Dr. Jean to me. Then he sighs and says, "For such a little place, there are an awful lot of secrets."

"Just get it over with," snaps Dr. Jean.

I struggle to a sitting position. Goodbye? I don't know what to make of that. Secrets? Well, that is true, but which ones does he mean? It would help if I knew what's happened up to this point. And the spinning room isn't doing me any favors.

A knock sounds at the door. Marcus frowns and waves away the guards. He points at Nurse Kathy. "Make yourself useful, will you, dear? Go tell whomever it is that you are closed for the day."

"I certainly will not!" retorts Nurse Kathy with a sniff. She crosses her loose, freckled arms in front of her.

"Take the key," Marcus says quietly, holding Dr. Jean's

copy out to her, "and tell them you are closed for the day. That is the message you will give, Kathy."

Nurse Kathy's mouth puckers, but she gets to her feet. She grabs the key and shuffles over to the door. From where I sit, I can see her hands shake as the lock unclicks. She pokes her head out the door. I hear her reciting the instructions in Torundi and, after a pause, a familiar voice mumbles its assent. I recognize the voice immediately. It is Ibu Heti, coming for more medicine for her baby. She asks if she can return first thing in the morning. Nurse Kathy says that she should, and then closes the door.

"Lock it," says Marcus.

Nurse Kathy turns the key.

"Thank you." As Marcus points Kathy back to her seat, I notice that he holds a gun in his left hand. He waits until she is seated, then crosses his legs and glances around the room. When he gets to Dr. Jean, his gaze stays there. Dr. Jean returns his stare but says nothing.

"I don't know how to tell you this," continues Marcus, picking something from his sleeve. He turns to me, contrite. My head is killing me. I don't know what is going on, but now is hardly the time to make dramatic soliloquies. He says, "I really did think a smart girl like you would have already figured it out ...."

"What?" I say through gritted teeth.

Marcus raises his brows. "Why, it's obvious, Sam. I thought you'd want to bid adieu to your father."

I've been sitting still this whole time, concentrating on the silk kerchief at Marcus's throat, trying to make the room stay still. But at this pronouncement, everything freezes. A strange buzzing fills the air, and I see Marcus look back at me, that disorienting smile in his eyes.

"I've always wondered, Dupuy: Where were you when Merpati brought your newborn daughter to the mission? Did you see her coming? Did you watch Merpati die or did you just hide until that nasty business was over?"

Dr. Jean says nothing. Trudy and Nurse Kathy stare.

Merpati.

Doctor Jean Dupuy.

Me.

I feel the exam table paper crinkle under my hands, I hear that buzzing sound again, and I see faces swimming in front of me, swirling with the room.

"Well," Trudy finally says, her voice sounding forced, "that can't be the reason why we're all here."

"You are absolutely right," agrees Marcus. He uncrosses his legs and leans forward. "Sam, I'm sorry about the way you've had to learn this, but you're not the only one your father has betrayed. Aside from the unfortunate Merpati, your mother, he's completely disregarded us, the very organization who founded this mission in the first place! We did everything for him. We provided a home, we facilitated his purpose in life – who else gets an opportunity like that? We even protected his little secret, and all we ever asked in return was a small favor that would only benefit the island and everyone in it."

"How would it benefit anyone in Torundi?" growls Dr. Jean. Even in my stupor, I think it peculiar that this is the thing he chooses to respond to. "If the Tanah Yatim were conveyed to your company, what then, Marcus? You've exposed me for what I am, so don't lie to them now. Let's just pretend for a moment that I'll go along with your plan. Tell them what would really happen!"

"Calm down, Dupuy. You still have a chance to show your appreciation—"

"What are we *talking* about?" interrupts Trudy.

Marcus sits straight in his chair, the palms of his hands pressing against his knees. "We are talking about an act of solidarity, Ms. Wallace," he answers while continuing to stare at Dr. Jean. "That is why I have you here. I want all of us in agreement. From now on, your secrets are my secrets; mine, yours. If one goes down, we'll go down together, so to speak. And I won't tease you along anymore. In short, we have a new plan. We will no longer be asking Dupuy to persuade the sultan to bestow the holy site to our very deserving environmental group. We've found a much simpler solution."

"What's that?" says Dr. Jean.

Marcus smiles. "We have located the sultan's half brother, Harim, who is more than willing to fill that void. He and Djadrani were equals in another life, as you may know, both administrators under the king and queen." Marcus lifts his right hand, palm up and open, as though he is weighing an invisible stone within it.

"But Djadrani was more ambitious, even then. He managed all those years ago to have Harim appointed over the southeast side of the island, based near the reclusive lands of the Tagolis. Out of sight, out of mind. When the king died, Djadrani stayed close to the palace, currying favor with Her Majesty. After her death, Djadrani's appointment seemed a natural transition, but many believed it should have gone to Harim. He was the older of the two, and his father's blood linked more closely to that of royalty. Djadrani knew this, too, and tried to have him killed off. Fortuitously for us, something went amiss. Harim managed to escape and has been in hiding ever since." Marcus drops his hand. "We are eager to help him achieve his rightful position."

The room is silent for at least a minute. The clock on the wall ticks steadily, and with each second that passes, the tick grows louder.

"You want me to *help* you get rid of Djadrani," Dr. Jean finally says.

"We do. It isn't asking much. All you have to do is deliver a certain medication on your next scheduled visit, which I believe is, quite conveniently, this afternoon. He trusts you. He'll take whatever dose you prescribe."

I look from Marcus to Dr. Jean, not knowing what to expect next.

"When you go to your motorcycle," Marcus continues, "you will find what you need already placed in your bag. All you have to do is show up at your regular time and do the deed."

"And if I don't?"

Marcus adjusts the silk knot at his neckline. "Then one of these trained marksmen," he nods toward the guards by the door, "will be forced to shoot not only the sultan, but you as well. We'd prefer not to. It makes people ask too many questions. So unnecessary. Of course, you'll only be injured, because I do insist that you live to watch what will happen back here, should you choose to be recalcitrant."

"If that's all it takes, why not do it yourself?" Trudy snaps. I blink at her, stunned. Trudy's got guts. Even when she's held captive at gunpoint and facing a rather steep learning curve that includes the disillusionment of one Dr. Jean Dupuy's character and the dubious future of her precious Global Medicine Solutions, she's tough. Marcus does not share my sentiment.

"Because," he answers slowly, as if speaking to an especially obtuse individual, "as you know, Djadrani is a bit of a hermit these days. No one would suspect Dupuy's presence, however, and as Djadrani's health hasn't been stellar of late, his demise will appear to be of natural causes. The same could not be said of a stranger who forces his way into the palace."

As if on cue, the two guards walk toward Dr. Jean.

Marcus nods. "Time to go now, Dupuy," he says.

15. THE WHITE PALACE

Marcus scoots his chair so that he is only two feet away from me. He turns slightly and stretches out his legs, like a cat basking in the sunlight. He looks so comfortable here. Nurse Kathy and Trudy remain behind him, fixed to their seats as the sound of motorcycles fade into the distance.

"I'll let you in on another secret," he says after a while. "You'll like this one."

I glance up into those cool, blue eyes. How could I have ever thought that he might be my father? How could I have ever *not* considered that Dr. Jean was?

"What if I told you ...." He pauses, as though thinking something over. "What if I told you that it was you who tipped us off about Gabriel?"

My fingers dig into the exam table.

"I see your confusion," he continues sympathetically. "But after all, he is exceptional; you didn't really think *he'd* made the mistake, did you?"

The room starts spinning again, faster and faster.

I put my head down for a moment, lowering it between my knees. I feel dazed by the painful truth of his statement.

"How did you know I'd go to the fort?" I finally ask. I lift my head and force myself to sit upright. Better to get this over with.

"I do like you, Sam," he says with a sigh. "So I'll answer your question, but then I'll expect you to answer one of mine. Agreed?"

I merely look back at him. I want to hide the panic clawing under my skin.

"Well, it is quite simple," he continues, straightening in his seat. "After your little picnic with Dupuy that day when you and I first met in the cave, some of my friends and I decided to stop by Gabriel's place at the end of the holidays. But when we got there, he was gone. We waited two days! By the third day, there was still no sign of him. There was, however, a certain taxi driver outside his apartment. We questioned him. He said he was looking for work and had learned the address after watching Gabriel walk home one night. He didn't seem to know much, but what he did know, he was more than willing to share .... Gabriel's penchant for hibiscus and fort-side *tête-à-têtes,* for instance. We finally managed to track him down days later. Truth be told, I think we pushed him too hard too fast. The boy was tired. I think he was almost relieved to get caught."

I swallow, trying to sort that out.

"And the note?" I ask. "The one left in my locker, with his handwriting?"

"That is a separate question, Sam. It is my turn now."

Another knock sounds at the door.

"These *people,*" Marcus growls, twisting in his chair. He waves his gun. "Up you go, Kathy. The same as before."

Nurse Kathy doesn't protest this time. She hobbles to the door, now turning the key that's already in place there. She pokes her head out and begins the standard explanation. And then she stumbles backward. Everything happens at once.

At first, I think I'm seeing things. A gun goes off. Then another. But I'm still not sure because my head is so foggy. Maybe it's a side effect from whatever it is that Marcus gave me, or a reaction to all that has hit my mind today; a defense mechanism; I only see what I most want to see.

But no.

He is definitely *here*, holding a rifle similar to that of the guards'. Marcus staggers backward, clutching a pant leg that mushrooms with blood. Gabe is behind him now, jamming the rifle butt into his head. Marcus crumples to the floor, his gun clattering beside him. Only Trudy has the sense to reach for it. Nurse Kathy is screaming at the top of her lungs. I'm babbling something, too, I don't even know what. Then Gabe's voice: calm and quick. Trudy understands, I think. My brain feels like it's grabbing at words that only fall between fingers.

Gabe throws a rope to Trudy and then grabs my arm. He pulls me through the door. Moving seems to help clear my head. I wobble to a stop as we pass a guard who lies sprawled on the ground, just outside the clinic. His head faces the wrong direction.

"Di-didyudothat?" I slur stupidly.

But Gabe doesn't answer; he pulls me toward a large motorcycle – shiny and black. It looks incredibly out of place. And it's too big. I don't see how it can fit through the trees, but in the next moment, we're on it.

"Hold on tight, Sam."

The engine roars in my ears as we catapult into the rain forest. I didn't know bikes could go so fast. The trees whip by so quickly that the entire world is nothing but a blur of green. I hold on tighter, gasping at the fresh air until I realize that I am crying. My arms wrap so tightly around Gabe that it would be impossible to press closer, my face against his back, my sobs disappearing into the roar.

The tangle of forest continues to rocket past. It feels like it matches the manic blur of my mind; the mute terror of Gabe's disappearance, the confusion of my abduction, the revelation of Dr. Jean, the horror of Djadrani's planned demise, and then … Gabe. He is here. It all wrings out of me and I clutch him so hard that my arms ache from the pressure. I don't know how far we've gone or how fast we are going. It is wild and terrifying. It is everything I feel.

We begin to slow down. By the time Gabe cuts the engine, the swell of relief and anxiety has been cried out of me. I may look like hell, but I am calm now.

I lift my head and look over his shoulder. Before us gleams a large, white complex. It stands apart from the rain forest, is surrounded by palm trees and perfectly placed palmettos and faces a high cliff that looms over the sea.

"Djadrani's palace," I whisper.

I've never seen it before. All my life I've heard tales of its magnificence. I've always wondered if it could really be so.

Gabe rolls to a stop just outside the outer wall. He drops his feet to the ground, steadying the bike for me as I slide off. My joints wobble under my weight as though they've been replaced with tapioca pudding. I clutch the bike seat for a moment, trying to regain balance without giving myself away.

"You've got to go up there," he says, pointing to the left. I can just make out a wide, marble staircase that leads into the main building. "Tell them who you are and that you need to see Dr. Jean immediately. I am sure they know of you; they should let you through. Get Dupuy and then get out of there."

I let go of the seat. "What about you?"

His eyes flick from the palace to me.

"I've got to find the other guard who followed Dupuy. And you need to get up those stairs before he sees you. Sam, you can do this. But we have to move. If all goes well, I'll meet you there," he says, gesturing to the outside of the palace's main entrance. A little further to the left, I can see Dr. Jean's Yamaha parked under the shade of a palm tree.

"And if it doesn't?"

"Then I'll find you. But no matter what happens, make sure you get back to Penang as soon as possible. You can't stay in Torundi. And don't let Djadrani know you'll be leaving."

But I can't turn away. I feel like if I stop looking at him, he will disappear again.

"Sam, you have to go now," he says, and the urgency in his voice shakes some sense into me. I swallow, forcing my gaze from him.

"Okay."

And then I am running.

"Sam ...."

I turn. He stands just outside the entrance to the complex, and when our eyes meet, that same look is there as it has always been, fierce and steady and endless.

"Be careful," he says. "And remember what I said about Penang."

"I … I love you," I say. Or at least I think I do.

A smile twitches at his mouth. "About time you admitted it, Clemens."

And then he is gone. His steps fade around the perimeter wall as I force my legs back into a run, now stumbling toward the gleaming white steps of the palace, my heart throbbing in my ears.

I nearly slam into a palace guard.

He holds his hands firmly at my shoulders and pushes me away. His eyes narrow.

And I have some explaining to do.

"Selamat Siang," I greet him. He is dressed all in white. A long sword is slung over his shoulder. Just behind him, another guard, also dressed in white, brandishes what I believe to be a machine gun.

"Who are you?" the first guard demands in Torundi. "From what place have you come?"

I explain as quickly as possible. I am from the mission, I say. I am here for Dr. Jean. It is an emergency.

The man continues to examine me for a moment before nodding briefly.

"I have heard of you," he finally says. "You are the mixed-race whom no one wanted to claim, raised by the outsiders."

An unflattering summary, certainly, but – for once – it actually comes in handy. "Yes," I pant, and then I repeat the urgency of my visit.

The guard considers me for another moment. Then he turns to the marble stairs that lead to the palace. He gestures for me to follow.

When we step through the ornate doorway, I am immediately struck by the grandeur, by the still coolness. Everything here is made of white marble; the sounds of our footsteps echo off the smooth, high walls that curve over us into a rounded arch.

"How long has Dr. Jean been here?" I ask in my best palace murmur.

"Not long," replies the guard, his voice unhurried. But his tone warns me to keep my silence.

We make our way up the staircase that curves from the foyer onto a semi-circular landing on the second floor. The guard moves with deliberation, each step slow and careful. I bite my lip, trying to control my impatience. When we finally reach the landing, I note more men dressed in white standing along the walls with such perfect stillness that I would have assumed they were statues had their dark eyes not shifted toward me. The guard pays them no mind as he leads me past them and through the main hallway of the second floor.

I follow behind, dazed by the opulence. While white marble reaches up and over everything, the floor is now covered with rich carpets and the ceiling above glimmers with warm, radiant light. The ceiling appears to be gold-plated. It is adorned with chandeliers that drip with gemstones, only the light in the hall isn't actually coming *from* the chandeliers. I gaze up at the open skylights that allow sunlight to beam into the hallway. The sun's rays are diffused through the dangling gemstones of the chandeliers, sending shafts of emerald and amber and ruby over the walls and the glowing, gold ceiling.

The guard stops at a gilded archway at the end of the hall. Beyond this, I can see that the hall opens up into a brightly lit room. A young woman, more beautiful than anyone I've ever seen in my life, bows gently to the guard as she shifts her soft, wide eyes to me. The guard explains my relation to the mission and asks her to show me in. I notice that he calls her Citra.

She says nothing. She bows again and then gestures for me to follow.

I instantly feel ungainly. Citra practically floats over the floor, her bare feet moving soundlessly across the mosaic marble of the room. When we reach the far side, she pauses beside a wide window, indicating for me to stay there. An ornate canopy bed stands twenty feet away. Delicate mosquito netting drapes over the teak frame that is accented with gold filigree, and beside the bed, now turning with a look of complete astonishment, is Dr. Jean.

"Sam! What are you doing here?"

I glance from Dr. Jean to the bedside table, where his bag sits open. It takes some doing, but I push down the sense of indignation that wells up from the sight of him.

"Gabe brought me," I answer quickly, looking around. "He's out there now, looking for Marcus's other guard . . . ." I stop. My gaze flits uneasily to the bed. Through the haze of mosquito netting that surrounds the bed I can make out a form reclining inside. I know this must be the sultan. And I know I should look away.

I stare back at him instead.

In my disjointed state of mind, all I can think of is that he looks nothing like I'd imagined. He is surprisingly ordinary, slightly overweight and older than I'd thought – maybe sixty-five or so. For some reason, I'd always imagined him around the same age as Dr. Jean. He has a pleasant, round face, high cheekbones and bright, alert eyes that are currently looking back at me in amazement.

The sound of shattering glass hits my ears.

"Djadrani, take cover!" yells Dr. Jean.

I grope confusedly at a stream of gauzy curtain that has somehow tangled up with my arms. Someone tackles me – it must be Dr. Jean, I'm not sure – but I hit the floor, pulling the curtain and its golden rod from the wall in the process. The rod clangs against marble, bouncing a cacophony of echoes all around, but the echoes I hear aren't just from that. Noises ring from everywhere . . . sounds of screams and gun shots and more shattering glass fill the room. Within seconds, so do a hundred white uniforms. I lie with my face smashed against the cool marble floor, the weight of Dr. Jean pressed over my back.

I do not know how long this lasts. It could be seconds, it could be minutes. The shooting inside the room eventually stops. Citra's screaming joins the frantic exclamations of the guards, and I feel Dr. Jean's weight lift from me. I raise my head. I look toward the bed.

Nothing but a cloud of white feathers floats inside the battered netting. I do not care. All I can think of are the random shots I hear in the distance.

"Sultan Djadrani," calls Dr. Jean, "are you all right?" A low moan replies from somewhere on the other side of the bed.

"Stay here," Dr. Jean commands me. "Don't dare get up."

And then he slips across the floor towards the sultan.

At this, the guards yell in alarm. Four white uniforms rush forward and drag Dr. Jean away. "Get the girl," bellows another.

I feel several hands on me. I am dragged to the other side of the room, my three guards joining Dr. Jean's four. Seven guns point at once.

"Don't move," orders one guard, quite unnecessarily, but then he turns his attention back to the bedside.

"Marcus is tied up – Trudy's watching him – the other guard is dead," I blurt frantically. "Gabe's looking for the sniper now; you've got to let the sultan know that he is out there, that he is protecting him!"

"How can they tell them apart?" whispers Dr. Jean.

"The sniper was – was wearing a black jacket," I say; all of this is taking far too long. "Gabe only had on a T-shirt, dark green, I think. His hair is brown, not blond like the sniper's. And the sniper is taller—"

A guard growls, "Be silent!"

"There is something I need to discuss with the sultan," Dr. Jean replies loudly. "It can not wait."

All I can see from where I sit is the ring of guards and guns, but in the next moment, one of the guards indicates for Dr. Jean to get up. Dr. Jean scrambles to his feet and moves toward the bed. Between the guards and Citra's sobbing, I can not hear what he is saying.

A minute or two passes, but to me it feels like an eternity; every second lost is another chance at Gabe's life. Finally, the sultan barks several orders to his guards, telling them to fan the property and to be sure no harm comes to the man of my description. As they scurry from the room I close my eyes and fight the pounding in my head. Even now, with the sultan's command, I know it may be too late.

"So, this is your Sam, is it?"

My eyes fly open at the sound of my name.

Through the shredded mosquito netting I can see the sultan situating himself against the pillows. Citra must have left with most of the guards, leaving only a few who stand watch by the windows. One by one, they draw the shutters, leaving the room in increasing darkness.

"I need to go outside," I answer, getting to my feet.

The sultan chuckles. "I'm afraid I can not allow you to leave just yet. Please be patient while my guards track down the shooter; this should only take a few more minutes."

I lower my gaze to the floor, trying to still the rush of my pulse. I think I hate this man before me. I think I may have wanted to find him dead after all. But his voice is so kind, his demeanor so calm. Almost gentle. He is nothing like the monster in my mind.

But those are the most adept ones, aren't they?

He's still speaking, his English perfectly articulated, his vocabulary fluent and easy, but I am not hearing the words. My gaze locks instead on the used syringe on the floor. My eyes move from it to Dr. Jean.

"He knows, Sam," he says. "I've told him everything."

I feel myself draw back. I am too shocked to respond. Djadrani smiles in understanding.

"It is not what you think," the sultan continues. "It is merely an anesthetic. We planned for it weeks ago. Coupled with another drug, it would have given me the appearance of passing." He continues to regard me in his serene manner. "And *that*," he adds, "is a Ming Dynasty."

I look from him to Dr. Jean and, from the bulging

motion of Dr. Jean's eyes, gather I shouldn't be standing where I am. I glance over my shoulder, just now realizing that I've been leaning against an enormous, porcelain vase.

I wobble away from it.

"I understand from your father that we have your friend to thank for our preparedness," the sultan continues. "After we have found my brother, I will see to it that your friend is properly rewarded."

I do not like that idea. I don't know if it is wise for the sultan to have anything to do with Gabe.

Another shot echoes from somewhere in the distance. My heart double-times from the sound.

"And the tantalum?" I say. "What are your plans for that?"

The sultan shifts in his bed, now folding his hands over the white sheet that stretches across his abdomen. I'm suddenly reminded of a frog. I know it is ridiculous, but I can't help but wonder if he wears one of those old-fashioned nightcaps to bed, too. The ones with the little tassel.

"*That* is a matter that will take some time to decide upon," he replies, turning his gaze to the nearest window. The shutters are latched, but cracks of light beam through the slats. He pauses for a few more moments, as if waiting for another sound, but none comes. My pulse rages in the silence. "Dr. Dupuy might just make a philanthropist of me yet," he resumes. "These recent events have shown me that perhaps I have been myopic in my approach. We are a small nation. And the world has changed since the time I took power. I can see now that it is time to consider new ways of thought."

The room falls quiet. There have been no shouts or shots for several minutes.

"I should go now," I say.

The sultan looks back at me. His expression remains serene, his eyes calm and bright, but there is a void to them as well. A stillness that makes my skin ripple.

"Run along," he says smoothly. "And Jean, please go with her. Go home and get some rest. I'll send Alen and Sahala with you as an escort. They can collect your captor once they reach the mission, and I am sure you will be hearing from me in the next day or two."

Dr. Jean nods. He silently reassembles his bag and then picks the syringe up from the floor. He examines it for a moment before slipping it back into his things.

"Be safe, Sultan," he says, and then he walks toward me, his eyes troubled.

16. GABRIEL

He isn't here. I look again, following the perimeter of the wall in either direction, but there is no sign of Gabe and no sign of his bike. I run toward the nearest guard.

"The man that the sultan sent everyone to look for, the one who is helping us, has he been seen?"

"Two foreigners went that way," he says, calmly gesturing to the jungle. "Other guards went after them."

I turn without another word and sprint toward Dr. Jean's Yamaha.

"Sam, stop!" calls Dr. Jean. "What are you doing?"

But I've already cranked the starter. The gas lever twists in my hand as the engine roars under me. I circle the bike around, nearly running over Dr. Jean's foot in the process.

He lunges forward. I half expect him to knock me off his bike, but instead he scrambles behind me, clapping one hand over my shoulder as he tucks his bag in front him.

"Let's go!"

I rev the gas and dart through the outer gate, leaving a trail of dust behind. We are in the jungle now, zooming past trees, faster and faster. Dr. Jean's exclamations do nothing to slow me down. I follow the path Gabe and I took on our way in; I have to reach him before the palace guards mistake one for the other. I have to, I have to, I have to, and it is all I think as the trees blur with the engine's roar.

When we reach the mission, I kill the engine and shove the kickstand to the ground. Dr. Jean slides off the seat and wobbles forward two steps before freezing to a stop. He stares down at the ground, at the dead guard with a twisted neck. And then he turns and stares just as dazedly at something else to the right of us. It is the other guard – the sniper. His body lies sprawled to the side of our path, a tidy trail of blood oozing from the center of his forehead.

Trudy runs toward us. "Jean! Sam! I-I'm so sorry!"

"Trudy! Thank God you are all right!" says Dr. Jean. "And Kathy?"

"No! I mean, we're fine. It's that man, Marcus!" she replies hurriedly. "I wanted to check on Heti's baby, so I left the gun with Kathy. I-I know I shouldn't have, but everything seemed safe enough …."

Nurse Kathy appears in the doorway.

"Well, what was I *supposed* to do?" she snaps. "He had to

use the bathroom. I do declare, he was threatening to just go where he was if I didn't comply!"

"And then he got away," Trudy cuts in, looking frantically between Dr. Jean and me. "He shot his own man as soon as the guard arrived on his bike. I saw it – I was just coming back to the clinic. He took the bike and headed that way," she says, pointing to a narrow path that leads to a sheltered bend in the river. "And then, just after he left – seconds later – we saw that other man …."

"Gabe?" I barely manage.

"He followed him—"

But I don't wait for her to finish. Up goes the kickstand and down goes the starter. The tires bump over a short, rough-hewn bridge that arches over the mission's main storm drain and then I'm springing down the path before Dr. Jean can hop on.

I see tire marks before me and follow them as quickly as I can, ducking to avoid the dry, reedy grasses that whip at my face as I pass. Soon I approach a fork where the trail splits in two directions. I take the one to the left and continue on until I finally reach the sheltered bend of the river and its wide, flat bank. I am surprised by several people standing here – including Pak Siaosi – all of them staring downstream, as if in a trance.

I screech to a stop and run toward Pak Siaosi, leaving the Yamaha on its side.

"What's happened?" I demand in Torundi. Even as I ask the question, I see one of the bikes sprawled over the muddy bank, but no sign of Gabe or of Marcus. I follow Pak Siaosi's gaze to the bend in the river, where the alcove joins with the river's deep stream. Just there, I see the other bike. It bobs on its side, slowly sinking into the depths of the murky, brown water.

Pak Siaosi lifts his arm in its direction.

"I have never in my life seen such a sight," he announces slowly, his voice filled with awe. "It was some sort of vessel, it looked like one of your flying machines ... it had wings, and yet, I saw it float on the water."

"The motorcycle?"

"No. It was another thing. I could see it from where I was on the river bank." He turns to indicate a trail of trampled footprints leading from farther upstream. "It was this thing, this flying machine, that the first motorcycle was discarded for," he explains, shaking his head in disbelief. "At first, I did not even see that the machine was there, because it was hidden behind the grove of trees, but when the first motorcycle came to a stop, I saw a man throw it down and leap toward the grove. In the next moment, I heard an incredible sound and then I saw this vessel floating out from the shallow water by the grove and heading to the deep end of the river."

I nod, understanding now. I was unconscious when Marcus brought me here, so of course I wouldn't remember where he'd hid the seaplane. How very clever of him. He chose one of the few places on the Mokanan where Dyeens usually don't go.

"And the other man?" I press. "The other bike? Did you see what happened there as well?"

Pak Siaosi is still staring downstream; his hand remains raised and pointed in the direction of the slowly disappearing bike.

"That is the most incredible part," he almost whispers. "I was running toward the vessel, to see what all of this was about, when another motorcycle darts from the tall grass, just like the first one." He pauses to motion between the bike sprawled on the bank and the one submerging below the water. His gaze lingers on the sinking bike, his eyes somber and troubled.

The rumble of engines sounds behind us. I turn to look. Pak Siaosi turns, too, just when two more motorcycles appear. These, I recognize at once, are the sultan's guards. I also see that Dr. Jean is with them.

"It seems that today is destined for strange things," Pak Siaosi notes in his patient, accepting manner.

"And then?" I prompt, turning back to that particular spot of river. "What happened then?"

Pak Siaosi slowly follows my gaze. "I was still running," he answers, but with caution, as if he cannot believe his own words, "and I saw that the vessel was increasing in speed as it moved into the main body of the river. I called behind me, to the other men fishing upstream." He gestures to a group of men huddled together; they are speaking in hushed tones. "I called to them and exclaimed that they must come see this sight before me."

"And the second bike?" I gasp, staring desperately into the elder's face. He shakes his head back and forth.

"The motorcycle flew from the bluff, just over there, into the air, as if chasing the vessel. Of course, as everyone should know, this is not possible, for motorcycles do not fly. It fell into the river as the machine increased in speed, and I could not believe what my eyes showed me next, because I saw the machine lift from the water and soar into the air. Well, I am an old man, I told myself, and my mind has fallen prey to old men's thinking. I am dreaming in the middle of the day, seeing impossible, foolish things . . . ." He pauses, still shaking his head.

"What happened?" I cry. "To the bike driver, I mean?"

The elder turns his gaze from the river to my face, and his warm, brown eyes seem as fluid as the water before us.

"I could not see at first," he says. "There was a large splash, just after the flying machine lifted away, and then I saw him struggle in the water. I called out to those who were near me to help. We ran into the river, but the water is too deep there to see, and the current moves things quickly. We could not reach him. Shortly after that, we had to return to the banks for it was not safe for us to continue," he finishes, inclining his head once again toward the deep end of the river.

I follow his gesture. A sickening dread rolls into me, squeezing the air from my lungs. My eyes lock on a long, knobby form, barely perceptible from where we stand. But I've seen it before. It is a thing not often seen on our banks. When it is seen, we know to stay away. And then, just seconds after I've spotted it, the crocodile disappears once more into the deep.

I am frozen in place. I continue to stare at the far side of the riverbank. The meaning behind Pak Siaosi's words settles in.

"One of the men found something floating nearby," he says, fishing into the woven bag slung over his side. He pulls out a piece of dark green cloth.

"Sam," comes Dr. Jean's voice, and I feel his hand over my shoulder. "Oh, Sam! I'm so sorry!"

"That is not all that they found," Pak Siaosi adds quietly. "The other is … not to be mentioned, for his spirit will be angry at our words. We knew then why his struggle had been a short one, and we dared not stay in the water any longer after seeing that."

I look from the scrap of cloth to the river. No.

I grab the cloth from Pak Siaosi's hands.

No.

No.

No.

I can hear the sound of Pak Siaosi's voice; he is still speaking, and I can feel Dr. Jean's arms suddenly around me, but the river and the bank and the sky all around become one and my lungs twist with the scrap of Gabe's shirt in my fingers and I can't breathe, I can't breathe, no, no, I can't breathe.

"Sam, can you hear me?"

The sound of it cracks something in my mind, as if, just before, my thoughts had been sealed inside my head, made water tight. The peaceful, sailing feeling I have awakened to is instantly replaced with despair. The memory of the river – of the strip of T-shirt I'd clutched in my hand – floods back.

"No," I groan, and this, too, surprises me. I feel as if inside, I am shouting, I am raging. But my voice sounds so feeble.

Something warm presses my face, and I know without even turning that it is Dr. Jean's hand. I hate him.

"Sam, are you hurt? Are you in pain?" his voice calls again.

I keep my eyes closed and pretend not to hear.

"I don't know what to do," whispers Dr. Jean. "Please, tell me what you think I should do."

"She just needs to rest," replies Nurse Kathy.

"Rest," echoes Dr. Jean.

"Rest," a voice inside me mocks. And it is joined by a chorus of screaming voices. *Rest and the rest and the rest* pounds my heart in return, harder and harder, until it feels as if it will break free. Yes, yes, break free and burst into the river.

"She needs to calm down."

Rest and the rest and the rest and the rest and the rest, rest, rest....

Something pricks my skin, and a warm cloud rushes up my arm, leaving me once again in that white, floating silence. I don't know how long I stay there, if it is hours or days. And when I finally open my eyes to see Dr. Jean seated beside me, the urge to look away has lessened.

"Hi." He smiles.

I look around the room. Flowers are everywhere.

"It is good to see you awake," Dr. Jean murmurs, squeezing my hand. "I've been so worried."

"How long?" I say. I stop to swallow, and Dr. Jean lifts a glass with a plastic straw angling out of it to me. I take a sip. "How long have I been like this?"

"Two days."

"Two days?" I repeat, surprised to be surprised by this.

"You've been through a lot, Sam. I think you needed the time."

I nod, only partly listening. Time. I can't think of a way, of a means to justify what has happened. *Time.* And here is another word:

Gone.

Just like that.

"Here," Dr. Jean says, placing something in my palm. "I took it off you earlier. You were so agitated – you kept grabbing at it in your sleep. I was afraid you might hurt yourself."

I look down at my hand, at the gold glint of his locket.

"Yes," replies Dr. Jean. Carefully he lifts the necklace from my hand, brings it forward, and clasps it around my neck. "Here we are, see? Just like before."

I close my eyes, remembering that perfect, starry night. Nothing will ever be like before.

"I've called your school," Dr. Jean is saying. "I've told them as much as I felt was appropriate regarding what's happened. Mr. King was very understanding and very concerned."

The clock ticks loudly on the wall. I say, "When do I go back?"

"Go *back!*" repeats Dr. Jean. "I told Mr. King you'd be staying here. Isn't that what you want?"

What I want. What an idea. "I think I should go back," I say.

Dr. Jean squeezes my hand again, his brows creasing together. "You sure?"

I nod and close my eyes, reaching up for my locket, holding it tight in my fist. We don't say anything for a while.

"I know this is the wrong time to bring it up, Sam," Dr. Jean says eventually, and I open my eyes. He rubs his hands over his face. "I know you feel betrayed by me, and I understand that, but you have to know that what Marcus said the other day, about Merpati … about your mother … he doesn't know what he's talking about. It wasn't like that at all. I don't want you to think that, especially not with everything else you're dealing with right now."

I swallow and look around the room again. Frangipanis float in glass tumblers, orchids in empty bottles. There's even a bowl of Nurse Kathy's gardenias. I can smell their pungent, jasmine-and-honey fragrance from here.

"What was it like then?" I say.

He turns to me, hopeful. "Really?"

"I'd like to know."

He nods slowly. Then he says, "Your mother … well, Merpati was the bravest person I've ever known." His words come out in a rush, as though spoken by a person who has been holding their breath for too long. "You remind me of her so much sometimes. She didn't care about the things that most people do; she never calculated, she was just ... well, she had this clarity. She was brilliant and original and kind."

His words sound strange to me. And I've never thought of myself that way, actually. It is an odd comparison.

"So what happened?" I ask.

He searches my face. "You sure you're ready to hear this?"

"I've been ready for seventeen years."

He takes another breath, his hand pushing over the stubble on his chin. "Well then," he says, his voice growing bitter, "I was young and stupid, that's what happened." He shakes his head and stares at the floor. I notice his hands. They are balled into fists, but I don't think he realizes. "When I first arrived in Torundi, I was introduced to Merpati. She had a reputation for healing, as many Tagolis do." He stops for a moment and clears his throat. "Unlike most Tagolis, though, she actually agreed to teach me some of the medicinal properties of various flora here, showed me how to use them. Things between us changed somewhere along the line. But no one knew about it but us, mostly because Merpati was very careful. I resented her for that, actually. I did not understand why we couldn't be more … open." He glances over at me.

"And then?"

His voice is flat, matter-of-fact:

"When she found out about ... you, she told me that it would be better if we didn't see each other anymore. She said it would be easier for her, that her village would find a way to accept her again. She explained to me that, if our relationship were discovered, I'd be sent packing. I'd never be permitted to stay on in Torundi. There were several groups of Westerners who had come to the island around that time – Marcus's expedition was one of them – and she convinced me that it would be easy to blame her situation on one of them. Well, we had a fight about it. I think she provoked me on purpose, in retrospect, but at the time, I was too self-absorbed to see anything beyond my own anger. It doesn't excuse things." He shifts uneasily in his chair.

"So, you didn't know about her banishment?" I ask.

"I had no idea!" he says angrily. "I wish I could go back and change it all. Perhaps if I had returned to see her, if I had put more thought into her actions that last time we spoke, I might have realized her sacrifice. But I didn't. And when she came to us after you were born, it all happened so fast. It was in the middle of the night; Kathy was so busy trying to help her that she didn't come and get me until it was too late. Merpati was already gone. And then, later, when the shock wore off, I was afraid that if I told anyone the truth, that I'd be sent away, leaving you behind. I knew GMS wouldn't tolerate such behavior. I also knew enough of Torundi law to understand the position I'd put them in. And I knew that if I left the mission, I wouldn't be permitted to take you with me."

I let his words sink in.

"So there you have it," Dr. Jean says quietly. "To be honest, I'm relieved it's finally out. When Marcus threatened me with revealing the truth several months ago, it forced me to tell Djadrani about it myself. He was surprisingly composed and accepting of the matter. I wonder if he already knew, actually."

I reach for my glass and poke the straw into my mouth, taking a long sip. Djadrani. I remember the way he looked at me the other day, just before I left the palace. Something about it doesn't sit right. I put the glass down.

"I meant to tell you over Christmas," Dr. Jean adds. "But then everything else came up and I thought, under the circumstances, it would be best to wait ...." He stops and glances at me, a question in his eyes.

"And Marcus? How did he find out?" I say.

"You know, I'm not sure." Dr. Jean frowns. "I think he guessed it; I certainly never said anything, and the Tagolis think Merpati and her child passed away in the forest, so it couldn't have been from them. They don't know she came here. No one does. As far as everyone outside the mission knows, your mother was just a young woman from a nearby village who died while giving birth. Your parents remain a mystery. Those were the instructions your mother gave Kathy right before she passed."

I watch him as he says all of this. I do not know how to respond. There are still so many questions. Too many. Questions like: *Did you love her?* I don't know how to ask that. Or, on a less personal level: *Why would my mother be so concerned with hiding her identity? Why did it matter, especially if she knew she was going to die? Why all the secrets?*

Dr. Jean looks so miserable I think he may actually cry. I have never seen him cry. I do not want to see it now. "Have you heard from the sultan?" I ask instead, changing the subject. "Has there been any progress as to the holy site?"

Dr. Jean stares blankly at the floor for several more seconds. "He's promised to assemble a team of advisors, some with experience in these matters," he finally says. He shakes his head distractedly. "From what I've heard, we can even have hope Torundi citizens may be shareholders in the enterprise – just as your Gabe suggested – so that every person benefits from its resources. With that wealth …." He pauses for a moment, still shaking his head. A knock sounds from the door. We both turn to see Pak Siaosi come in, holding a glass jar filled with white jasmine.

"Ah!" he cries, his face breaking into a smile. "She is well! It is a good thing to see you, *Mata Hantu.*"

I try to smile. "Thank you, Pak Siaosi. The flowers are beautiful."

This pleases him, and he strides across the room, placing the jar next to another one filled with moon orchids before pulling up a chair beside us. He beams down at me, and then he turns to Dr. Jean and announces they've caught a wild boar that morning.

"That is a good omen, is it not?" replies Dr. Jean in Torundi, and Pak Siaosi answers that it is. His soft, low baritone grows more animated as he relays the details of the hunt. I listen between the two, suddenly feeling as if I am watching a play, and realize that I still clutch Gabe's necklace in my right hand.

I nod to myself in understanding. So this is how it will be from now on, as if I have been removed from all that once felt real. And that sense of being alive with wonder, that feeling that life can be everything I hoped it could be … *that* is gone forever. It is wrapped up tight in my locket. And I will hold on to it, just as my locket will hold on to those memories, and it will be golden – pure and irreplaceable – something never to be felt again.

17. THE QUEST

It takes a week before a flight can be arranged to bring me back to Penang. Dr. Jean meets with Djadrani again in the interim, only to return to the mission far less optimistic than when he'd left.

The sultan has had a change of heart, Dr. Jean reports wearily, and he is now fearful of taking any action that would further inflame the citizens. The Tanah Yatim is a place untouched for centuries, and the prospect of any development might prove a violation reprehensible enough to evoke rebellion. As it is, unrest ripples through the villages and the half brother, Harim – whose destiny had come so close to usurping Djadrani's rule – has slipped once more into shadow. Perhaps it would be best, the sultan tells Dr. Jean, to simply wait and see.

I don't believe a word of it. Djadrani is planning

something else; I am as sure of that as the brown of the Mokanan's waters. Equally obvious is the fact that Dr. Jean is being left in the dark. It is a time of uncertainty for everyone.

In the mission, we have our own problems to contend with – the most obvious being the fact that our sponsoring company has turned against us. We don't know what has happened to Marcus, if or when he might return, or what UnMonde might do next. Our enemy has gone from a constant, overbearing shadow to completely invisible. Not a trace of UnMonde can be found: no evidence of their base on the island, no knowledge of their presence from other villages .... The only vestiges left behind were the bodies of the two deceased guards, which Djadrani's men have already removed, and the motorcycle on the riverbank. The latter proves bereft of any identification.

Even Dr. Jean's old correspondence records to GMS are, in this light, entirely unsubstantiated. Our research reveals that Global Medicine Solutions dissolved seven months prior, and nothing can tie that little NGO to an enterprising corporation on the cusp of global dominance. In fact, UnMonde – by name at least – can not be found anywhere. It is as if they never existed, just like Gabe had said.

Which brings me back to Penang. I told Dr. Jean that I couldn't face the banks of the Mokanan – and that is somewhat true – but there is another, much more important, reason for me to return to school, a reason fueled by the white, hot fury inside me that grows every day, stoking my resolve until it takes up every bit of space inside.

I know it is a long shot. I know I am just a high school student, and my enemies exist in a world beyond my reach. But there may be something they left behind in Penang that can change that. Something Gabe left behind. The taxi driver, for instance. If I can find anything at all, it might prove to be just the evidence Dr. Jean needs to dig up the truth behind UnMonde.

And that thought?

That thought is the only thing that keeps me going.

My first days back are difficult. No one on campus knows anything helpful about Gabe: where he'd lived, what he'd done in his spare time, with whom he might have socialized … nothing. Even Krikorian is a no-go. Worse, everyone treats me as though I'm some sort of delicate flower. No one knows what happened in Torundi, of course. All Dr. Jean has divulged to Mr. King is the part about my abduction. But still, my roommates shadow me everywhere, and it isn't until Saturday that I am finally able to sneak over the lower campus seawall.

The water is tranquil that day, the air steamy and low, and as I dart toward the large boulders of the eastern beach, I catch sight of the red canoe, still leaning on its side against the edge of the seawall. Something hard bobbles into my throat. I swallow it down and head for the path that leads into the jungle.

When I reach the trees, I look around, trying to recall which way Gabe took me that day. It takes a little searching, but I eventually find the right tree. After a few trial-and-error attempts, I locate the rope twisted under rattan and, a few tugs later, a ladder swings down beside me. My heart thumps at the sight of it. I climb with deliberate care, trying to master that rush between hope and dread.

When I reach the top, I crawl onto the platform and look around. Most of the *tikars* are still rolled up neatly in a corner, and the rattan shelf remains untouched but for one book that lies in shreds about the floor. Perhaps some macaques have made mischief here, because a few water bottles sport gnawed caps and, in addition to the paper strewn about, some sort of animal feces lies on the left side of the platform. I skirt around this and head to the books. My hands shake, I notice, but I pick up the first one anyway, riffling through the pages for any kind of clue. An address or a note maybe.

Nothing.

I go to the second book, then the third. There has to be something here. A business card, perhaps, or a phone number scribbled down. Still nothing. I open the small box on the shelf, only to find a few cobwebs. I close it and pick up the last book. We've read this one in English class: *Walden, or Life in the Woods*, by Henry David Thoreau. It falls open to the second chapter.

Just then a noise comes from somewhere below. It's the rope ladder – I'd forgotten to bring it up. I don't know who or what could possibly be coming up here, but I know I should be prepared. I put down Thoreau and turn, waiting, just when a familiar face pops above the platform.

"*Gajendra?*"

Sweat trickles down his temples as he crawls onto the floor, panting the whole way.

"What on earth are you doing here?" I ask.

"What are *you* doing here?" he demands with a gasp, looking about uneasily. He grabs his handkerchief and dabs frantically at his face.

For some reason, this makes me angry. And then I realize why. This is *our* place, the one place no one has ever been to but Gabe and me. I've thought about coming here since that day I woke up in the clinic with nothing left of Gabe but a strip of green T-shirt and an empty locket. And now here is Gajendra, sweating all over the floor.

"This is ridiculous," I say. "You've no right to stalk me!"

Gajendra freezes mid-dab. "I most certainly am *not* stalking you! I do have better things to do with my time than to follow you about for the fun of it!"

"Then why are you here?"

"Well, if you must know, I am here because I consider myself your friend!" he snaps, indignant. He starts dabbing again. I've never seen him sweat so much. "I am here because I am worried about you, because I care about you and because, as incredible as it may seem, I might have some idea as to what is going on."

"You have no idea, trust me."

Gajendra lowers his handkerchief as he takes a deep breath and looks around, apparently just now noticing the animal droppings a few inches from where he sits. He springs to his feet, stalks over to the rolled-up *tikars* and unfurls one over a clean space on the floor. He settles onto it, crossing his legs with composure. "I mean that I have known for quite some time about you and … Mr. Jones," he finally says, his mouth twisting in distaste. "I suspected you were meeting him that day at Thaipusam. And I blame myself for whatever happened. I should have stopped you."

I sink against one of the bamboo pillars.

"I can understand your surprise," he resumes with a sniff. "However, it does not change the fact that I feel it my duty to help you now. I can put the two and the two together! I can see what he did to you!"

I turn from Gajendra and look through the trees. I can see the campus, my dorm, and I remember that day when I'd come here, a whole lifetime ago. I say, "Gabe is dead, Gajendra."

The words are so hollow. It feels like it is breaking some sort of natural law, to be able to pronounce such a thing with no repercussion, no reaction from the wind or the trees … or from me.

"Surely not!" gasps Gajendra. "You—"

"He died saving my life. Saving my home."

Gajendra murmurs something by way of response, but I just stare off through the trees.

"Do you know anything about him?" I ask after a while. I glance to where he sits. "He wasn't just here to study. There are people involved who are responsible for his death. It's very important I learn anything I can about his life outside PACA."

Gajendra looks back at me, his deep, dark eyes warm with worry. "What happened, Sam?"

But I can't tell him. That is mine. It is the only thing I have left, and no one else can touch it.

"Whatever happened," Gajendra adds quietly after a while, "he would want you to continue on, you know."

I clamp my jaw, fighting the urge to scream at him. *Continue on?* "I need to find out where Gabe lived," I say instead. "I need to track down anyone who knew him off campus. Will you help me with that?"

"You're trying to find the people who are responsible for his death?" he says.

"Yes." I breathe, calming myself.

"And you will not tell me what happened …."

"I can't."

"But you are looking for clues, searching for a way to locate them?"

I nod.

"Then you will be putting yourself in danger, surely!"

"I'll be leaving campus a lot," I say, intent on ending this conversation. "I'll be looking for a taxi driver who knows something about ... Gabe's employer. It would be very helpful if you could cover for me."

Gajendra exhales loudly. His eyes stay on me, thoughtful. His forehead and neck are slick with sweat.

"I will help you," he finally answers. "But in return, you must promise to let me know where you are going first. I do not want you wandering about in this secretive manner, agreed? If these people are dangerous, then you can not be so solitary. You have no idea how much my poor Lily has listened to my moaning over the past few weeks. The guilt I have felt when you disappeared and *I* was the one who saw you last! I will not allow that to happen again! So you must promise me that. You must promise to include me."

I blink at him in surprise. How could he possibly feel responsible for what happened? The idea is preposterous.

"Promise me," he says with a glare. "And promise me you will try to move on with your life, too. Spend time with your friends – have more fun! In return, I will help you however I can."

It is no use.

"Okay," I say. "I promise."

That evening I creep over to the school office and unlock the door using keys I've lifted from Aunt Janie's apartment. I slip into the dark interior, unlock another door leading to the file room and click on my flashlight. Staff records are to the right; I scan down to the drawer labeled "J-M." Gabriel Jones. Second file.

It is surprisingly thin. One page, in fact, with a passport photo, fake last name, a transcript from a university he never attended and letters of reference from people I am certain don't actually exist. No address or contact information, though. Of course not. I grab the photo, shove the folder back into the drawer and head to my dorm. My Saturday has been more or less a waste, and the disappointment pushes into me. I fight it back. I have three months before graduation. I do not have time to wallow in failure.

On Sunday evening I sneak past the night guard and over the campus wall, the whole time resisting the twinge of guilt for leaving without telling Gajendra. This time I head down Tanjung Bungah Road, catching the bus toward Georgetown until it approaches a familiar bus stop on the right with the apartment complex just behind it. I get off the bus and walk down the narrow road that branches off the left side of the street.

Soon I arrive at the outdoor Chinese theater, dormant as it had been that last time. I continue down the road until the glow of kiosk lights warms the night. The tables and chairs have regained their positions under the banyan trees, and even the little gibbon with the red and gold vest is back, swinging back and forth between the hanging roots.

I recognize the vendor closest to me; dried squid hangs from the glass windows of his cart, and steam curls from an aluminum pot on his left.

"Selamat Malam," I greet him, walking over. He bows his head slightly in return. "Do you remember me?"

His expression tells me that he does.

"Do you remember the taxi driver – the one with the Lat cartoon bumper sticker – that would bring me here?"

A pause as he looks from me to the haze of the beach beyond, uncertainty crossing his face.

"Why?" he says.

"Because I need to talk to him, to the taxi driver. He … has something of mine."

The man busies himself with lifting the lid off his pot and stirring the broth inside.

"Many drivers come here to eat," he says. "Maybe he eats here, maybe not. You are too young – go home!"

"What about this man?" I ask, fishing out the passport photo of Gabe. "Have you ever seen him?"

The man sighs impatiently, puts down his ladle and grabs the photo from me. He glares at it. "No!" he snaps, shoving the photo back and returning to his soup.

I feel my face burn hot with frustration, but I try to stay calm. I am here now, so I might as well make the most of it. I turn and walk to a table, sit down and wait.

I sit there for a whole hour. The empty space under the trees gradually fills with diners: families, working men, groups of teenagers and even what appears to be a chess club. But no sign of my taxi driver. Another hour goes by. It is now almost nine o'clock, time for curfew. I rise to my feet and leave.

From that day on I hunt for the driver everywhere. I watch for him when I accompany my roommates to Hillside, I look for him when we go to Batu Ferringhi, I search the narrow streets of Georgetown when we take our school outings. And I show Gabe's picture to anyone who will look at it.

Nothing.

Weeks go by.

And then one Wednesday, school shuts down for PACA's Teacher Appreciation Day. My roommates head to the beach for the afternoon. I stay behind, half-heartedly feigning a fever. Unaccountably, they buy it – EJ only rolls her eyes and Tess looks annoyed – but they don't question it; they don't question anything anymore.

After they leave, I slip off campus and catch the bus to Gurney Drive. I get off and walk the sidewalk that parallels the pedestrian zone until I find what I came here for: Penang Environmental Society. It is my last unexplored connection. But thirty minutes later I leave the PES building as uninformed as I when I'd entered.

My skin prickles and sticks to my clothes; it is hot, probably over a hundred Fahrenheit, and the midday sun glares from the concrete walkway. I walk on, and each step doubles the frustration brimming inside. It is now late April. I have one month left until graduation and exactly five ringgit to my name. I've spent every dime I've earned from waitressing on buses and taxis in useless quests that have led to nothing. I've gone to the Cathay Hotel, all over Batu – I even approached fishermen on the beach outside our school – I've gone everywhere and approached anyone who might remember Gabe, but all my efforts have proven to be equally useless. Now I just want to scream until my throat bleeds.

I walk to a bus stop and sit down, exhausted. My temples pound behind my eyes. I put my head down for a moment, closing my eyes to the loud, sticky world all around.

When I look up again, I gaze miserably in front of me. It takes at least a minute until I realized I'm staring at a familiar yellow cab sporting a Lat bumper sticker; it's parked along the curb not fifteen feet away. The man inside is eating a curry puff while his radio blares retro pop music. I feel like I've been hit by a Hin bus. But in a good way. For half of a Whitney Houston song, I forget to breathe.

Then, finally, I fumble for my bag. I grab a pen and paper, my pulse thudding in my ears. I blink through the sunlight and scratch down the license plate number, watching as the driver finishes his lunch. It is definitely him: middle-aged, straight black hair slicked back without a part, a slight pot belly, longish nails on each pinky, a jade ring on his left index finger.

The man has his head back now, apparently taking a snooze while he waits on his next ride. I grab my bag and, as quietly as possible, creep toward the taxi. The passenger window is down, so I tiptoe to it and peer inside at his badge pasted to the dashboard. The plastic laminate curls at the corners, clouding the small letters. I creep closer. I can hear the driver's soft breathing.

"Yong," I make out. I squint, trying for his first name, but then the driver snorts and bolts upright in alarm. His eyes meet mine and, just as he reaches for the ignition, I land on the seat beside him, slamming the door closed.

"Remember me?" I say, ripping his badge from the dashboard. I shove it into my bag before he's recovered enough to snatch it back. I dig out Gabe's picture. "Remember him?"

Yong's eyes bulge in disbelief. "What are you doing?"

"It's what *you're* doing," I answer, clicking the seat belt. "You're taking me to his apartment."

"But I don't—"

"You know exactly where his apartment is. I know you know, because you're the one who betrayed him. How much did they pay you, Mr. Yong?"

He swallows, his hands never leaving the steering wheel. His forehead pops with sweat.

"I hope it was worth it," I say, my pulse beating against my temples. My voice shakes when I say the rest of it: "Because he's dead now."

Mr. Yong turns to me, his face drained to white. "Mr. Jones?" he whispers.

That ache in my throat comes back so forcefully I can't speak. I nod.

"But he ... he told me to cooperate! He said if they came, I should tell them where I'd taken him!" He moans, his hands covering his face. I do not believe him.

"Please take me to his apartment," I repeat. "Unless you want me to report to the police that you assisted in my abduction, I suggest we go *now.*"

Yong swallows hard, then the engine rumbles to life and the car rolls from the curb. His hands shake as he shifts into second.

"I can take you," he says once we're heading down the road, "but you will find nothing. They cleaned out the place three days later. I ... saw them do it. I thought he had moved."

"Who is 'they'?"

"His friends – from the company," he says, wiping his forehead. "But there is something I—"

"Can you describe them?" I say, cutting him off. "What they looked like? Did they give you a business card, anything?"

Yong shakes his head slowly, his hands still trembling. "They gave me five hundred ringgit to tell them what I knew and then two hundred more to bring you ... there," he finishes uneasily.

"And what did you know?"

"Only … only the trips I did for him. Several times I took him into Georgetown – I know he caught the ferry to Butterworth, the port terminal for the mainland, at least twice. And I took him a few times to Batu Ferringhi. Then you, of course ...."

"Their names?"

"I do not know! They were all businessmen, well dressed, very polite, so I thought ... they just gave me the money. I did not ask questions!" The agitation in his voice sounds real. He keeps driving, his eyes glued to the road. I watch him, frustrated.

Soon we are approaching Hillside. He turns left just before the stalls and heads down a side street lined with houses and shops. He turns again, then slows to a stop beside a little park with a rusty swing set, a teeter-totter and a neglected conglomeration of monkey bars. The street wraps around the park, and all along the other side run modest, single-story duplexes squared off by little fences.

I look from the park to Yong … just as his eyes widen with interest.

I follow his gaze, noticing a young woman open a door two duplexes down. She holds a baby in her arms and a toddler tugs at her skirt. She reminds me a little of Leila. Seconds later, a man appears through the door. Mid-thirties, maybe. He turns and closes the door, locking it behind him.

They stroll down the cement walkway, headed to the park. Yong points with his thumb and quietly says, "That is where he lived. I told you – you would find nothing."

I gulp back my breath, his words floating about my ears. I can't quite accept them.

"But I ... do have something," he adds, his tone uncertain. Nervous. I jerk my gaze from the duplex to Yong.

"What do you have?"

"If ... if I give this to you, will you leave me alone?" he hedges, his voice barely a whisper. "I have a family. Whatever this is about, I do not want any more trouble."

"I have no interest in bothering you, believe me!" I say. "I'm just trying to find out who those people are."

Yong only exhales loudly through his mouth. "Give me my badge first," he says.

I feel around in my bag, my gaze never leaving him, until I clasp the square piece of plastic. I pull it out. Yong snatches it from my grasp. He looks back at me once more, as if still debating something in his mind.

"The police," I remind him.

"Yes, yes, I know!" He ducks below the dashboard and roots about in the recesses behind the steering wheel. Seconds later he straightens to a sitting position. A small, sealed shipping envelope is in his hands. "I only did what he asked me to do," he repeats … pleadingly, I think. "I never imagined things would go so badly."

I swallow, trying to control the leaping in my chest. I stare at the envelope in his hands. "Is that … that's from *him*?"

He nods, handing me the envelope. I take it, still too full of amazement to really think straight.

"And ... why do you have this?" I manage.

"That's just the thing," Yong says, his expression matching my own bewilderment. "The last time I saw him ... his instructions ... he wanted me to hold on to it. He trusted me, you know." He pauses and shakes his head, gazing from me to his badge to the shipping envelope. He takes another deep breath, squeezing his eyes shut.

"He told me he did not know if he would return," he continues with increasing agitation. His eyes are squeezed so tight that his face contorts comically. When he speaks next, his words come out in hiccups:

"I did not believe him; I thought it was just another one of his strange things. But he said that I should hide this someplace where it would be ready at a moment's notice; that I should tell no one. And I have done just what he asked; it has been over three months and I was beginning to believe his words after all. In two more weeks' time, on the date he'd given me, I was prepared to take this to the place he had instructed – until today! It was as if I saw a ghost when you showed up like that, because it is what he said would happen. It took a moment for me to recover from the shock, I think ...."

"I don't understand!" I practically shout. "What did he say would happen?"

Yong opens his eyes and gazes back at me. His pupils remain dilated as he whispers, "He said that you would come looking!"

18. THE HIDDEN KEY

Gajendra turns in surprise as I run through the cafeteria door. It is only 1:30 but, since it is a school holiday, all the cooks except he and Saul have left.

"I thought you were sick!" he exclaims.

"Healed," I pant excitedly. "I need some ringgit for a ride into town! Yong won't take me and—"

"What are you talking about?"

"The taxi driver!" I repeat impatiently. "I found him, Gajendra, and I was right! He *did* know something, something that ...." I let my words trail off, distracted by Gajendra's glare.

"You promised me, Sam," he hisses slowly. "You said you would not go gallivanting about without my knowledge!"

"I lied."

"You—"

"Look, I said I'd try to have fun. I've never had more fun than today. Happy? Now, can you lend me the money? I've got to get to the bank before it closes!"

"What bank?"

"Ach! Please, just—"

"NO!" snaps Gajendra, waggling his finger at me. "What bank? That is the deal!"

I sigh, dig into my bag and produce the envelope. I hand it over.

Gajendra takes it, still scowling, and peeks inside. He scowls more and tips the envelope until a thin tablet computer slides into his hand. "What is this?"

"It's the directions! See?"

"I see nothing of the kind. How does it … there is no button," he continues irritably, turning the device this way and that. The glossy surface flashes in the light, but otherwise remains inanimate. "Is it a phone?"

"No, it had directions!" I say, grabbing the tablet from him. I am starting to panic when suddenly the screen ripples to life. "See, I told you! It—"

He grabs it back and says, "It is blank."

I take it, flicking it to me once more, only to find the directions neatly taking up the first two-thirds of the screen. I hand it to Gajendra, impatient. "Look, Gajendra. I told you, it's—"

"Turn it to you!" he cries, staring at the tablet.

I do.

"Turn it to me!"

I do.

"Ayo! Turn it back to you!"

This is getting ridiculous but I need that ringgit, so I comply. As before, the lit screen glows back at me.

Gajendra gasps once again. "It is just like the movies!" he whispers, his eyes wide with wonder. "I have seen this displayed in the most convincing of manners, but I never—"

"What *is* it, Gajendra?"

"It is using facial recognition!" he announces, scuttling to my side.

This discovery shocks me more than him, I think. I flick the tablet away once again, now noticing the fading screen as soon as it turns from me. I flick it back and it instantly glows to life.

"What does it say?" he asks.

Dazed, I angle the tablet so he can read over my shoulder. Gajendra's lips move silently.

"I told you," I say, recovering. "It's the address to a bank, with instructions to ask for a Mr. Tan when I get there!"

"And the bottom part?"

"I don't know, some kind of password or code, I guess."

Gajendra nods. His eyes are still glued to the tablet when he says, "Meet me at the Hillside bus stop in fifteen minutes. I will be wearing a disguise, but you will know me by my Donegal tweed cap. I will take you there."

I blink back at him, wondering what part of that announcement makes a modicum of sense.

Gajendra whips around and marches to the kitchen, instructing Saul to take over until he's returned. "Fifteen minutes!" he calls to me. "Do not be late!"

I sigh in defeat. I'm not getting my money, that much is obvious. And I've no choice but to go along with whatever Gajendra says if I want to get to that bank today. So I head upstairs to my dorm room to change. Whatever is at that bank, it might help if I show up in something more respectable than flip-flops and cut-off army fatigues.

I am midway into my paisley, circa-1970s pants when Tess, EJ and Sandy stroll through the door.

"I thought you were at the beach!" I say, hobbling on one leg.

"And *we* thought you were *sick,*" says Tess, grimacing. "You never wear those things."

"For good reason," EJ adds with a shudder.

"Thought I'd see how they fit," I improvise. "You guys headed out again?"

But this does not have the effect I'd hoped for.

Sandy crosses her arms in front of her and says, "Aunt Janie just asked us if we knew where you were. Funny, don't you think? Especially if you've been sick with a fever all day."

I glance from Sandy to my roommates. Tess arches an eyebrow. EJ and Sandy slowly step backward, taking positions by the door.

"Where are you going, Sam?" Tess asks, but it isn't really a question, not really.

"Don't think we haven't noticed you sneaking out all the time!" EJ chimes in.

"What we're trying to say," says Sandy, looking inappropriately enthused by the pronouncement, "is that this an intervention."

I stare back at her.

"So you've got two choices," she continues. "Either we go wherever it is you're going … *together* … or we inform Aunt Janie that you're about to sneak out all alone again and we're just super worried—"

"Fine!" I sigh, squeezing into my other pant leg. I zip up the side-fly of my disco pants and slip into my sandals. "I don't have time for this! Let's go!"

Tess, EJ and Sandy exchange glances, by all appearances shocked by their rapid success.

"We should have done this earlier," says EJ.

I roll my eyes and grab my postal bag.

Three minutes later we are hoofing it up Tanjung Bungah Road. By the time we reach the bus stop, a tiny, off-white vehicle chugs to a halt beside us. A man with an olive tweed cap, dark glasses and a very unusual, red-tinged beard peers through his window, head twitching from me to my gaggle of friends, his expression aghast.

I shrug back at him.

"Get in," I say, hopping into the front seat.

"Why are *they* here?" hisses Gajendra as we clamor into the car. "It is bad enough that I am taking you. Do you know how much trouble I could get in?"

"They insisted on coming," I say. "But I'll take that ringgit if you'd rather."

"Hit it!" laughs Sandy before Gajendra can reply. "And hurry! There's Mr. King!"

The car's engine roars to life, the wheels smearing rubber on the curb. I duck my head just as we pass Mr. King while my roommates and Sandy do the same in the back seat, giggling hysterically the whole way.

"This is not funny!" wheezes Gajendra through his beard, but it does nothing to sober the mood in the back seat. Gajendra drives faster, now passing Gurney Drive, and soon we are weaving through the cluttered streets of Georgetown. He slows to a stop when we reach the bank, an imposing colonial-style building catty-corner to an alleyway.

"Where are we going?" asks EJ.

I scan the area for a distraction. That's one great thing about Penang: No matter where you go, you can count on some kind of viable, street-side commerce. "There," I say, pointing to the alley, where several stalls selling clothes and leather goods are set up. "I was … just going to do some shopping. Gajendra told me about this place – super-cheap prices. I need an outfit for graduation." I glance at Gajendra, but he stares straight ahead, refusing to corroborate.

"Shopping," repeats Tess. And I hate the way she arches that eyebrow.

EJ points to a polka dot dress hanging from the nearest stall rafters. "So cute!" she squeals, and I could just hug her on the spot. Suddenly she's out the door with Sandy, Tess and me following her across the street. Gajendra stays put.

"Good luck finding your *outfit,"* he says with a sneer.

I ignore him … and Tess's suspicious glare … and head to the stalls, feigning interest in a green dress next to EJ's polka dot one.

Soon EJ's trying things on in a makeshift dressing room made of sarongs hung from a clothesline while Tess and Sandy argue over whether or not the knock-off Gucci bags could pass as genuine. Clearly I am of little use as far as that goes. I duck behind the stall's tarp wall and dart to the bank.

I race up the wide steps, heart pounding, and glance back. There is no way my friends can see me from where they are. Perfect. I step through the bank's revolving door, still giddy from the rush of events. The door spins me into a grandiose lobby full of dark wood and grey marble. I look around, instantly subdued.

Conservatively dressed men and women move about. I glance from them to the ghastly anachronism that is my pants and cringe, wishing I'd worn my granny skirt instead. But that feeling only lasts for a second because suddenly a man in a dark suit stands before me, politely asking if he can be of any assistance.

"Yes, I'm …." I pause to swallow the tremor in my voice. "I'm looking for Mr. Tan, please."

The man considers me for a second, surprise flitting through his eyes.

"I see. Please wait here," he says after another moment. Then he walks off, leaving me in the middle of the lobby.

I try to act natural. Several employees glance my way, curious. I suppose I can't blame them. I am definitely out of place here. If I was nervous before, I am now positively shaking. I quickly look down at my feet, concentrating on keeping my toes still, and begin to wonder if that polite man is merely directing security to escort me out. Then he returns, another man at his side.

"This is Mr. Tan," he announces.

"Please follow me," Mr. Tan says with a nod, flicking his gaze my way. We cross the lobby and pass through a door that leads to a hallway with two elevators. He pushes a button and, seconds later, a ding reports the arrival of one of the elevators. Mr. Tan indicates the opening door.

"Shall we?"

I step inside. He follows and swipes a card through a reader. The doors close and down we go, until another ding announces our destination. We step out of the elevator and into a large, dark room with wood-paneled walls interspersed with closed doors. The room smells of lemon-scented cleaning agent and a hint of mildew.

Mr. Tan strolls across the room, his polished shoes clicking against polished tile. He stops at the second door, takes out another card, swipes it through the reader and then punches in a code. The door groans open.

"Here you are, Ms. Clemens," he says, disappearing for a moment into the room. "Take as much time as you need. Just press that button when you are ready to leave."

"You … know my name?"

"Of course."

I swallow again and walk after him, peeking about the room. It is empty except for a long, wooden desk, a lamp, an adjustable swivel chair and a wall lined with small, square drawers. A chest-like box, for lack of a better word, about one foot in length by eight inches in width and height, rests on the desk. I gaze from it to Mr. Tan, wondering.

"He said you'd have the key," he adds.

"The key?" I repeat, walking toward the desk.

"That is what he said," Mr. Tan says with a bow. He steps away and closes the door, leaving me alone.

I stare down at the chest, then back to the closed door and the green button just to its left. I am suddenly terrified. Terrified of what I will find, because this is the moment I've been living for and now … what will I have left? The thought drains every ounce of excitement from me, stark reality filling its place. This search has pushed me forward for the past three months. When it ends, I won't have a reason to go on. I won't have anything.

I turn back to the chest and put my hands to the sides of the lid. The box opens easily, yawning back on two hinges, revealing a dark, small box inside. I lift the box out and place it on the desk. It is entirely seamless except for a hairline ridge just below the top surface. It feels cool to the touch, like metal and glass … similar to my tablet. I pick the box up, carefully examining the entire surface, and put it down again.

Anxiety rolls over me.

The possibility of coming this close is too awful. I don't have an actual key, I know that. And I see no apparent need for one; there is no keyhole.

I pull the chair over to sit and place my bag on the desk, digging around inside it for the envelope. I slip out the tablet and its surface instantly glows to life.

As before, the tablet displays the bank's name and address, plus directions to ask for Mr. Tan. And the bottom of the screen still displays the nine short lines in a row that I assume form some sort of password or code.

Nine characters. It isn't Gabe's name and it couldn't be mine. It isn't my birthday and I don't know his. It isn't anything I can think of.

I wave the tablet all around the box surface, feeling ridiculous, justifiably so because nothing happens. I place the tablet on the desk beside the little box and sit back, still staring. Nothing. I can think of absolutely nothing.

But I have the key. Or so he'd said.

I glance down at my fidgeting fingers and then the realization hits me like a live wire. My fingers spring apart from the shock as his locket thumps against my chest. Of course! It has to be. It is the only thing I have of his.

I can barely unclasp the chain around my neck with my shaky fingers, but then I have the locket in my hands. I glance from it to the box, still wondering how it could be used as a key. I run it all along the sides, searching for any sign of an indentation or place in which the locket might fit, but every inch of the box is smooth and flat. I groan, frustrated, and put the locket down. Clearly I am missing something. But what? I grab the tablet once again, staring blankly at those nine lines.

And then I remember.

"It's different than most. It slides open, like this …."

What was inside the locket? An empty frame. An empty frame filled with a glossy, dark material. Just like my tablet.

With clumsy fingers I slide the locket apart, then turn the bottom half so the empty frame faces the box. I catch my breath as a little panel with pale blue lighting flickers to life on the surface of the box. The panel has five squares arranged in a pattern that's obviously intended to accommodate a set of fingerprints.

"Oh!" I whisper.

And then I lift my hand to the glowing squares.

19. DJADRANI'S SECRET

I'm not sure what I expected.

But it isn't what I found in that box.

It holds four cards, three passports and cash in five different currencies.

After I've calmed down enough to think clearly, I decipher that three of the cards are credit cards, with names matching those in the three different passports. The fourth card contains no name, only a sequence of letters and numbers on a solid, tan background. The three passports contain stamps from previously visited countries, all with three different names, birth dates and nationalities. A surprising, yet not entirely bizarre, inventory … until the following fact is included: *all* of them have my photograph.

I am still staring at the last passport – apparently a Canadian named Fiona Taber who bears a striking resemblance to me has recently returned from a trip to Australia – when I notice a scrap of paper at the bottom of the box. I pick it up.

"Your eyes," it says.

I stare at those two words for several minutes, the silence of the room buzzing in my ears. I look from it to the tablet resting on the desk.

Your eyes.

I take a deep breath, the memory of that perfect night sinking in with an ache that I haven't allowed since three months ago. The rocking boat, the stars above, the sound of his voice; it squeezes everything inside.

But how could this clue translate into a nine-character password? I sit for a moment, letting my mind consider all that Gabe knows about me, about my upbringing in Torundi, about the mission, about the people who worked there and went there for medical help, about what the Dyeens called me because of my lighter eyes: *Mata Hantu.*

I grab for the tablet. I put my finger to the first line, which immediately enlarges to take up the width of the tablet. I am not sure what to do.

"M," I trace with my fingertip. As soon as my finger leaves the tablet the line minimizes to its previous position at the bottom of the screen, but an asterisk now floats just above it. I hit the next line.

"A"

Again the line minimizes and an asterisk appears. My pulse throbs in my ears. I continue on until *Mata Hantu* has been spelled out. Nine asterisks float above the dotted lines toward the bottom of the tablet's screen for a moment.

Then the tablet pales to a perfect, pearlescent white. A few seconds later, Gabe's face appears. "If you're watching this," he begins, "it means that I am gone ...."

I don't remember pushing the green button. I don't remember walking out of the bank. I wouldn't have remembered sitting in Gajendra's car had he not turned to me, his warm eyes wide with alarm.

"Sam, what happened!"

I stare at the bag in my hands.

"Sam, are you all right?"

I look from the bag to Gajendra. It feels like everything is in slow motion, and the sound of Gabe's voice still rings in my ears.

"Did you find anything?"

"Yes," I hear myself say. "I found something."

"And it is what you were looking for?" Gajendra presses.

I can hear the worry in his voice. I think I nod. It is difficult to know. Gabe's message echoes in my mind, louder and louder, pounding into my brain until two things feel stamped inside forever.

The first is the most bizarre, and yet the easier to accept. Gabe explained that, somewhere in the days between my leaving for Christmas break and returning to school, he'd discovered the truth about UnMonde's interest in me. And the truth wasn't even close to what he'd been told when assigned to his babysitting mission.

Quite the opposite.

Because, in fact, UnMonde held no independent motivation for keeping tabs on me at all. They were, however, very much interested in exchanging favors with someone else in order to gain access to the Tanah Yatim.

And that is where the shocker comes in:

UnMonde has been watching me at the request of someone else altogether!

I'd replayed Gabe's message three times, though I was certain I had not misheard it. But it remains difficult to fully process what it said. Because the "someone else" with whom UnMonde is working … is none other than Sultan Djadrani.

I can't comprehend what this means or why Djadrani should care one way or another about my existence – it is all too random. Even so, Gabe's revelation makes plain that UnMonde has been in cahoots with Djadrani all along and that Djadrani, in turn, has thoroughly duped Dr. Jean. How this fits in with Harim and his plot to overthrow Djadrani remains a mystery, but it is clear that UnMonde plays both sides. My head swims with possibilities – none of them lucid – but I don't have time to sort it out at the moment because I'm still grappling with the rest of Gabe's message.

He'd continued on to explain that, some months prior, he'd developed a contact in Kuala Lumpur. He told me the name and address. I am to use that contact as needed after I graduate – and before, if necessary. But I can not return to Torundi. The sultan, for whatever bizarre reason, clearly does not have my best interests at heart. Hence the contents of the safety deposit box. Gabe had put some things in place – time should take care of the rest, he'd said, but if I noticed anything unusual, I was to use that contact. Until then, I should stop my search. I should keep my head down, carry on at PACA and graduate. I should attend college. I should move on with my life, he'd said. And then he'd said the second thing, the thing I know I can't do, and just the sound of his words saying it burns inside me until I feel as though my chest might actually crack open.

"Sam!" Gajendra persists, and I realize he has me by the shoulders. "What is it? What is wrong?"

I blink, not caring that the tears I haven't cried in three months are flooding down my face. Because I can't do what Gabe told me I must do. It is the cruelest command, and it rips inside until his words feel as if they will bleed out of my mouth.

"I can't!" I hear myself sob.

"Can't … what?" says Gajendra.

I wipe my eyes, trying to stop the flow, but I can't stop it. "I *can't* let him go!" I hear this from somewhere in the roar of my mind. I'm saying it. It is my voice. "He can't just *tell* me to do that. It's not right, it isn't fair!"

"No, it isn't fair," Gajendra murmurs.

"But he's *gone!*" I wail. "How can I just *get rid* of that, of the best thing I've ever known? I can't just *wipe it away!* He can't just say that; he has no right because he's *gone* and it *won't* be okay, nothing will *ever* be okay … and now my home …." I can't finish because I am choking on my tears. I cry and cry until nothing more will come out, and the whole time Gajendra sits there with me, patting my head as though I'm a little girl.

I sit up straight after a while, embarrassed. My head throbs in an empty sort of way, as if I've cried out all the stuff inside.

"I'm sorry," I say.

Gajendra pulls a handkerchief from his shirt pocket. "He is a part of you now," he says gently, dabbing at the tears. "*That* is real and can never be taken from you, unless you choose to let it be taken."

I know his words are supposed to help. I know I shouldn't be angered by them; that his intentions are good and kind. But that platitude ….

I turn my face to the window, squeezing my hands into fists, forcing myself to calm down.

It isn't Gajendra's fault.

And I can't tell him the rest, the part that is almost as hard to bear: that my home is no longer my own, that I have nowhere familiar to return to. I have no idea what will become of me now.

I am alone.

Most people get some kind of choice, don't they? Most people can choose one thing or another; like conformity or individuality, safety or adventure, love or money, career or family. Isn't that how it works? Mine was all or nothing, and I didn't even get to choose.

"It isn't the same," I say, fighting down the anger. And I suddenly think of Dr. Jean. Even that – the idea of my father; the hope that someone of my blood was out there and that perhaps, someday, I would find him. That, too, has been taken from me, leaving in its place a unique sort of disillusionment that I'm still trying to comprehend.

"Of course it isn't the same," Gajendra agrees. But he has no idea. No one who hasn't been through it can possibly know. "But you can take his memory with you – you don't have to get rid of it. Take all that he brought and honor it with your own life, Sam."

"What life?" I whisper.

Gajendra gazes back at me. I turn again to look out the window. People are everywhere, threading between the usual flurry of traffic. The sun beats down on the dark streets, warming the oranges and greens and reds of nearby stall tarps and umbrellas. A soft breeze rustles the long fingers of palm fronds that line the street median. A bus chugs by. It is just another day in Georgetown.

"You feel things so very deeply, Sam," Gajendra says with a sigh.

"Yes," I say. Because there is nothing left to add.

I blow my nose again and then breathe deeply, feeling calmer. Not better, but calmer, and I start to think through Gabe's message once more. I still have the contact in KL. Perhaps I'll discover something useful when I meet them. If I can just hold on for another month, maybe then I can go there and discover something new. Maybe then I can have my purpose returned to me, and it will be enough just to know that, somehow, I will avenge Gabe's death. Somehow I will expose UnMonde for what they are ....

The car doors fling open.

"Sam! Where on earth have you been? We've been looking ...." EJ stops short, glancing from Gajendra to me, as Tess drops her new, fake Gucci bag and leans in, worried.

"Sam, you okay?"

I take a deep breath, trying to compose myself. I attempt a grateful glance at Gajendra before turning.

"Yeah, sorry," I say. "I ... I just got sad over the idea of graduating, I guess."

The fib comes out easily enough. So have the other lies I've been telling quite consistently of late. I know, in my case, they are always for good reasons. Considerate reasons even. But still, I have to wonder: Is that what life does to you? Make it so the truth becomes too difficult to acknowledge anymore, so that lies become the paint to hide what's underneath?

"What did you guys get?" I ask.

"Get?" EJ gushes happily. She bounces into the back seat, brandishing a skirt, a pair of leather sandals and a woven belt. No polka dot dress, I notice. Tess and Sandy tumble in after her. "You totally missed out!"

Gajendra sighs and raises his eyes to the sky. Then he starts the car. We roll down the road as my friends babble on. Even in my numb misery I have to admit that, at this exact moment, their shopping spree commentary is exactly what I need to hear. And I realize something else, too.

I realize I've never, ever had friends like them before. They've made me something more than myself in so many ways. Before them, I only had one side to me. They've changed that. I am no longer the girl I was when I first arrived at PACA. They've forced me to adapt and grow in ways I'd never have done without their influence; they've helped me understand how their world works. And although they don't know it, they are helping me cope with my present circumstance.

Admittedly I don't know how things will end up just yet. The idea of my world without Torundi is too painful to process, and Gabe's message spins in my mind like shrapnel, ripping away raw parts. I don't know how I will reconcile that, but I do know that, without my friends sitting here with me right now, I wouldn't be able to face anything.

But here's the thing:

I also know I am not the person they see me as. Perhaps it will always be that way for me, because the world I come from is completely different than theirs, completely different from their culture. And I realize they'll never get that.

To them, I am just a girl in their class, in their dorm, at their school, speaking their language and, aside from my unfortunate wardrobe, more or less look like them on the outside. That is how this reality bubble that is PACA allows us to live. It is change that will illustrate our differences.

When they go home, they'll go home to their families, to parents and siblings with whom they've grown up, who share a name and a sense of identity, a nationality. A sense of belonging. I've never had that. It isn't Dr. Jean's fault – I know he's done his best – but I'll never be able to look at him quite like that, either. Like I belong.

And their towns – in Thailand or Indonesia or wherever else – are metropolises filled with malls and theaters and all the modern amenities I've never known in my quiet little life. And when it comes time to go to college they'll go to places to which they are at least somewhat adapted, places they've been raised to identify with, maybe even visited a few times.

I am not like them.

Even if I really wanted to be and gave it everything I've got, I know I would never succeed. There will always be another side of me that runs rivers through my being.

Those rivers are my home in Torundi and the rain forest where I collect my orchids, the mission cemetery where my mother lies, the banks of the Mokanan and the Tuafi trees I've grown up studying, all of my Dyeen friends with whom I've shared most of my life; I'll miss them as much as I'll miss Dr. Jean and Nurse Kathy and Trudy. And now those rivers also include something else, the most sacred thing of all, and it will carve its roots into me until it is as deep and as beautiful as the Tanah Yatim.

That river belongs to Gabe.

20. DESCENDANT

I know what you're probably thinking:

That was supposed to be the end of my story.

I was supposed to graduate, go to college, study, graduate again, maybe go to medical school. Life would intervene. Who knows, perhaps someday, a long, long way down the line, I would get married. Have kids. I was supposed to grow up and grow old.

But that's not what happens.

The day after graduation, I say goodbye to my friends. After the summer, Tess will be going to school in Minnesota, near where her aunt lives. Aaron already has plans to visit her over Christmas. Sandy is off to Toronto, where she hopes to pursue a career in acting – an announcement that surprised all of us a little, I think. EJ is attending university at Pepperdine, just as she'd always planned.

Another plan EJ announces as we hug goodbye? We are all to meet in New Orleans nine months from now for Mardis Gras. She makes us swear to it. They'll all be staying with me, she announces, so I'd better have a big room at Tulane.

Later that morning Dr. Jean, Trudy and I head downtown to catch the ferry over to the mainland port of Butterworth. From there we'll take a bus to KL and stay in town for a few days before flying off to New Orleans, where we'll spend the summer settling me in. Obviously, Trudy is coming with us. Ever since she and Dr. Jean showed their faces at PACA for my graduation, it was almost laughable at how poorly they disguised their feelings for each other. Sometime between Thaipusam and now, a romance between them has not just blossomed, but run completely riot. It is about time, as far as I am concerned. I wonder if any ceremonies are planned in the near future.

When we arrive at the ferry terminal, we have about twenty minutes before our scheduled departure. Gajendra and his wife, Lily, are seeing us off, but since they aren't here yet I run across the street for one last iced coffee. I feel a little sad as I pay out my change. I may even be teary-eyed because the vendor looks at me kind of funny. I thank him and walk off, sipping my magical elixir-in-a-bag while adjusting my new backpack with my free hand. It was a graduation gift from my roommates.

"You need to have something that's *not* embarrassing to use at your new school!" EJ had said.

My things are heavier than usual today. In addition to its normal contents, my bag also holds all of my passports plus the cards and money from the safety deposit box. Dr. Jean and Trudy are completely clueless about my plans, of course – I've managed to convince them to take our little detour to KL as a final adieu to Malaysia – but I am planning on chasing down my contact later that day, as soon as we get settled in. I've already worked up an excuse to justify an excursion from our hotel that afternoon, and I expect I can make it to the address by four o'clock.

I am nervous about the venture. I have no idea what to expect.

I wander over to a magazine kiosk, still thinking my plans over. I peruse the selection before me … a few local papers, a plethora of fashion magazines hailing from every corner of the globe … and I have just spotted an interesting travel pamphlet on Kuala Lumpur when someone tugs at my arm. I spin around.

"Go, lady!" hisses a man, probably not much older than me.

"What?"

"Down there, go now!" he whispers, taking me by the arm and pulling me down the sidewalk. I glance from him back to the ferry terminal, a little stunned, but there is something about his demeanor that keeps me from resisting.

"What is it?" I ask, quickening my pace.

I look around again. At first, nothing seems the least bit unusual. The streets bustle as they always do; people and cars and motorcycles zip here and there in a hectic buzz that actually has its own sense of order.

The man beside me suddenly grabs my bag.

"Let go!" I yelp, jerking away, but just then I realize he isn't taking it, he is slipping it over my shoulders! Unusual behavior, to be sure, but I am done trying to suss it out. This is getting creepy and, besides, I shouldn't have wandered over here in the first place. I turn, resolved to head back to the terminal, but the man grabs me again and then, with a surprising amount of strength – because he isn't much bigger than me, really – he pushes me into an alley.

"Lady, please, you must—"

A shot rings through the traffic. The man beside me crumples to the ground. I stagger back for a moment, shocked out of my wits, and it is just registering that I need to help him when a motorcycle roars into the narrow street.

"Get on!" shouts the driver, but he doesn't give me much time to think it over because another shot shatters the wall behind me. Dust filters in the air and I can taste the powdery residue of cement in my mouth. I freeze for a moment, staring at the driver. I don't know him. The man on the ground isn't moving.

"GET ON!" the driver repeats, just as a third shot hits the wall, and in that moment, I feel myself yanked toward the motorcycle. I am not all the way on when it roars down the alleyway, turning a corner, carrying me with it.

"What's happening?" I scream, but the motorcycle only howls in reply, now joined by another sound. I struggle to sit properly on the back, clinging to the driver for dear life. When I'm firmly on the seat, I look behind us. A second motorcycle is taking chase. Its driver wears a shielded helmet and is dressed in dark clothing. He could simply be on an errand, I suppose, but circumstances suggest otherwise. This is confirmed in the next second, when he flips a strap over his shoulder and I see what he carries.

"Someone's behind us! He's got a gun!" I yell, just as our bike turns another corner. I don't know where we are going, of course, but I know that soon we'll run out of road. We are only a block or so from the sea. This realization is cut short by another, much more terrifying, one because suddenly, we turn down a tiny alleyway, fly through an open apartment door and, to my astonishment, proceed up a flight of stairs. I hold on, unaware of anything but the walls of the apartment and the landing ahead. When we reach it, we don't stop. We zoom down a hallway, into another room, the wheels skidding around a corner, and then we bump down another flight of stairs that leads out the back of the apartment. We're on a terrace of sorts now, surrounded by water. The bike skids over the terrace, screeching to a stop just where a speedboat bobs in the water.

"Get off!" the driver bellows, which is quite unnecessary. I slither off all on my own, sort of a combination of slipping and fainting, I think, with the only difference being I am still conscious. Before I can make sense of my surroundings another man picks me up and lugs me to the boat. I try to gain my footing, but my legs have turned to rubber. I try to twist away instead, but he holds me fast and practically throws me onto the deck, jumping on after me. I scream something, I don't even know what. I'm clawing at the boat rail, trying to climb out when I turn to look at my captor just as the engine rumbles to life.

"Stay down, Sam."

Another unnecessary command, because now, I know I have lost it. I couldn't have moved if my life depended on it. It is all too surreal, just like in a dream, and I am not sure what part of this scenario is the most fantastical.

Water sprays in my face and spreads all around as the boat roars away from the landing. Condos and the toppling, colonial shops of Georgetown race backward as, to my left, the ferry terminal recedes by the millisecond. I look again to the driver, but no, no, no, it is impossible. I look away. The Penang Bridge stretches across the Malacca Strait, into the distance.

I turn back to the driver.

He is still there, the sun shining over his shoulders and glinting off his hair, sparking copper. Exactly as I remembered.

"Don't worry about Dupuy and Wallace," he says, his voice clipped, urgent. "I've sent someone to warn them, but they're not the ones these people are interested in. The more distance from you, the safer it is for them."

I blink again.

I have just heard his voice, haven't I? I've imagined his face a million times, but actually *hearing* his voice say a whole sentence, not just a hint before flitting away ….

"Gabe?"

But I don't think it actually comes out.

He stands at the wheel, eyes fixed before him.

"I thought you were dead!" I say. I'm sure of it this time.

"I know this must be difficult, but I'll explain later, Sam," he shouts, throwing a glance my way. "Right now, I need you to look behind us. Do you see anyone?"

"I thought you were dead!" I repeat, the words finally reaching the right volume. We are exploding past fishing boats and small, industrial vessels. We are halfway between Georgetown and the mainland of Butterworth.

"It was Marcus," he replies loudly, battling over the engine noise. "He's the one who fell into the water. You weren't the only one – UnMonde believed it, too – I had to let them think it, it was the only way I could – never mind, later, we don't have time! There's something much more important I need to tell you."

I blink, not quite trusting myself, but I see his face. I hear his voice. When the wind blows against his shirt, I can still make out the scar running up his back. All real.

"I came back as soon as I could. Djadrani's found out you're not returning to Torundi," he continues, his voice strained. "These are his men – they're after you, Sam. Djadrani's half brother, Harim, he—"

"I THOUGHT YOU WERE DEAD!"

"Yes, I know! Now, please, look behind us and …."

I don't hear him. I am breathing too quickly but the air seems thin and heavy all at once. "I can't believe this, I don't understand!" I gasp stupidly, and my ears pound with hard, angry rain. No, it isn't rain. It is something else. It is gunshots.

The boat screams over the water, and I can see that we are headed toward an alcove near the Butterworth ferry and train terminals, but from this same direction another boat curls into the water and races toward us.

"Change of plans. Sam, the vest down there, put it on!" Gabe commands, which is enough to prompt my attention to the black object on the floor. I stagger to it, shrugging it over my shoulders and fitting the clasps together just as our boat whips a right angle, now blasting north along the coastline. I nearly topple face-first onto the deck, and the scramble helps clear my head a little. There is no way I can make sense of what is going on, but I have one fact to cling to:

"What … why is Djadrani after *me?*" I cry over the roar.

Gabe keeps his gaze ahead.

"Because his half brother, the one behind the palace attack …," he yells, his voice quick, stilted. "UnMonde used them both. And now Harim is bent on retribution. He wants the sultanate, now more than ever since he knows about the Tanah Yatim. But it isn't just that. He knows Djadrani's secret—"

More gunshots.

"Sam, take the wheel!"

"What?"

"Take the …." His voice disappears within the sudden pounding. I stare from him to the boat chasing behind us, then to the whirring thrum overhead. A helicopter slices through the sky as shots fire from above. "TAKE THE WHEEL!"

I stumble over, too dazed to argue. I must have grabbed it because, in the next moment, Gabe is bent down and unzipping a large carrying bag, now fastening parts of a gun to each other with an efficiency I have all but forgotten.

"What is going on?" I scream. "Why are they shooting at us?"

"That's what I came back to tell you – it's …." His voice drowns out for another second, then "your mother!" is all that I hear.

"My mother?" I repeat, but then the boat lurches, knocking Gabe to the side.

"You've got to focus," he yells, grabbing the wheel for a second. "Look! No, not to the shore! That way!"

I swallow, back to the present, gripping the wheel and steering us north. Shots rain overhead, spraying into the water. I try to keep a straight line as Gabe lifts the machine gun to his shoulder.

"What does my mother have to do with *this?*" I hear myself saying; maybe I say it several times, I don't know, but the only response is the volley of gunshots all around us, pinging off the boat and tearing into the sea. A round of fire rips from our side of things, drilling into the sky, and it seems as though the whole world explodes with fury.

I keep driving, hot with fear, pain stabbing my shoulder, but I dare not glance away from my course as a second bout rages into the air. This time, a terrible shriek replies and at that, I turn to look.

The helicopter howls into a freefall behind us, like an injured beast, its rotor blades moaning into the sea, churning smoke with foam.

"Don't look, DRIVE!"

"What about the other boat?" I gasp, correcting my course, but my entire body shakes so much that I clasp the wheel even tighter, feeling certain it is the only thing keeping me upright.

"BRATATATATATAT," rages the machine gun.

A few single replies.

And then, nothing.

Gabe is taking the wheel again. I stagger away, glancing from him to the straits behind us. The helicopter lists sideways in the water, some distance off. Its blades thrash futilely, slower and slower, and the other boat has turned from us, now racing to its aid. I feel a shudder leave me as I turn again to Gabe. His face is tight with worry.

"In the bag! Get the orange sack out," he orders.

"What?"

"Sam, you're hit. Find the bandages – we've got to gain some distance."

I look down and see my sleeve blooming wet with color. I blink at it for a few seconds, shocked. I hadn't even known ….

"Sam, are you okay?"

"Yes, I … yes."

"Then get the bandages!"

It takes a few more seconds before I realize what he is saying. I scramble to the bag, fishing around until I find the orange sack. I fumble at the zipper, now sorting through a collection of first aid items. I pull out a pressure dressing just as Gabe slows to a stop, shifting the boat into neutral.

He grabs the bandage, then rips the sleeve from my arm. I follow his gaze.

"I … I don't think it went in," I stammer, staring at the blood. It doesn't seem real or, rather, it feels like I am looking at someone else's shoulder.

He grimaces as he wipes the wound clean.

"Yes, I think you're right," he says, wrapping the dressing around it, and before I've comprehended that the deed is done, he's already shifted back into gear. We head once more over the water. I glance from my gauzed shoulder to where he stands at the wheel. His calm unsettles me. I don't know whether I should scream or cry.

"Where … where are we going?" I say instead.

"We'll have to head north, maybe hit somewhere near Perlis, cross the Thai border. We'll regroup from there. I had transport waiting at Butterworth, but it looks like Djadrani's men knew about that, too. KL will have to wait." He is saying all of this quickly and clearly, but he might as well be speaking Swahili.

My head feels as if it might explode. I don't understand any of this.

"Why?" I hear myself say.

Gabe keeps driving, but he glances toward me. There is something about his expression … uncertainty, I think. I've never seen that in him before.

"Because you are not safe. Not here, not anywhere, so long as Djadrani and Harim can reach you. UnMonde must have known, too. You're the card they're all playing."

I look down at the seat beside me. For the first time, I think to sit in it. So I do. It is warm, the rubber-like canvas sticking to my skin. It is the only thing on this boat that feels real. Far behind me, in the wake of gunshots, a helicopter sinks into the sea. And all around us, bullet holes festoon our craft. I suppose nothing should seem so strange by comparison. But it does, because the most incredible, the most strange thing of all stands beside me, piloting us up the Strait of Malacca, risen from the dead. I know he is real, but I still can not grasp it.

"No," I say, but it sounds hollow, like an echo. "I mean, why are *you* here?"

"What?"

"I thought you were dead!" I say for the umpteenth time. I know it is redundant. But now the words grow angry, and I don't care if I sound stupid or if tears gather in my eyes, because it hurts to look at him, to see him here, and the question sobs out of me:

"It almost killed me! No, I *died* inside! You let me believe it, you told me to let you go – why would you do that! And now you just show up, and you're telling me things that make no sense … *why* are you *here*, Gabe? I—"

"Sam!" he yells, cutting me off. "I'll tell you anything you want to know, but right now, just listen to me!"

"WHAT?"

The engine roar sinks to a loud murmur. We still travel north over the water, but our speed slows to an ordinary pace.

"Your mother," he replies after a moment, glancing over at me again, "held a secret, one known only by Harim and Djadrani. One that finishes the tale … that, until now, Djadrani has kept in complete silence …."

"NO!" I snap, springing to my feet. "Why are *you* here? Tell me that first!"

"Why do you think!" he bellows in return.

"Tell me! I want you to say it!"

"I *have* said it!"

The engine revs once more over the water and I stand, clutching the seat edge, glaring at him.

"I've said it every day – before I even understood what it was – since that first moment I saw you, I think – isn't it obvious? I've said it until everything has fallen away but that, until nothing else is left. I love you, Sam, is that what you want me to say? Because it doesn't matter now! It doesn't matter how I feel or even how *you* feel! Everything has changed for you, but you have to know!"

"*What* do I *have* to know?" I yell back.

Gabe does a quick back-and-forth from me to the water. The boat roars faster, his hands on the wheel, eyes straight. A muscle jumps in his jaw.

"Remember when we spoke of your scar?" he asks after another moment, but he doesn't turn, he keeps looking before him, and his voice is strangely calm, determined.

"Remember you said that it showed you were taboo, that your mother brought shame to the Tagolis?"

I think I say yes. In any case I nod, bewildered by this turn in conversation.

"And you said that your existence had never even been made known to them? That, as far as everyone in Torundi was concerned, you were simply an orphan from a nearby village to the Dyeens, left at the mission steps?"

"Yes," I say again, and a sense of foreboding creeps through me.

"Your mother gave birth to you in secret, Sam. No one ever saw you; even the Tagoli elder who administered the brand did so at night, in the darkness. All that the Tagolis knew was that your mother and a baby swaddled in a *ta'omala* – the traditional dress for male infants – had been exiled. She negotiated to be left with you in the rain forest, Sam. She must have known."

"I ... don't understand," I say. "She must have known what?"

Gabe keeps driving, the engine slowing again, but I can see the tendons stretch over his hands just like they did that night we met at the fort. Right before he told me the truth.

"Your mother was also an illegitimate child, Sam – but you already knew that. What you didn't know is that your mother was the only offspring," he answers, his voice increasingly calm, like words read from a teleprompter. "It is what Djadrani and Harim helped hide all those years ago, by sending your pregnant grandmother to the Tagoli village in the most eastern part of the island, then under Harim's administration. Your mother was illegitimate but, according to Torundi law, a direct line all the same."

"Direct ... what?" I sputter, but Gabe is still speaking:

"Until a year or so ago, Djadrani believed that line had been dealt with. He didn't know you were her child. It was believed that heir was a male, a firstborn who was brought to a neighboring village after being exiled from the Tagolis, after your mother supposedly perished in the rain forest. It was the whole point behind Djadrani's purge. But UnMonde must have discovered the truth through Harim. Do you understand what I'm telling you?"

I continue to stand there, a million thoughts hitting me at once. "And … that's why Djadrani wants me killed?"

"Why he wants you and Harim and anyone else who might know killed. Because the truth is threatening to come out and, if that happens, the sultanate will be moot for both of them. You weren't supposed to know about it. No one was. And now, you're of age. You weren't supposed to be here for that."

"For … the truth?" I stammer. My mind feels thick, like it moves through jelly.

"Don't you see?" he says, turning to me. "Your mother was the sole descendant of the king, Sam. That makes *you* the rightful ruler of Torundi!"

I think I've sat back down, but am not sure.

We continue through the water, everything around spinning with the hum of the boat. Gabe still speaks, I think, but I don't hear him. I don't hear anything. I look down, trying to make that pronouncement stay still for a moment, to make the world stay still.

The dark, fern-like shape of my scar meets my gaze.

There are so many things about those last words that I don't understand. A hazy past no one has ever told me. A past only my enemies understand. I am taboo. My mother had been taboo. Taboo from existing, even, without my ever having suspected why. And now, here I am, unwittingly the link to a kingdom I hold so dear.

It doesn't seem possible.

Yet there is no denying the chase I've just witnessed – the death I've just escaped. My mother wasn't so lucky. She must have brought me to the mission, knowing. My strange, adopted life saved me. My strange, Western name clothed me in a new skin. For seventeen years I was the mission's child, a mystery to the Dyeens and to most of Torundi.

A mystery to me.

And now everything I've known about myself, about my life – about Torundi – has changed.

Gabe turns, as if sensing my thoughts. The sun catches the flickering glow of his eyes, teal to golden green. And it is like that night of the scavenger hunt, I realize, when I saw him in the Cathay Hotel. The slow click of a puzzle rotates in my mind, bits and pieces of random facts and feelings – instincts that have never had a home – and here is the key piece, finally snapping into place.

I don't look away. His eyes are as deep as the straits around us, deep and alive and full of unknowns. But I've already jumped in. I've jumped in and I swim to that thing I believe in.

"Yes, that does change everything," I whisper.

"Yes," he replies. His voice is hollow, detached.

The air smells saltier all of a sudden, the wind whips harder and the sound of the boat returns with a rumble in my ears. Far to my right, the shores of Malaysia stretch north to south; far to my left, nothing but sea.

"Everything," I say, turning back to him, "but you."

Anticlimatic !!

THE END

ABOUT THE AUTHOR

J.L. McCreedy was born in New Jersey, grew up in Indonesia and Malaysia, graduated law school in Mississippi and currently lives in Borneo. She is also the author of *Liberty Frye and the Witches of Hessen.*

Please visit her at *www.TongaTime.com.*